Zev Chafets

THE
BOOKMAKERS

RANDOM HOUSE
NEW YORK

Copyright © 1995 by Zev Chafets

All rights reserved under International and Pan-American Copyright
Conventions. Published in the United States by Random House, Inc., New York,
and simultaneously in Canada by Random House of Canada Limited, Toronto.

Grateful acknowledgment is made to Jobete Music Co., Inc. for permission to reprint two lines
from "The Way You Do the Things You Do" by William Robinson, Jr., and Robert Rogers.
Copyright © 1964 by Jobete Music Co., Inc. Reprinted by permission.

Library of Congress Cataloging-in-Publication Data
Chafets, Ze'ev.
    The bookmakers / Zev Chafets.
      p.   cm.
    ISBN 0-679-41456-8 :
    1. Authors and publishers—New York (N.Y.)—Fiction.
  2. Novelists, American—New York (N.Y.)—Fiction. 3. Murder—New
York (N.Y.)—Fiction. I. Title.
PS3553.H225B66 1995
813'.54—dc20   94-32159

Manufactured in the United States of America on acid-free paper.
98765432
First Edition

BOOK DESIGN BY TANYA M. PÉREZ

For Lisa, with love

THE BOOKMAKERS

One

At 3:15 on the morning of his forty-fifth birthday, near the corner of West Seventy-sixth and Columbus, Mack Green received a gift from a stranger. The gift—unexpected and startling—came wrapped in a revelation: that he was a man capable of seriously contemplating his own suicide. And although it was something that had never occurred to him before, he instantly recognized it as the idea that would save his life.

Mack was on the street at that hour because he dreaded the prospect of discussing the future of the American novel—especially his own American novels—in bed, buck naked, before breakfast, with a woman whose name he didn't know. Brenda or Glenda—she had only said it once, and her Indiana accent made it hard to catch—claimed to be a literary critic from Indianapolis. This wasn't entirely improbable; the Flying Tiger Polo Lounge, described in an outdated guidebook as "New York's hottest literary hangout," where Mack had been celebrating his birthday with double bourbons, attracted a disproportionate number of literary ladies from the Big Ten states. Over the years, Mack, whose resistance to sexual temptation was close to zero, had succumbed with amiable ease to the charms of countless Brendas and Glendas looking for a one-night stand with a once-famous author.

In bed, half drunk, the bookish groupies of middle America comported themselves like high-priced, low-minded hookers. But in the morning, with sleep-putty still clogging the corners of their eyes and tequila on their breath, they underwent a frightening transformation into serious-minded free-verse poets or assistant professors of creative writing. What was Updike really like? How does one find a really fine New York publisher? And, inevitably, why had so much time passed since Mack's last novel?

Mornings, he had learned, were best spent alone, asleep on the perennially unmade mattress in his West Side studio apartment. And so Mack, who tried hard never to hurt people's feelings, waited until the literary ladies snored off before slipping out of bed, scribbling an affectionate note and fleeing into the night.

Most times he took a taxi home, but tonight he decided to walk. A few days earlier he had been given a harsh lecture by Dottie Coleman, who, combining the internist's natural alarmism with the brutal frankness of an ex-lover, had warned him that his cholesterol and liver enzymes looked like "a Molotov cocktail in a test tube," that he had every risk factor for most of the diseases common in the industrialized world and that his lifestyle was twenty years too young for his body. She had used hard words—"alcoholic," "lung cancer" and "drop dead at any minute" were the ones that lingered in his mind—and while he detected a certain fond malice in her attitude (ending their affair had been his idea), the dire picture she painted was not entirely unfamiliar. Mack was too allied with his bad habits to abandon them, but he was willing to moderate their evil effect by sporadic acts of medical virtue, such as a salubrious postcoital hike.

And so he had walked from the Waldorf, arriving at the corner of Columbus and Seventy-sixth in a sweaty, self-congratulatory state. He was thinking about calling Dottie later to let her know he was taking her warning seriously when he heard a thick, furry voice from a doorway next to his brownstone.

" 'Scuse me, mister, you got the time?"

Mack turned and saw a thin young black man in a crummy-looking imitation-leather jacket. In the dim light of the doorway he could see dulled, yellowish eyes peering at him. Though the kid looked no more than sixteen, Mack immediately understood that he was about to get robbed.

"I said, do you have the time?" repeated the boy, who suddenly darted in front of Mack, blocking his way.

"I heard you," said Mack.

"You too good to talk to niggers?"

"Naw, I talk to niggers all day long," said Mack. The smart-ass answer startled him. After twenty-five years in New York, he knew better.

"Gimme your watch, you nigger-talking motherfucker. And your wallet." The kid was trying to sound threatening, but his voice wobbled nervously. When Mack didn't move, he reached inside his jacket, pulled out a Smith & Wesson .32 revolver and pointed it at him. "Right now, man. I ain't playin'."

Mack noticed that the kid's arm was trembling. He saw it with a kind of intense but distant interest, as if the hand holding the pistol belonged to one of his fictional characters. Suddenly he felt the once-familiar hunger to mold and craft a great scene. The feeling gave him a sense of fearless control.

"Beat it, Junior," he said, watching the kid's eyes widen in disbelief.

"Man, you must be crazy," said the mugger, waving the gun. "You give it up right now or I'll shoot your motherfucking ass for real."

"Go ahead," said Mack. "Let's see you do it."

"Man, give me the wallet," the kid said, his voice rising. "Give me that motherfucker, man—"

"Hey, don't shout," said Mack. He was surprised to see that the kid instinctively lowered his voice. He took a sudden step forward, not knowing exactly what he was planning to do. The kid retreated, stumbling slightly. While he was off-balance, Mack lunged and grabbed him by the forearm. Even through the jacket sleeve the arm felt thin and weak. Mack shook it hard, and when the Smith & Wesson clattered to the pavement he put his foot on it and pushed the kid back against the building. Then he bent down and scooped up the gun. The whole thing took less than ten seconds.

"Man, you're the worst fucking thief I ever met," said Mack, breathing hard from the exertion. "This your first time or what?"

"Don't hurt me, man, I'm sick."

"Sorry to hear it," said Mack. "You should take better care of yourself. I know an internist I could recommend if you don't mind a woman doctor."

The kid looked at him through scared yellow eyes and said nothing.

"I have this theory," Mack continued in an easy, conversational tone he barely recognized as his own. "People get the mugger they deserve. You think I deserve you?"

"Man, what you gonna do?"

"I'm talking to you, son. We're having a late-night chat. Answer my question—you think I deserve you?"

"You a cop?"

Mack laughed and shook his head. "I'm a writer. I can talk like a cop, though. I make up dialogue. You know what dialogue is? Like in the movies, when people talk to each other? What I'm doing now is bantering with you, cop style." Green was aware that he was babbling, but he didn't care. It was three in the morning, he was flying on adrenaline and he had already begun to grasp the significance of this encounter.

"Let me tell you something else," he continued. "People get

the mugger they deserve? Well, muggers get the muggees they deserve. You got me and I'm the wrong one. Know why?"

The kid shrugged. Green could see that he was no longer frightened. In fact, he looked a little impatient.

"Because I wasn't afraid to die just now. Usually I am, just like everybody else, so don't blame yourself. You just happened to catch me on a bad night."

The kid shifted his feet and looked at Mack. His nose was running and he wiped it with his sleeve. Suddenly Green felt very tired. "Okay, Dillinger, split," he said. "I want to go home and get some sleep."

"What about my gun?"

"I'm keeping the gun," said Mack. "It's a souvenir. In the morning it will remind me of you."

"Oh, man, I need that gun. I ain't gonna do you nothin'," moaned the kid with soft, hopeless urgency.

"Nosiree, bob, this here six-shooter stays with me," said Mack. "That's cowboy dialogue I'm doing now. Recognize it? You go to the movies ever?"

"Shit," said the mugger.

"I used to go every Saturday, in Oriole. That's where I'm from, Oriole, Michigan. Name's Mack Green but they call me the Oriole Kid and I'm confiscating your shooting iron, pardner. Now run your ass back uptown before I make you dance. And tell them up there that the Oriole Kid is back in town."

The young man gave Green a long look, appraising his chances of grabbing the pistol. Then his shoulders slumped and he started trudging up Columbus. Green watched him for a moment as he absently emptied the bullets from the revolver and tucked it into his waistband. After years of inexplicable bad luck and frustration, Mack knew that he had been given the gift he had been waiting for: the return of his creative imagination.

"Hey, kid," he called out. The boy stopped and turned, facing Mack.

"Yeah? What?"

"What's your name?"

"Shit," said the boy defiantly.

"Good name," said Mack. "It fits you. When the new best-seller by Mack Green comes out, be sure and steal a copy. It'll be dedicated to you."

Two

When the phone on Tommy Russo's nightstand rang he awoke instantly, a reflex from his days at the seminary. He checked his Rolex, saw it was just past nine—too early for a call from the Coast on the movie deal—and let the machine answer. "You have reached the residence of Tomas Russo," said the refined telephone voice, which belonged to one of his actor clients. "Please leave a message and I'll return your call as soon as possible."

"Tommy, pick up the phone. It's me, Mack."

Russo leaned over and pressed the speaker button. "Yo, Mack, what's the deal?" he said in his Brooklyn honk.

"We've got to talk," said Mack excitedly. "What time are you going into the office?"

"I'm not," said Russo. "I'm working at home for a few days."

"You sick or something?"

"Naw, just trying to avoid the rat race." He didn't mention

that the rat was Herman Reggie, to whom he owed eighteen thousand dollars.

"I can't wait a few days," said Mack. "This is a big thing. Meet me for lunch." The invitation was at once friendly and imperious—the tone Mack had used with Tommy Russo from the beginning.

"What kind of big thing?" Tommy asked cautiously.

"A book idea, the one I've been waiting for. It came to me last night."

"A book idea," Tommy repeated in an expressionless tone. In the old days, when Mack was a hot writer, Russo had made a lot of money on his book ideas; nowadays they just cost him drinks and lunch—and with Mack, that could be an expensive proposition. Still, he owed Mack, and Tommy Russo had been raised to respect his obligations. "I'll meet you at one," he said.

"Where?"

"How about the Tiger? I haven't been there in a while."

"I thought you hated the place."

"I'm in a nostalgic mood," said Tommy. The Flying Tiger would be perfect, he thought; Reggie would never think of looking for him in a dive like that. Besides, it wouldn't cost a fortune.

"Okay," said Mack. "The Tiger at one. And Tommy? This time I've really got something."

Russo climbed from between his satin sheets and padded into the bathroom to shower. Twenty minutes later, shaved and powdered, he returned to the bedroom and stood in front of his open closet, trying to decide what to wear. In the years since Tommy Russo had left the priesthood, he had never lost his pleasure in the simple act of dressing himself as he pleased. He had Mack to thank—or blame—for that.

The Flying Tiger was nearly deserted when Mack walked in just past eleven. As usual, Otto was behind the bar polishing beer glasses and breaking rolls of quarters into the old-fashioned cash register. The jukebox played Ray Charles's "The Night Time is the Right Time." Mack loved oldies, especially fifties R&B and the Tiger had a great selection, thanks to Otto, who shared Mack's taste in music. What he thought of as their friendship had begun one night, years ago, when he overheard the bartender remark to someone that rock and roll died the day the Beatles stepped off the plane in New York.

The Tiger had a shifting clientele. The daytime customers were mostly construction workers drinking their lunches and reporters lubricating their gossip with Irish whiskey. Next came the businessmen, slurping up happy-hour courage for the miserable commute home. And then, around ten, the young writers began to arrive. Otto, a creased, rumpled man in his late fifties, ministered to them all, dispensing big drinks, greasy food and bland patter with a detatched impartiality that bespoke a fine Catholic understanding of human frailty.

When Mack first started coming to the Tiger it was as a member of the daytime journalist crowd. He was fresh from Ann Arbor, where he had been sports editor of the *Michigan Daily*, a credential that got him a reporter's job at the *New York Post*. One day, sitting at the bar, he fell into conversation with a tattooed guy about his own age who claimed to be a Vietnam veteran. "I killed me fifty-seven gooks over there," said the man. "If I was a pilot, that'd make me an ace, like Jimmy Doolittle and them."

Mack looked down the bar, noticed a bottle of Heinz 57 Varieties near the man's plate and instantly recognized it as the source of the body count. "What're you going to do now that you're back in civilian life?" he asked.

"I'm going to re-up, go back and get me an even hundred," said the guy. "I promised my girl. Then I figure I might run for public office in my native Wisconsin."

"Otto," Mack called to the bartender, "put this man's lunch on my tab. He's a great American."

That night Mack went home, sat down at his Smith-Corona

portable and began to write the story of Ace Fletcher, a good-natured, dim-witted farm boy who tries to impress a girl by joining the army and killing a hundred Vietcong. Eighty thousand words later he had a novel, which he called *Bragging Rights*.

The book came out in 1972, and it was greeted enthusiastically by critics who saw it, in the words of *The New York Times*, as "a bitingly funny satirical send-up of the war. Vietnam may have found its Joseph Heller." The book didn't quite reach the bestseller list, but on the strength of reviews like this it became a minor campus classic and made its author a celebrity spokesman for his generation.

Mack was bemused by his status as an antiwar culture hero. As the only son of a widowed mother he had a draft deferment, and he hadn't really given Vietnam much thought. He saw *Bragging Rights* as a story about a weird guy, nothing more. But if America wanted to consider Mack Green an idealist, and rich and famous, he had no objection.

With his royalty money, Mack quit the *Post* and became a full-time novelist. During the days he worked on a new book, *The Oriole Kid,* about a sportswriter from a small Michigan town who talks the Yankees into giving him a tryout and actually makes the team. At night he enjoyed his newfound celebrity as a welcome guest at boozy, druggy parties; in countless beds; and at the Young Authors' table at the Flying Tiger. In those days he would often catch the stares of the tourists and bask in their envy, a successful young man in a glamorous profession, like a private eye or an international diamond thief.

But Mack was no longer young and nowadays he did his drinking at the bar with Otto. Sometimes, when it was quiet, they watched a few innings of a ball game together, or shot the breeze about movies. They never discussed Mack's books because, as far as Mack knew, Otto never read books. He had been serving liquor to writers long enough to surmise that he wasn't likely to be entertained or enlightened by their printed thoughts.

Otto Kelly had owned the Tiger as long as Mack had been going there, and he remembered the days when Mack sat with the writers. He recalled him, a good-looking, sandy-haired kid, always with a girl, singing snatches of R&B hits along with the jukebox and dancing in the narrow aisle between the tables. Mack was still good-looking—Otto thought he resembled that actor, Jeff Bridges—but he was starting to thicken around the waist and to take on the deceptively outdoor rosiness of the habitual indoor drinker.

Still, Otto was nobody's judge. That morning he greeted Mack the same way he had for twenty years, with a smile and a wink and a friendly, "Hiya, kid, what'll it be?"

Mack consulted his watch and ordered a Bloody Mary. "I want to ask you a question," he said when Otto set the drink in front of him. "What would you do if you had a million dollars and one year to live?"

Otto wiped a spot off the bar and smiled. "Somebody gives me a million? I buy two Mercedes, one for me and one for Betty—a hundred thousand bucks. A house on the beach in Fort Lauderdale—half a mil. Hundred thousand in the bank for each of the two kids. And I'd blow the other two hundred on a trip around the world. That makes an even million."

"You've got it all planned."

"It's not exactly a rare question in the bartender business," said Otto. "You serve booze, you get a lot of what-ifs."

"Yeah," agreed Mack. "I guess. You must get sick of it."

"Nah, goes with the job," said Otto. "At least it's better than the all-time white team."

"What?"

"You know, who's the greatest white basketball team in history. That's the one gets me. I mean, I like basketball and all, but who gives a shit?"

"Right," said Mack. He thought for a moment. "I guess you'd have to say Bird, Walton, McHale, Cousy and West."

"Stockton. They all say Stockton instead of Cousy. Half the kids come in here these days, they never even heard of Cousy."

Mack shook his head. "Cousy was a better outside shooter—" The door opened and Mack saw the squat, impeccably tailored reflection of Tommy Russo in the mirror above the bar. Otto scowled, not trying to hide his disapproval of the agent. "To be continued," Mack said to the bartender, sliding off his stool. "Right now I've got to tell a priest about a miracle."

Tommy Russo's first thought was that the Flying Tiger hadn't changed. The jukebox still played old-fashioned jigaboo music, the air stank of grease and stale beer and Otto gave him his usual Mick fish-eye from behind the bar. Mack looked the same too, dressed as always in a pair of faded jeans and a flannel shirt. Over the years Tommy often wondered how he lived the way he did, suffered so many disappointments and still looked so young. Protestant genes, he decided.

Russo himself had changed considerably. He had added forty pounds to his five-foot, seven-inch frame, weight that even his two-thousand-dollar suits couldn't disguise. His thick black eyebrows had grown together, giving him the look of a well-groomed, roly-poly ape. And 10 percent of anything no longer seemed like a lot of money to him. He had become one of New York's most successful agents—and, because of his passion for gambling, one of the least solvent.

Most of the ex-priests Tommy knew had gone sex-crazy after leaving their calling, but he was no more interested in women now than he had been at St. Fred's. He had never married, and visited expensive prostitutes when the need arose. Luxury and high-rolling excited Tommy Russo—the thing that turned him on about sex was knowing that he was paying five hundred bucks an orgasm.

On the other hand he was willing to admit that gambling had become a real addiction. Wagering large sums of money gave him

the kind of thrill that no woman ever could. Unfortunately, he had
been on a bad run lately. The eighteen grand he owed Herman
Reggie was just one of his debts; he was into bookies all over the
country for more than a hundred thousand bucks. He had no
doubt that he could eventually pay up, and most of his creditors
were willing to wait. Herman Reggie was different, though, and
Tommy needed to do something about him quick.

"Father Tomas," said Mack, taking Russo's hand and bowing
in mock reverence. He had never lost the habit of treating Tommy
with the proprietary superiority of an author for one of his characters. At one time this had annoyed Russo, but as Mack's career
slipped, he had forgiven him. The arrogance was good-natured
and, Tommy thought, even a little brave, like a down-at-the-heels
aristocrat sporting a fresh carnation in the lapel of a frayed suit.
Russo felt a genuine affection for Mack, mixed with gratitude, pity
and a nagging sense of guilt. Of course it wasn't Tommy's fault that
Mack's books no longer sold; there was no way he could have
halted his client's long slide down. At least that was what he told
himself, and usually he could make himself believe it.

"Sorry I'm late," Tommy said. "The cab ran into a demonstration on Broadway. Reverend Abijamin and some of his homeboys
are picketing the theater district and it tied up traffic for a mile."

"No enjoyment without employment!" Russo intoned.
"These rhyming shakedown preachers make me want to puke."

"Spoken like a true man of the cloth," said Mack. "Sit down,
Tommy, have a drink. I want you relaxed when you hear my
idea."

"Yeah, yeah, I'm relaxed," Russo said as he took a seat at a
table near the window.

"You want to hear some music?" Mack asked, gesturing toward the jukebox. "Little Hank Ballard and the Midnighters
maybe?"

"Midnighters my ass, this is the twentieth century. Motown's
dead, in case you didn't know."

"He wasn't Motown," said Mack. "He was from Detroit, but he wasn't a Motown artist. He came a little earlier, around the time of Little Willie John and—"

"Come on, Mack, I'm not in the mood for rock-and-roll 101 today. What's on your mind?"

"Okay, here goes. Last night I was walking home about three, all alone, and guess what happened?"

"You got mugged," said Russo.

"How'd you know that?"

"Are you kidding? What else could have happened at three in the morning in this city?"

"Yeah, well, anyway, this kid jumps out of a doorway and pulls a gun on me—"

"What kind of kid?"

"How the hell do I know? I never saw him before," said Mack. "Probably a crackhead."

"I meant what color," said Russo. "What color kid?"

"He was black," said Mack, "but that's not the important—"

"Yeah, right," said Tommy with sour irony.

"Anyway, the kid says, 'Give me your wallet or I'll shoot,' something like that. At which point, what do you think I did?"

"Gave him the wallet," said Russo. "What's the point here?"

"Like hell I did," Mack said triumphantly. "I grabbed the gun, knocked him on his ass and sent him home."

"What are you, a fucking moron? You got a death wish or something?"

"That's just it—for one split second I did," said Mack. "I was looking down the barrel of the gun and all I was was curious what would it feel like if he pulled the trigger. In a way I even wanted him to. You ever have a feeling like that?"

"Hell no," said Russo.

"Anyway, there I am, standing in the street with the kid's gun in my hand and all of a sudden a whole novel popped right into my head."

"It popped into your head," echoed Tommy.

"Right. It begins when this guy, a middle-aged writer, gets mugged and he suddenly realizes he doesn't give a shit if the guy shoots him or not. Only in his case it's not just a momentary thing, it's real. He's burned out, beaten down and just generally tired of living. So he decides to keep a diary about his last year on earth, sell it to a publisher for a shitload of money and then, at the end of the year, actually kill himself."

"Why would he need the money if he's gonna kill himself?"

"Let's say he needs it for his kids. Or maybe he just wants to blow it on a last fling. The motivation will come later. The point isn't the money. Maybe he doesn't even get any money. The thing is, he sells the idea to a publisher and sets out on an adventure that's supposed to culminate in his suicide. What do you think so far?"

"It gives me the creeps," said Russo.

"It's supposed to. Everybody wonders what he'd do if he only had a year to live. And suicide books are big these days. It can't miss, Tommy, I'm telling you."

"So then what happens? What does the writer end up doing?"

"I don't know yet," said Mack. "What I want to do is put myself in the guy's place, really try to get into his mind, see what happens. Maybe he'll go through with it, maybe not. My not knowing will give it freshness."

Russo paused, staring into space. Then he said, "I don't like this. I may not be a priest anymore but I'm still a Catholic and suicide's a mortal sin."

"Hey, Tomas, this is me, the Oriole Kid. I'm not going to kill myself, I'm talking about a novel. Fiction. As your buddy Reverend Abijamin would say, no simulation without stimulation."

Tommy looked at his friend and wondered. Mack was reckless about the way he lived and he had suffered the kind of disappointments that would have tempted the average guy to reach for the gas pipe a long time ago. Maybe he was finally cracking up. "Going around thinking like somebody who might off himself, that's playing with fire. A man shouldn't dick around with fate like that," he said slowly.

"Jesus." Mack laughed. "You and your Sicilian superstitions. Just tell me, in your professional opinion, is that or is it not a fantastic project?"

"Yeah, it's a good premise, but—"

"No buts. I've been waiting for a great idea for years and I'm not pissing it away. The only question is, are you going to sell it for me or do I have to find some other defrocked priest to pick my pocket?"

For a long moment Russo remained silent. Then he sighed. "Yeah, all right, write up a proposal and I'll try to find you a publisher."

"I want Stealth," said Mack.

"Wolfowitz? I don't think so," said Tommy. Six years earlier, when Mack's last novel, *Light Years,* had bombed, Arthur "Stealth" Wolfowitz, editor in chief of Gothic Books, had dropped his old pal Mack Green with a thud.

"I know we had bad luck the last couple times out, but he's the only editor in town I trust to do this thing right," said Mack. "Take less money if you have to, but get him to do it."

"You trust him," Tommy repeated in a flat voice.

"Nobody can market a book better than Stealth," said Mack. "I know that from experience."

"He didn't do such a hot job on the last ones."

"It wasn't his fault, it was mine," said Mack. "I didn't have the right story. Now I do." He reached across the table and put his hand on Russo's stubby arm. "Please, Tommy, do this for me. Convince him."

There was a note of desperation in Mack's voice that Russo had never heard before. "Okay," he said, "I'll talk to him if you're sure that's what you want. Just remember one thing."

"What's that?" asked Mack, signaling to Otto for menus.

"Going to Wolfowitz was your idea," Tommy said.

Three

The editorial staff of Gothic Books was gathered around the long mahogany table in the boardroom when Arthur Wolfowitz arrived at precisely nine and called the meeting to order. It was his custom to meet with the editors every Monday morning to discuss new acquisitions. He enjoyed the sessions because they gave him an opportunity to display leadership, foster team spirit and appropriate the good ideas of his colleagues.

"Good morning, everybody," he said crisply, rapping his Mont Blanc pen smartly on the polished table. Wolfowitz was a man of little emotion; in its place he had developed a repertoire of artificial body language to express what he did not feel. He pursed his lips to show surprise, slapped his palm on tabletops to simulate anger, furrowed his brow to convey concern. Tapping his pen on the table was meant to signify businesslike efficiency. "Let's get started. John, what have you got?"

John Quinn, a pudgy young man trapped in a tight-vested three-piece suit, was the junior member of the staff, entrusted mostly with insignificant fiction. Wolfowitz had hired him because his father worked in the book review section of the *Times*.

Quinn cleared his throat and looked at the others. "I've been reading a terrific proposal by a new writer from Mississippi named Terry Harper," he said. "It's a definite one, three, five and six and probably an eight, too."

The numbers were a Wolfowitz innovation, a code designed to prevent editors from getting too windy about the books they wanted to sign up. The editor in chief, who had little tolerance for idle literary chitchat, had concocted a numbered checklist of attributes that he encouraged his editors to use at all times. Automatically he interpreted Quinn's figures: one meant the book was commercial, three that it had humor, five that it contained kinky sex, six that a similar book had been a bestseller in the past two years; and eight that it could be acquired cheaply.

"How much five does it have?" asked Wolfowitz.

"Big-time five. It's about this far from hardcore," said Quinn, holding his fat thumb and finger an inch apart. Wolfowitz noted approvingly that Quinn's gesture was an imitation of his own body language. The editor in chief liked obsequious young subordinates.

"Fine. What's the eight on this?" he asked.

"He'll take twenty-five thousand," said Quinn.

"Okay, knock him down to twenty and make the deal. Brad?"

Bradley Knox was a tall, reedy, professorial man in his late forties who had been brought to Gothic by publisher Douglas Floutie. Wolfowitz distrusted Knox's ties to the boss and dealt with him gingerly.

"I've got the Smith book that we talked about on the phone the other day," he said. "I think it's very amusing. Lots of three."

"Right," said Wolfowitz, arranging his mouth into a collegial smile. "Why don't you tell everyone what the gimmick is, they'll get a kick out of it." Like most of Knox's projects, this one was a sure loser, which is why Wolfowitz was encouraging it. His plan was to wait until Knox's track record got so bad that Floutie would be forced to get rid of him.

"It's called *The Big Book of Smiths*," said Knox with a waggish grin. "It's a sort of humorous guide to everybody and everything with the name Smith. Some of the categories are quite clever, I think. For example, Word Smiths—Smiths who were writers, such as Adam. Or Tune Smiths, such as Bessie or Kate. There's Black Smiths—"

"Like Willie Smith," Wolfowitz said helpfully.

"Exactly. The list goes on and on. And there's also a history of the Smith name and a Smith geography with little-known facts. For instance, did you know that Smith County, Kansas is the exact geographical center of the United States?" Wolfowitz shook his head in wonder as Bradley Knox bubbled on. "Well, you get the point. The idea, and I think it's a sound one, is that there are eight million Smiths in America. If even one in ten buys the book, we stand to make a fortune. Not to mention people who might give it as a present."

"The perfect gift for the Smith in your life," said Wolfowitz.

"And then we could go on to other names," said Knox, missing the mockery in Wolfowitz's tone. "It could become a series: Jones, Johnson, Williams—"

"Crosby, Stills and Nash, Martin and Lewis, Merrill, Lynch, Pierce, Fenner and Smith—here we are right back to Smith again," said Wolfowitz, spreading his arms, palms up, in theatrical admiration. "You've really got something here, Brad. I want you to handle it personally. Dorothy?"

Dorothy Ravitsky was a thin, nervous woman with a sharp tongue and a very good eye for commercial fiction. Wolfowitz, who was a CPA by training, relied on her professional judgment, although the sound of her intense, high-pitched voice never ceased to grate on him.

"We're still trying to sign up the Kleinhouse trilogy," she said.

"He wants a bundle, though, especially now that Hollywood is buying his books."

"How much?"

"A million, five."

"Who's the agent?"

"Tomas Russo."

"Let me speak to him," said Wolfowitz. "He's tough but maybe I can talk him down."

No one around the table doubted that he could. The editor in chief was a legendary deal-maker. Like all great negotiators, his success was based on a keen understanding of human nature. Early in his career he had discovered that most writers knew nothing about money and, amazingly, were proud of it—so proud, in fact, that they were willing to fork over 10 percent of their income to literary agents whose main job was to preserve the illusion that their clients were too artistic to deal with mere commerce.

This simple insight had led to another: agents, unlike writers, were in it for the money. And since even the most prolific writer rarely turned out more than a book a year, agents who wanted to prosper needed to sell many books by many authors. That, in turn, gave Wolfowitz leverage. It meant that he was negotiating with people who needed him more than they needed their own clients.

There were, of course, ethical agents who refused to sell out their authors, but Wolfowitz tried to avoid them. Idealists made him uncomfortable. He preferred the realists, men and women who knew where their real interests lay. Tommy Russo was among the most realistic. Wolfowitz made a note to phone him and then quickly went around the room, calling on each editor in turn. When the last one had spoken, he gathered up his notes, popped the cap back on the Mont Blanc and clapped his hands decisively. "Okay, meeting's adjourned," he said. "Let's go make some money."

As usual, the first thing Wolfowitz noticed when he returned to his spacious corner office was the framed wedding photo of

Louise on the shelf behind his desk. Visitors often commented on her youthful beauty, but to Wolfowitz she was, after almost twenty years of marriage, even more lovely—and more maddeningly desirable—than she had been as a bride. He glanced quickly through the messages on his desk, picked up the phone and buzzed his secretary. "Claire, get hold of Tommy Russo, see if he can meet me for lunch at Antonelli's at one."

"Will do. By the way, Floutie called. He wants to see you today."

"Did he say what he wants?"

"Nope. You want me to fix a time?"

"Nah, blow him off. I'm not in the mood for His Nibs today."

When Tommy saw Wolfowitz enter Antonelli's crowded dining room he breathed a deep sigh of relief. He had been waiting for fifteen tense minutes, aware of the fact that the restaurant, one of the most popular luncheon spots for the publishing crowd, was exactly the kind of place where Herman Reggie might look for him. Now, with Wolfowitz here, he felt safe and hopeful that the deal they were about to make would net him enough to get him out of trouble with the giant bookie and his midget sidekick.

"Sorry, I got caught up in some last-minute crap," Wolfowitz said with an apologetic smile as he slid into a seat across from Russo. "The Secretary of State called. This is between us, okay?"

Russo nodded gravely. At lunch, Wolfowitz never failed to drop names or pick up the check. It was, as far as Tommy was concerned, good physics.

"He's getting ready to resign—apparently he's pissed off about Bosnia or something—but he wants to get a book deal first."

"Very statesmanlike," said Russo. "Just out of curiosity, what are you paying him?"

"Too much," said Wolfowitz sourly. Actually he was delighted by the Secretary's book proposal, which was full of nasty gossip about the President, the First Lady and assorted world leaders. He was even happier about his acquisition of a retired secret service agent's memoirs—he was planning to reveal that the Secretary had engaged in oral sex with a Latin American ambassador at an OAS conference. The books would promote each other nicely. "Speaking of paying too much, let's eat." Wolfowitz waved over a waiter and, without consulting Tommy, ordered two hundred and fifty dollars' worth of lunch.

"They must love you in this place," said Russo.

"Spending money on you is good business. I want to get this Kleinhouse thing done. Ravitsky says you're asking a million and a half."

"It's a fair price," said Russo. "The guy's hot. You cleaned up on his last novel and he knows it. Besides, we'd be tying up three books here, not just one."

"Oh, so that's what a trilogy means," said Wolfowitz with a wintry smile. "I'll pay nine hundred thousand. That's plenty."

Russo shook his head. "He won't go for it, no way. Honest to God, I come back to him with that he'll switch agents."

"Well, what'll it take? Don't fool around, just give me the number."

"I could swing it for one point two, I think."

"Okay, but I'll tell you frankly, the only reason I'm going that high is because Floutie wants it. Personally, I can't see a trilogy about the Spanish-American War selling diddly-shit."

"If it's Floutie's project, let's make it one and a half," said Russo. "What the hell, it's his money."

Wolfowitz shook his head. "His father-in-law's money. And my reputation. One point two."

"Your reputation, my commission," said Tommy. "The difference between 10 percent of one point five and one point two is—"

"Thirty," said Wolfowitz. He loved doing business with Tommy Russo. Most agents were willing to bend a little to stay on his good side, but Tommy was ready to flat out break the law.

Wolfowitz attributed Russo's flexibility to his years in the priesthood; he was a man who knew the difference between a mortal sin and simple larceny. "I'll make sure you get it," he said.

"In that case, we've got a deal," said Russo. He reached across the table, exposing two inches of starched white cuff, and took Wolfowitz's hand. The money would be enough to pay off Herman Reggie and the rest of the sharks and still leave him a nice piece of change.

Wolfowitz freed his hand and raised his glass, which contained eleven dollars' worth of sparkling water from Belgium. "To literature," he toasted.

"To literature," said Tommy, and took a gulp of water. "Which reminds me. I've got another project I want to talk to you about."

"Shoot," said Wolfowitz, tilting his head slightly to convey attention.

"It's Mack. He's got an idea for a new book."

"Sorry," said Wolfowitz blandly. "He hasn't earned out an advance in years. He's washed up."

"This is different," said Russo. "At least give me five minutes to tell you about it."

Wolfowitz sighed with resignation. "Five minutes," he said, consulting his watch.

Tommy began talking fast, describing Mack's mugging, his momentary death wish and the book idea it had inspired. As he spoke he saw that Wolfowitz was listening raptly. "You gotta admit, it's a helluva notion," Tommy concluded, pressing his advantage.

"Yeah, not bad. He's right about one thing—now that the baby boomers are figuring out that exercise and fiber aren't going to keep them alive forever, death's going to be big in publishing. But I don't know if it's for us—"

"He wants you," said Russo. "Says you're the only editor he trusts. You know how Mack is."

"I do," said Wolfowitz in a neutral tone. "I also know he hasn't written anything bigger than a *Sports Illustrated* piece in years. He spends all his time chasing girls and getting loaded at the Tiger like it's still 1975. I don't care how good the idea is, it's worthless if he doesn't produce."

"He'll produce," promised Tommy. "Look, I'm asking you as a favor. I'll give it to you for seventy-five thousand—"

"Plus how much for you?"

"Nothing," said Tommy waving his hand. "Just the regular 10 percent commission."

"Nothing?" said Wolfowitz. "This must mean a lot to you."

"It means a lot to him. He won't admit it, but he's desperate. He knows this is his last chance."

"He said that?"

"Not in so many words, but yeah, basically that's what he said."

Wolfowitz stared down at the snowy white tablecloth, lost in thought. "If I agree," he finally said, "it's on two conditions. First, I want to see his pages as he goes along, make sure he's actually working."

"Mack doesn't like to show his work until it's finished," said Tommy. "You know that."

"In that case—"

"No, no," said Russo quickly. "He'll agree this time. What else?"

"I don't want him telling anyone what he's working on."

"He probably wouldn't anyway, but why not?"

"Because I want to do it as a surprise. The return of Mack Green. Great media. Besides, if it's no good and we decide not to publish it, I don't want him humiliated."

Russo looked at Wolfowitz and saw a tight smile on his lips. He thought he knew the editor's full repertoire of fake expressions, but the hungry satisfaction he saw now was new and disconcertingly authentic. Tommy chose to interpret it as the look of a man happy to help out an old friend.

"I'm glad you're doing this," he said to Wolfowitz. "When you come down to it, neither one of us would be here if it wasn't for Mack. I owe him, you owe him. It's sort of our chance to pay Mack back."

"You're absolutely right," said Wolfowitz, taking a sip of water and wiping his mouth daintily with his crisp napkin. "Now I think about it, that's exactly what it is."

Four

One sweltering August afternoon in the summer of 1959, when Artie Wolfowitz was fifteen years old, he walked into Mike's Corner Grocery and asked Mike Stanislaw, a grumpy old immigrant in a dirty white apron that smelled of herring, for a vanilla Drumstick.

Mike thrust his left arm into the freezer and came out with a paper-wrapped Drumstick. "Cost you ten cents," he said, his right hand outstretched. The store was just down the street from the tiny clapboard house where Artie lived with his widowed mother; he had been shopping there ever since he was a small boy, but the old guy didn't care—he had an inflexible policy of holding on to the goods until he was paid.

Artie dug into his jeans, came up with a dime, all the money he had on him, and tossed it on the Formica counter. He took the Drumstick, began unwrapping it and saw that it was solid ice cream.

"Hey, Mike, there's no cone," he said, as the Drumstick began melting on his hand.

Mike shrugged. "That's the way it come," he said.

"There's supposed to be a cone. Look, I can't even hold it this way," said Artie. "Give me a different one."

"Another ten cents," said Mike, watching impassively as the ice cream dripped through Artie's fingers. "You got a problem, write to the factory, they give you the money back."

Artie stood facing the grocer, literally speechless with anger and frustration. Then he tossed the glob of ice cream on the counter and ran out of the store. He tried to tell himself it was only an ice-cream cone, but as the day wore on he grew more and more enraged that Mike, whom he had known all his life, would cheat and humiliate him for a dime.

The next day Artie got a small brown notebook and began a private boycott. He walked blocks out of his way to the Woolworth's in the shopping center to buy what he needed. When he passed Mike's, looked through the dirty windowpane and saw Mike inside, it warmed him to realize that the old bastard had no idea that he was the subject of a vendetta. He would find out, but only when Artie was ready.

The moment came in mid-October, when Artie walked into Mike's Corner Grocery for the first time in more than two months. He took out his notebook, laid it on the counter and looked the old man in the eye. "Remember that Drumstick you sold me? The one without the cone? You said to take it back to the factory."

Mike shrugged his fat shoulders, but it was clear from the look on his face that he hadn't forgotten.

"I decided not to shop here anymore," said Artie. "Maybe you noticed."

"Big deal," said Mike. "Who cares?"

Artie opened his notebook, where long columns of figures were neatly printed, a date alongside each amount. "Every time I buy something someplace else, I write it down in here," he said. "It's a record, like, of what it's costing you. Want to know how much?"

Mike peered at the notebook, trying to read upside down. Artie spun it around to make it easier. "Twenty-eight dollars and forty-six cents so far," he said, pointing to the bottom line. "Minus the dime you rooked me out of, that makes twenty-eight dollars and thirty-six cents."

"Big deal," Mike repeated.

"It will be," said Artie. He picked up his notebook and walked to the door. "I'll be back."

From then on Artie Wolfowitz made a practice of stopping by Mike's Corner Grocery on the first of each month to announce his updated total. At first, Mike displayed an exaggerated apathy, but as the amount began to grow he became visibly upset. In March, when the figure passed one hundred dollars, he lost control and chased Artie out of the store. "I'll be back next month, you dumb Polack," the boy yelled over his shoulder. "That Drumstick's going to cost you millions."

A few days later Artie was walking home from school when a blue Chevy pulled alongside and honked. He peered into the car and saw Mike's son, Stanley, behind the wheel. "Get in for a minute, I want to talk to you," he said.

Artie knew Stan, a pudgy, nearsighted guy in his mid-twenties, from around the neighborhood. "I'm here for a truce," he said. "This boycott of yours is driving my old man nuts."

"He asked for it," said Artie. "He screwed me out of a Drumstick."

"Jesus." Stan laughed. "A Drumstick costs a dime." He reached into his pocket and pulled out a five-dollar bill. "Here, that ought to make up for it, okay?"

Artie looked at the bill and shook his head. "First, let him apologize," he said, although he didn't really want an apology. The vendetta had become the most important thing in his life, and he had no intention of calling it off for five bucks.

"He's stubborn," said Stan, waving the money at Artie. "He won't apologize to a kid."

"Then fuck him," said Artie, reaching for the handle.

Stan put a soft, restraining hand on the boy's shoulder. His genial expression was replaced by a look of nearsighted concern. "He's an old man and you're making him sick," he said imploringly. "On the days you come in he can't even sleep. The doctor says it's bad for his blood pressure. What do you want to do, kill him?"

"I don't want anything," said Artie, pulling open the door and climbing out. "Tell him his Drumstick has cost him around a hundred and twenty bucks so far. I'll be in next week to give him the exact amount."

"Don't do this," said Stan, but Wolfowitz was already out of the car and running down the street, filled with a sense of triumph.

The following September, shortly after one of Artie's visits, Mike Stanislaw keeled over in the store: "Dead," in Gert Wolfowitz's hushed phrase, "before the poor man's head hit the meat counter." Artie was surprised to see that Mike's death deeply affected his widowed mother. "He was a good man," she said tearfully. "Despite his manner, he was always a gentleman."

"He was always a prick," Artie muttered under his breath so his mother wouldn't hear. He never used profanity in front of women, especially not her.

"I hope you'll come with me to the funeral," said Mrs. Wolfowitz. "We've known him for so long—"

"I need to take a walk," said Artie. He bounded out of the house, ran all the way to the park and collapsed on a bench near the baseball diamond. He knew he ought to feel remorse, but he didn't; in truth he was elated. Mike Stanislaw had humiliated and cheated him, and he, Artie Wolfowitz, had exacted justice. The fact that the war had started over an ice-cream cone meant nothing. Artie sat on the wooden bench feeling the cool September breeze on his face and experienced the exquisite satisfaction of total revenge.

After high school, Artie attended the local branch of the state university, near Buffalo, where he got an accounting degree. He was the first Wolfowitz to go to college, the first professional man in the family, and after graduating he took a job with a local firm, lived at home and supported his mother. It was a boring life but he didn't expect more.

Then, in the summer of 1972, Gert Wolfowitz discovered a lump under her left arm and eight weeks later she was dead. With nothing to hold him, Artie Wolfowitz moved to New York City, where he found a job monitoring sales figures in the marketing department of Gothic Books. He wasn't a reader, but the idea of working for a glamorous New York publisher appealed to him. He was especially drawn to the junior editors—graceful young men with carelessly elegant clothes and easy Ivy League manners, quick, good-looking women who dressed stylishly and joked about sex— but they made it clear with a cool politeness that they had no interest in socializing with a plain, unsophisticated bookkeeper from upstate nowhere.

One warm June evening after work, Artie wandered into the Flying Tiger, ordered a scotch-and-soda and sat self-consciously sipping his drink as he wistfully surveyed the scene. From his place at the bar, the Tiger seemed more like a clubhouse than a cocktail lounge. Everyone appeared to know one another, friendly insults were called from table to table and new arrivals got noisy, demonstrative greetings. From time to time Artie glanced at his watch to give the impression that he was waiting for someone, but nobody seemed to notice.

For something to do, Artie walked over to the jukebox and peered at the selections. His musical taste ran to Neil Diamond and Bobbie Gentry, and the songs, mostly by artists with names like Gatemouth and T-Bone, were unfamiliar. Randomly he hit some buttons and returned to the bar as a falsetto wail filled the room.

"All right! 'Mind Over Matter' by Nolan Strong and the Diablos!" he heard someone call with the exaggerated enunciation of a radio disc jockey. Artie turned and saw a tall, athletic young man with longish sandy hair and even, handsome features leap from his chair, pull the young woman next to him to her feet and begin dancing in the aisle. He was graceful and completely self-assured, singing along with the record so infectiously that several other couples rose to join him. He seemed different from the young sophisticates at Gothic, less Ivy League, more energetic and aggressive, like a high school homecoming king or the president of the student body.

When the song ended, the sandy-haired guy sauntered over to the bar, called out for a double bourbon on the rocks, climbed onto the stool next to Wolfowitz and slapped him lightly on the back. "Man, I love that song," he said in an easy, conversational way. "You must be from Detroit, right?"

"Upstate New York," said Wolfowitz. "A hick town you never heard of. What makes you say Detroit?"

"It's a Detroit song," he said. "An oldie. Most people around here don't know it, so I figured you might be from out there. I'm from a little hick town, too. Oriole, Michigan."

"Michigan," Wolfowitz repeated, unable to think of anything interesting to add. He was flattered by the guy's friendliness, but disconcerted and a little distrustful, too. It occurred to him that he might be getting hustled or, worse, laughed at.

"Otto, give this man a drink," the sandy-haired guy told the bartender. "Anybody who appreciates Nolan Strong and the Diablos deserves a drink." He extended his hand. "My name's Mack Green, by the way."

"Artie Wolfowitz. Are you Mack Green the writer?"

"Yep," said Mack without affectation. "That's me. What do you do?"

"I work at Gothic Books," said Wolfowitz, hoping that Green would mistake him for an editor.

"Ah, so that's how you know my name," said Mack. Wolfowitz took it for false modesty; *Bragging Rights* and its young author were the talk of the publishing world. "What do you do over there?"

"I'm on the, ah, business side," said Wolfowitz. "Actually, I'm an accountant." He expected a dismissive reaction but Mack surprised him by slapping him on the back once more.

"The only people I know in this town are editors and writers," he said. "And girls. I never get a chance to talk to anybody normal. An accountant. That means you know where the ninety cents goes."

"What ninety cents?"

"The ninety cents out of every dollar I earn that the publisher keeps."

"You only get 10 percent?"

"Other authors get more?"

Wolfowitz shrugged. "Some do."

"I knew I was getting fleeced," said Mack, although he seemed more amused than upset. "Hey, grab your drink and join us. I want you to explain this shit to me."

Wolfowitz followed Mack to his table, where he was introduced to half a dozen people whose names he didn't catch. "Artie's the vice president of the New York City branch of the Nolan Strong fan club," Green told them. "He also works at Gothic. Be nice to him and he'll tell you how publishing really operates."

Artie Wolfowitz never learned why Mack had singled him out that evening, and for a long time he suspected some ulterior motive. Eventually, though, he accepted the friendship and his role in it as Mack's sidekick. It was a role Artie didn't mind a bit, especially since Mack was a generous and charming patron. He called Artie "Stealth" in tribute to his supposed business acumen, brought him into the inner circle at the Tiger and included him in his restless midnight pub crawls and pick-up expeditions. Together they careened through the city meeting beautiful women, drinking with celebrities and eccentrics, crashing parties where they were always welcomed, Mack constantly running and laughing and emanating an aura of joyful exuberance, Wolfowitz trailing happily in his wake.

His friendship with Mack had a galvanizing effect not only on Artie Wolfowitz's social life, but on his career. The young snobs at Gothic began treating him with respect. Even Douglas Floutie, who had recently acquired a controlling interest in the firm, took notice. One day he stopped the heretofore invisible young accountant in the hall and asked him to tell Mack how much he admired his work. "Let him know that Gothic is the kind of house that appreciates fine writing," he said.

Wolfowitz debated a long time about delivering the message—he was afraid Mack might think he was exploiting their friendship—but in the end it was Green himself who brought up the subject.

"I'm just about done with *The Oriole Kid*," he told Wolfowitz one night at the Tiger. "You think Gothic might be interested?"

"What's the matter with the publisher you've got?"

"Not aggressive enough," said Mack. "Besides, the editor I want is at Gothic."

"Who's that?"

"You," said Mack.

Wolfowitz burst out laughing. "Me? What the hell do I know about editing? I haven't read ten books since high school."

"I don't need Max Perkins," said Mack. Wolfowitz nodded, although he had no idea who Max Perkins was. "Giving me a literary editor is like giving Willie Mays a batting coach, it'd just mess up my style. I can write the books without any help. What I need is somebody who can sell 'em."

"What makes you think I could do that? I don't know anything about marketing or publicity. I'm a bookkeeper."

"So become a book*maker*. Look, the editor I've got now at Marathon takes me to lunch and talks about the goddamn French existentialists. He told me that great books sell themselves. You think great books sell themselves?"

Wolfowitz shook his head.

"Fuckin' A," said Mack. "We're a couple of smalltown boys, Stealth. You know about money and you'll pick up the rest as you go along. The main thing is, I trust you. I know you'll fight for me."

"Even if I wanted to, they'd never go along at Gothic," said Wolfowitz.

"They'll go along," Mack assured him. "Set me up an appointment with Floutie and you'll see."

Much to Wolfowitz's amazement, Mack was right; Floutie, after reading part of his new manuscript, agreed to the arrangement. He invited his newest editor and his newest author into his wood-paneled office, poured them each a stingy portion of sherry and raised his glass. "My dear Green, my dear Wolfowitz," he said in his acquired British accent, "let us toast a long and artistically profitable relationship."

"Floutie's a real fruit fly," Mack remarked that evening at the Flying Tiger. "What'd he do, inherit the company?"

"Close," said Wolfowitz. "His wife's father is Harlan Fassbinder."

"Who's he?"

"You've never heard of the Prince of Poultry? He's the biggest chicken grower in the country."

"And he bought Gothic for Floutie? He must love his ass," said Mack.

"I think he just wants to keep him out of the poultry business," said Wolfowitz. "Floutie's an ex-prof from Princeton. He knows about money like I do about Shakespeare. The old man probably figured that he couldn't lose too much publishing books."

"As long as *we* don't lose, that's all I care about," said Mack with an intensity that surprised Wolfowitz; it was part of Mack Green's style never to seem too serious about anything, especially his own career. But there was no mistaking his seriousness now, or his determination. "I'm counting on you to make *The Oriole Kid* a bestseller."

Wolfowitz remained silent and after a moment Mack grinned. "You missed your line. You were supposed to say, 'I'll do my best.' "

"Not my best," said Wolfowitz grimly. "Whatever it takes."

Five

Wolfowitz kept his promise. He worked twenty-hour days, browbeating the Gothic sales force into pushing *The Oriole Kid,* cajoling bookstores and the chains into increasing their orders, fighting his former colleagues for promotional dollars and constantly screaming at the hapless people in the Gothic PR department to get Mack Green more ink, more TV guest shots, more attention.

Inexperience liberated Wolfowitz from the genteel conventions of the publishing business. Books to him were not literature, not art, not even entertainment—they were gym shoes, breakfast cereal, a commodity in a wrapper to be hawked and hyped. As he worked frenzied days and nights on behalf of *The Oriole Kid,* he found he had an instinct for seeing—or creating—marketing and promotional schemes and gimmicks that older, more traditional editors never would have imagined. His personal favorite was talking the PR guy of the New York Yankees into letting Mack, the Oriole Kid himself, pitch in an exhibition game and then buying enough drinks and dinners for sportswriters to turn it into a national media event and a segment on *Wide World of Sports*.

The day after Mack's baseball debut—which consisted of two walks, a wild pitch and a hilarious pick-off move to first that landed in the stands—Wolfowitz got a call from Harlan Fassbinder. "I hear you're the genius got some book writer of mine on TV last night," he said without preliminaries.

"It was my idea, yessir," said Wolfowitz.

"Floutie don't think it's dignified," Fassbinder said.

"He's probably right, but it's going to sell a lot of books," Wolfowitz replied.

"That's what you think is important, is it?" snapped Fassbinder in a challenging tone.

"Yessir, I do," said Wolfowitz, trying to keep his voice steady.

"Well, goddamnit Wolfowitz, so do I," squawked the King of Poultry. "It's about time I got myself a real rooster up there at Gothic. I'm keeping my eye on you." The phone went dead and Artie Wolfowitz sat at his desk with the receiver in his hand, feeling the thrill of the old man's approval. No one had ever called him a rooster before.

Unlike his father-in-law, Douglas Floutie was unhappy with the flurry of unconventional publicity surrounding *The Oriole Kid*. "Gimmicks, as you call them, are all well and good," he told Wolfowitz, "but you'll discover that serious reviews ultimately make a book and a writer's career. Mack Green is a considerable literary talent and with time he may develop into a truly important artist. I don't want him presented to the public as a buffoon."

Wolfowitz fought back an urge to tell Floutie about his conversation with old man Fassbinder. There was no point in making an enemy, and besides, he realized that Floutie had a point. The reviews would still be critical to the book's success.

"How do you fix a review in the *Times*?" he asked Leon Goldman, one of Gothic's senior editors, over lunch at Antonelli's.

Goldman stared at him for a long moment through filmy gray eyes and said, "Pardon me?"

"How do you make sure a book gets reviewed the right way over there?"

"I'm going to pretend I didn't hear that," said Goldman stiffly.

"In that case, I'm going to pretend I didn't hear myself invite you to lunch," said Wolfowitz. "Pick up the tab yourself." He hurried back to his office and called Fred Banner, an occasional drinking buddy who worked in the *Times* accounting department. "Who do you know at the *Book Review*?" he asked.

"You gotta be kidding," said Banner. "How would I know any of those Ivy League turds?"

"I'm talking about one of us, a secretary, a typist, somebody who would appreciate five hundred dollars."

"For doing what?"

"For telling me who's been assigned to review Mack Green's novel. It's called *The Oriole Kid,* and it'll be out in a few weeks."

"That's industrial espionage," said Banner.

"Seven fifty," said Wolfowitz.

"You'll be hearing from me," Banner said.

The Oriole Kid had been assigned for review to a novelist of good reputation and modest commercial success named Walter T. Horton. Horton was originally from Mississippi, but he now lived in Manhattan, in a dicey neighborhood not far from Columbia. Wolfowitz arranged to meet him in a bar called the Urban Pioneer not far from the campus.

"I've been wanting to meet you for a long time," Wolfowitz said. "I'm a fan of yours."

"That puts you in a small but distinguished company, sir," said the author in a stagy, effeminate southern drawl that didn't conceal his delight.

"Not so small," said Wolfowitz. "There's a lot of people who admire your books. There ought to be a lot more. Are you working on something now?"

"As a matter of fact I am," said Horton.

"I imagine you've already got a publisher."

"Several houses are interested," said Horton. "I really can't say more than that."

"Well, I'd like you to consider coming over to Gothic," said Wolfowitz. "I don't know what your last advance was"—he paused and scratched his head in a gesture meant to convey his embarrassment at talking to an artist about money—"and I'm not crass enough to ask, but let's say, for the sake of argument, it was in the fifty-thousand ballpark." He raised his eyebrows to show that he considered this a shrewd guess and Horton smiled coyly. Actually Wolfowitz was certain that Horton had never gotten half that much. "If the book you're working on now is as good as the last ones, I might be able to do better than that."

"I'd be happy to show you the manuscript," said Horton. "Truly I would."

"Would you mind if I gave it to someone else, for an opinion?"

"Well . . ."

"You probably know him. Mack Green?"

A cloud of doubt and suspicion passed over Walter T. Horton's face. "I've seen him at the Flying Tiger from time to time but I don't really know him."

"Mack's the one who put me on to you in the first place," said Wolfowitz. "He thinks you're the most unappreciated writer of your generation."

"Is that a fact?" said Horton, torn between ethics and ego, suspicion and greed.

"Truth is, I'm not really much of a literary expert," said Wolfowitz. "My thing is selling books and making money. I wouldn't even be an editor if it wasn't for Mack."

Walter T. Horton searched Artie Wolfowitz's earnest, innocent face and allowed himself to believe that the editor's sudden interest in him was a coincidence. "I guess it would be all right," he said slowly, "but I wouldn't want anyone to know."

"Mum's the word," said Wolfowitz, pressing his index finger to his lips.

The day *The Oriole Kid* came out, five hundred hired street peddlers dressed in Yankee uniforms passed out autographed pictures of the author in front of bookstores around the country. That night Green appeared on the *Tonight Show* with Mickey Mantle, who called him "a major-league scribbler." Floutie was almost incoherent with anger and embarrassment—until he read Walter T. Morton's full-page review in the *Times* on Sunday, which included these lines: "It's probably too early to compare Mack Green with Mark Twain, but in his remarkable new novel, Green has given us a fictional hero, the Oriole Kid, who is a contemporary cousin to Huck Finn and Tom Sawyer . . . "

The Oriole Kid hit the bestseller list in its first week, rose to number one and stayed there for four months. The day Mack's picture appeared on the cover of *Time,* Douglas Floutie promoted Wolfowitz to senior editor and Harlan Fassbinder sent Mack and Artie each a crate of frozen chickens. To Wolfowitz's he appended a handwritten note: "Goddamn," it said, "I knew you were a rooster."

A few weeks after the *Time* cover, an article on Artie "Wolfwitz" was published in *The Wall Street Journal.* It hailed him as "a new-breed editor who knows how to read a balance sheet as well as a manuscript." It was the first time that Wolfowitz had ever seen his name in the newspaper and even the fact that it had been misspelled didn't detract from his pleasure.

That night Mack arrived at the Tiger with a woman named Louise Frank. "I thought you two ought to get to know each other," he said. "Louise is a writer, too."

Wolfowitz tried to smile, but he felt as though his face was frozen. Louise Frank was the most beautiful woman he had ever seen. He stared at her and Mack, trying to figure out their relationship. With Mack it was never clear. He flirted with every good-looking woman he met, slept with most and refused to take any of them seriously. He would go to great lengths to charm and seduce a woman, but he was completely unpossessive about his conquests. "There's plenty to go around," he often told Artie. "If you see someone you want, just help yourself."

It was an offer that Wolfowitz had never accepted. He had a straitlaced, secretly romantic attitude toward sex and found the idea of swapping women like sweaters distasteful. Besides, he was sure that the kind of women attracted to Mack wouldn't be interested in him. Artie had accepted this as a fact, without envy or resentment. Until Louise.

"I think Stealth's in love," said Mack, looking at the stunned expression on his friend's face. Wolfowitz blushed deeply but said nothing; he didn't trust his voice.

"Well, that was quick." Louise laughed. "I can't wait to see what happens next."

From that night on, Artie Wolfowitz divided his energies and wiles between promoting Mack and pursuing Louise Frank. He tolerated her capricious independence and her infidelities, sent her exotic flowers and expensive jewelry, praised her writing and humbly obeyed her commands (a new wardrobe, a different haircut, replacing Artie with Arthur). He also bought a still-unfinished book of her short stories for fifteen thousand dollars. Luckily for Wolfowitz, Floutie was impressed with her Radcliffe prose and authorized the deal, but even if he hadn't, Wolfowitz was prepared to pay the advance out of his own savings.

On her twenty-fifth birthday, they went to dinner at the Rainbow Room. After three cocktails, Wolfowitz reached into his pocket and with a trembling hand produced her birthday gift—a diamond engagement ring.

"If I take this, it means I have to marry you, doesn't it?" she said lightly.

"Don't tease me," he said. "I can't take it anymore."

"All right then," she said, "here are my terms. I want a kid right away and a nanny to take care of him so I can go on writing.

And I don't want you to have any fantasies about the little woman waiting for you to come home at night. That's not me. If I marry you, I intend to have an independent career and an independent personal life. Understood?"

Wolfowitz nodded, so overwhelmed with emotion that he couldn't speak; so overwhelmed, in fact, that for the first time in his life he failed to grasp exactly what he was being told.

A less love-struck, less cynical man would have wondered why a woman as beautiful and desirable as Louise Frank would agree to marry him. Wolfowitz attributed it to his growing professional importance, his persistence and Louise's recent, almost obsessive desire for a child.

In this he was partly correct; Louise Frank was almost two months pregnant when she accepted his proposal. Of the possible fathers—a movie critic married to her cousin, a South American novelist named, she was pretty sure, Ramone, her tennis coach, her tennis coach's friend, who had been visiting from Denver, and Artie—Wolfowitz was the only one who would conceivably marry her.

The ceremony was held at City Hall, with Mack acting as best man. Afterward they repaired to the Tiger for a raucous celebration hosted by Otto. Wolfowitz, drunk on champagne, played "Mind Over Matter" on the jukebox, draped his arm over Mack's shoulder and pulled him close. "I love you, I just want you to know that," he slurred. "I love Louise and I love you. You're my family." He leaned over and kissed Mack wetly on the cheek.

"Yeah, right." Mack grinned, embarrassed by the uncharacteristic show of affection.

"No, I mean it, Mack, I really mean it. I love you. Honest to God, I really mean it. Do you believe me that I mean it?"

"Sure, I love you too, Stealth," he said.

"Naw, you don't love anybody," said Wolfowitz with drunken insight. "Everybody loves you but you don't love a goddamned soul."

Six

Not long after Wolfowitz's marriage, Mack met Tomas Russo. Their first encounter took place in the confessional at St. Frederick's, where Tommy was serving as junior priest and all-purpose workhorse under Francis X. Dorsey, the laziest pastor in New York. Tommy got all the parish scut work, but the job he hated most was hearing confessions. It infuriated him that shrinks and talk-show hosts got paid big money for listening to the same kind of sordid crap he had to hear for free.

And so Tommy Russo had been in a foul mood when Mack Green slipped into the booth and said, "Forgive me, Father, for I have sinned." Russo, who had perfect pitch for the sound of Catholic contrition, instantly recognized from the tentative inflection that the man on the other side of the screen had never been inside a confessional in his life.

It wasn't unusual for non-Catholics to turn up at confession—

the city was filled with nutcases, curiosity seekers and street people looking for a warm place to sit down. They filled Tommy with rage, because they were trying to beat the system—and since he was a part of the system, to beat him. It was one of his rules not to get beat and over the course of his short career he had developed ways of handling the deadbeats.

"What can I do for you, my son?" he said, stepping up the Brooklyn in his voice.

"I've sinned, Father," said Mack.

"Yeah, you already mentioned that. You wanna be more specific?"

There was a long pause. "I've, ah, had sexual intercourse with the wife of my best friend."

"How many times?"

"A few times. I'm not positive."

"A few times in the same night, or a few different times? Don't lie, I can tell."

"A few different times."

"Are you sorry?"

"Of course I'm sorry," said Mack. "That's why I'm here."

Tommy smiled to himself—he had the guy going now. "You gonna do it again or what?"

"I might. I don't know."

"Yeah, well, you sound real sorry. You got anything else?"

"Not really."

"Okay, close the door on the way out."

"Aren't you going to, ah, prescribe any penance?"

"For what, sthupping your buddy's old lady? Okay, I hereby sentence you to see *The Sound of Music* three straight times. That ought to take your mind off poontang."

"Hey, what kind of thing is that for a priest to say?"

"You got complaints, call the Vatican. The number's in the book."

"You're not really a priest, are you?"

"What's it to ya? You're not a Catholic anyway."

"What makes you say that?"

"Get outta here," said Tommy. "You think I don't recognize a Protestant voice when I hear one?"

"Protestant voice?" Mack said, laughing. "What does a Protestant sound like?"

"Very much like this," said Tommy, raising his gravelly voice an octave and flattening his vowels in a good imitation of Mack's Midwestern drawl. Green laughed again and the priest said, "Okay, pal, show's over. Scram."

"Wait a minute," said Mack. "I didn't mean to be disrespectful. I'm a writer and I just wanted to find out what going to confession is like. It's for one of my characters."

"Oh yeah? What kind of writer?" asked Tommy, suddenly interested.

"A novelist. My name's Mack Green."

"Mack Green," Tommy mused. "I've heard of you. *The Oreo Kid,* right?"

"Oriole," said Mack.

"Hey, nice to meet ya," said the priest. "I don't get too many celebrities in here. My name's Tommy Russo."

"Not Father Tommy?"

"I'm twenty-eight years old," he said. "You gotta be about that, right?"

"Twenty-nine," said Mack.

"Well, you wanna call me Father, go ahead."

"What I'd really like to do is buy you a beer and ask you some questions."

"You mean like a consultant? Yeah, why not? 'Course I can't mention names or anything—"

"I know that much," said Mack.

"I can spring loose in about an hour," said Tommy. "There's a place on East Broadway, Brady's. We could meet there."

"Great," said Mack. "How will I recognize you?"

"Just be on the lookout for a little Italian guy in a black leather jacket."

"A black leather jacket?"

"I don't go to bars in my clericals," said Tommy. "Besides, I wasn't born a priest, ya know?"

At Brady's, Tommy ordered a dry martini, which seemed to him like a sophisticated choice, while Mack downed double bourbons with seemingly no effect and grilled him about his life. Delighted to be in the company of a famous young author, pleased to talk about himself for a change, Russo eagerly told Mack about his boyhood in a spit-on-the-sidewalk part of Bensonhurst, his days at the seminary and his increasingly onerous duties at St. Fred's. "In the beginning I expected people to come in and confess to murders, like they do in the movies," he confided, "but all I get is: 'Father, I have impure thoughts, Father, I jerked off three times, Father, I told my kittycat a lie—' "

"You mind if I tell you something about yourself? Something personal?" Mack asked.

"Sure, why not?" said Tommy, feeling the gin. It seemed to him that Mack Green was the most interesting listener he had ever met.

"You don't seem like a priest."

"You mean like Bing Crosby in *Going My Way*? Yeah, I guess you're right, I'm not really cut out for it."

"Then why'd you become one?"

"Runs in the family," Tommy said. "My uncle's a priest, my older brother's a priest and I got two sisters are nuns. I never really gave it much thought. One day I'm hanging out on the corner with the guys, singing, "Run Around Sue," and then, bing-bang, I'm in the seminary. Just like that."

"You didn't have to go," said Mack. "It's a free country."

"Where *you* live maybe it is," said Tommy. "Not in my family. Besides, with the draft and all, the deferment seemed like a good deal."

"There were easier ways to get out of Vietnam," said Mack. "Get a letter from a shrink. Cut off your toe. Anything's gotta be better than—"

"What, celibacy?"

"Well—"

"Don't worry, everybody's curious," said Tommy. "It's a part of the mystique. Truth is, it's no big deal. I mean, I'm not a homo, I get the urge just like anybody else, but usually I can handle it okay."

"What happens when you can't?"

"Then I go outta town and get laid," said Tommy.

"Are you supposed to admit that?" asked Mack, slightly shocked; he had an atheist's awe of holy vows.

"It's funny," said Tommy. "You come to me for confession and here I am confessing to you. It doesn't matter, though; I'm quitting."

"When did you decide that?"

"Just now, when I said it. But it's been building up."

"Can you do that? Walk away?"

"Hey, we're not talking Mafia here. The pope isn't going to put out a contract on me. I'll leave just before Easter and let that lazy bastard Dorsey do some work for a change." The thought of Father Francis X. Dorsey chaperoning the St. Fred's High School spring hop made Tommy grunt with pleasure.

"Why not sleep on it?" said Mack with real concern.

"Naw, like I said, I've been thinking about it for a couple of years." He took another sip of his martini and smiled. "Ever since my draft lottery number came up 346."

"What about all your uncles and sisters and—"

"They'll survive," said Tommy. "It's like Sinatra says, I gotta do it my way. Ever since I was a little kid I've had guilt stuffed down my throat. And for the last few years I've been stuffing it down other people's throats. But, hard as I try, I can't feel guilty about this. I'm not priest material and that's that."

"What are you going to do? For a living, I mean?"

"I got a cousin in Jersey City sells life insurance. I can probably catch on with him for a while. After that, who knows? Other guys get by, I figure I can too."

"You ever think about becoming an agent?"

"Like James Bond? Double O Seven? I don't think I got the right accent."

"I meant a literary agent."

"A literary agent? I don't even know what a literary agent does."

"Not much," said Mack. "You basically negotiate for authors with publishers."

"What makes you think I could do that?"

"You'd be a natural. You're a smart guy, likable. And you know when you're getting bullshitted. Like today at confession."

"Yeah, but that comes from experience—"

"You've got the experience," said Mack, warming to the idea. "A literary agent's basically just a middleman, same as a priest. Only instead of making deals for sinners with God, you make 'em with editors who just *think* they're God. They'd be a pushover for a guy like you who's used to dealing with the real thing."

Tommy thought about it for a moment. "What kind of dough do they make?"

"Ten percent of whatever their clients get, usually," said Mack.

"Sounds like a piece of cake," said Tommy. "Providing you got clients, that is."

Mack looked at Tommy and wondered what would happen to a priest who quit and became a literary agent. Turning real people into fictional characters was instinctive to Mack, and when he came across the right ones, professionally profitable. Tommy Russo was one of those people.

"I'll make you a deal," he said. "Right now I've got a proposal for a new novel called *Light Years*. It's with my editor at Gothic, Artie Wolfowitz. He's offering an eighty-thousand-dollar advance.

I want a hundred. Get it for me and I'll take you on as my agent. How about it?"

"What the hell do you need me for?" asked Tommy. "You already know the guy."

Mack grinned. "He's my best friend, which is why I can't negotiate with him. I don't want to fight with him over money. You fight with him."

Tommy returned the grin, but his mind was on the phrase "my best friend." Earlier Mack had confessed that he was sleeping with his best friend's wife. "Just out of curiosity, aren't you worried about this Wolfowitz finding out about you and his old lady?"

"It's no big thing," said Mack, frowning. "Just recreational sex, that's all."

"Yeah, then why did you pick that particular thing to confess?"

Mack laughed. "I figured it was the kind of thing a priest would consider a sin," he said. "I didn't know I'd run into one who gets laid in Poughkeepsie."

"I'm not so sure you're right about this Wolfowitz," said Tommy. "I'm just a wop from Bensonhurst, but where I come from, when a guy buddy-fucks his best friend there's usually trouble."

"That's another reason you'll make a great agent," said Mack. "You've got primal Sicilian instincts. So, have we got a deal?"

"Yeah, I'll give it a shot," said Tommy, extending his hand. For years he had been dreaming of a way out of the priesthood and now a stranger named Mack Green was offering him one. He was drawn to the young author's careless charm, but it was the money that excited him—10 percent of a hundred thousand bucks seemed like a fortune. If the agent thing didn't work, he could always go into the insurance business, but for that kind of dough it was worth taking a flyer. Looking back later, Tommy Russo realized that it was at that precise moment that he stopped being a priest and became a player.

Seven

As a new husband, Artie Wolfowitz spent his time and money indulging his pregnant wife. He went into debt to rent a place on Central Park West large enough for a nursery and a study for Louise, took her to expensive restaurants and Broadway openings, watered and fed her supercilious artistic friends. She responded with an offhanded affection that more than satisfied him. Louise Frank was a prize, greater than any he had dreamed of attaining, and he never awoke in the morning without a feeling of intense love and amazement at his good fortune.

The birth of Josh, seven months after the wedding, brought changes. Louise, who had passionately wanted a child, now insisted that an English nanny move in to care for him, and she paid the infant what Wolfowitz considered scant attention. She also limited their sex life to an occasional, grudging quickie. And, for the first time in their marriage, Louise began to go out at night on her own.

"I'm a writer, Arthur, not a hausfrau," she told him. "I need stimulation."

"Why can't we be stimulated together?" he asked plaintively.

"You're such a dominant personality, I don't feel like myself with you around," she explained in an appeasing tone. "I need to have my own experiences."

Even in his love-besotted state, Wolfowitz understood that these experiences might include other men. He reminded himself that he had agreed to allow her an independent life, told himself that he was a bigtime New York editor now, and should be sufficiently sophisticated to accept his wife's liberated lifestyle. And then he went out and hired a private investigator named Edgar Conlon to find out what Louise was doing in her spare time.

Conlon's report took six weeks to compile and it was worse than anything Wolfowitz had imagined. It included dates, times and the names of five men. Four of those names meant nothing to Wolfowitz. The fifth was Mack Green.

"Are you absolutely sure?" Wolfowitz asked the detective.

Conlon, a retired New York detective with a large nose and bad dentures, nodded. "I got pictures," he said, with the impersonal cheer of a man selling hot dogs at a ballpark.

"I don't want to see any pictures," said Wolfowitz, feeling numb.

"They don't cost that much, especially when you consider what they could save you in a divorce settlement," said Conlon. "And you wouldn't need the entire gallery. Probably just one or two guys would be plenty."

"There's not going to be a divorce," said Wolfowitz, more to himself than to the detective. His numbness was thawing, replaced by a humiliated rage. At that moment he made two irrevocable decisions. He would forgive Louise because he loved her too much to lose her. And he would take his revenge by ruining Mack Green's life.

• • •

Wolfowitz's strategy for keeping his wife was to make himself indispensable to her. As an anniversary gift he published her collection of short stories, *Village Idiots,* lavishing on it the ingenuity, attention and money he had once given *The Oriole Kid.* The book sold well despite lukewarm reviews and Louise was astute enough to see that its success was due to her husband's efforts. That realization altered the balance of power between them.

"You've given me a wonderful anniversary present," she told him one night in bed. "I wonder what you'd like from me."

"I'd like for you to stop going out alone so much," he said. "I worry about you. Besides, I don't think so much socializing is good for your career."

"I wouldn't want you to worry," said Louise, aware that a transaction was taking place. She snuggled against him and kissed his neck. "I'll stay home more at night if you want me to."

Wolfowitz noted the "at night" but decided to let it pass; he didn't want to make life intolerable for Louise. He knew that there was something perverse about the overpowering passion he felt for her, but he didn't care. In a way he even took pride in it, the pride of a square man in his secret kinkiness.

Wolfowitz's campaign against Mack Green was more surreptitious. Since his marriage, the two men no longer spent their evenings together but they still met for lunch at least once a week. Wolfowitz was careful not to display any outward signs of hostility, and Mack's obliviousness to impending disaster sharpened the pleasure of anticipation; Artie knew it was only a matter of time before he got his chance to get even.

Opportunity arrived in the rotund form of Tommy Russo. "I wanna talk to you about Mack's new book," he said. "See if we can come to some arrangement."

"I don't see why not," said Wolfowitz genially. He was aware that Mack had recently picked Russo up the same way *he* had once been chosen and for the same purpose, as a combination servant-sidekick. He also knew that the little ex-priest didn't know a thing about the book business.

"Mack told me what you want to pay. It's not enough," Russo said.

"How much did you have in mind?"

"A hundred," said Tommy, as if he dealt with six figures every day.

"I'm not going to give you a hundred," said Wolfowitz. "I'm going to write my offer on this piece of paper and let you read it." He scribbled a number, handed it to Russo and watched his face melt into greedy amazement.

The number Russo saw was $250,000.

"It's a two-book deal. A quarter of a million dollars for each of the next two Mack Green novels. Fair enough?"

"Jeez," Russo said, fingering his shirt where his clerical collar had been. Wolfowitz could see his dark eyes calculating his $25,000 commission. "Jeez, I dunno."

"I know you don't," said Wolfowitz. "You're probably thinking that if I'm willing to pay this much, I might pay more, that maybe you asked for too little." He raised his eyebrows in a gesture that invited confirmation, peered at Tommy and saw that he had guessed right. "It's not too little, it's too much, but offering too much this time is smart business, for two reasons. Since you're just starting out, and because we're both friends of Mack's, I'm going to explain why. Don't worry, I won't bullshit you, you can believe me. All right?"

Russo nodded, watching Wolfowitz's face closely. His years in the priesthood had taught him to be wary of people who said "believe me."

"First, I've got a huge investment in Mack and I want to keep him here at Gothic. The book business is changing, authors are starting to get big money. If I sign Mack for too little this time, he'll feel like he can do better someplace else. I wouldn't want that to happen."

"Makes sense," said Tommy. "What's the second reason?"

"The second reason is you," said Wolfowitz. "I want to do you a favor."

"What for? If you don't mind my asking?"

"Because I want you to owe me," said Wolfowitz. "When word of this deal gets around town, you're going to be a hot agent. I want to see your best books first, to negotiate with you in the spirit of mutual understanding."

"Mutual understanding meaning?" The phrase reminded Russo of the oily euphemisms of the Bensonhurst wise guys.

"Just that," Wolfowitz said smoothly. "I'm sure as you get to know the business, you'll see the value of a good relationship with a publisher like Gothic."

"Two hundred and fifty thousand," said Tommy, his eyes drawn back to the number on the paper.

Wolfowitz arranged his face in a friendly smile. "Don't worry," he said, "I'll get my money's worth."

There were many ways that Wolfowitz could have killed Mack Green's career, but he opted for slow strangulation. He brought out *Light Years* the same week that Norman Mailer and John Updike published their new novels, guaranteeing it secondary reviews. He allowed the PR department to do a slovenly job, booking Mack on second-rate shows and locking him into a long, pointless book tour. And he discreetly hinted to several friendly journalists that the book, if not exactly a turkey, was not the masterpiece Mack's fans had expected. Predictably, the bad word-of-mouth and Gothic's indifferent effort made an impression. The bookstore chains, for example, halved their initial orders. Wolfowitz made sure this fact leaked out, along with a rumor, which he strenuously denied, that Gothic was thinking about canceling the second half of Green's contract.

Despite Wolfowitz's assurance that the recession was to blame, Mack was taken aback by the poor showing of *Light Years*. Outwardly he maintained his usual self-confidence, but he had never experienced failure before and he didn't quite know what to make of it. For months he did little but hang around the Tiger, drinking too much and trying to get up the energy to write.

A year or so after the *Light Years* debacle, Mack met Wolfowitz for lunch at Antonelli's. "I've got some great news," he said. "I started work on the new book, *Three to Get Ready*. It's about three buddies who go off to Vietnam, come back to their hometown and kill the members of the draft board one by one. What do you think?"

"A murder mystery?"

"Come on, Stealth, since when do I write mysteries?" Mack demanded. "It's a Mack Green novel. I've got ten thousand words already and it's the best thing I've ever done. You're going to make back what you lost on the last one and then some. I'll send over what I've got, let you take a look at it. Maybe you can come up with some brilliant marketing ideas."

"I can't wait to get my hands on it," said Wolfowitz.

When the uncompleted manuscript arrived, Wolfowitz saw that Mack was right—it was terrific, funny and scary at the same time, full of improbable characters and vividly written scenes. He put it in his desk drawer and waited three days for Green to call.

"You read it?" he demanded in an exuberant tone.

"Yes," said Wolfowitz flatly. "I did."

"Well?"

Wolfowitz let the question hang in the air for a long moment and then cleared his throat. "I, ah, think we might have a problem. I'm no literary expert, you know that better than anybody, but the thing just doesn't seem to flow. It's kind of ponderous."

"Ponderous? That's not one of your words. Did you show it to somebody by any chance?"

"To tell you the truth," lied Wolfowitz, "I did show it to a couple of people and they thought—"

"That it's ponderous?"

"Fuck it, Mack, they don't have to be right, you know—"

"Who'd you show it to?"

"I'd rather not say. They're at other houses and I don't want to embarrass anybody."

"You showed my manuscript to editors from other houses? What are you, looking for someone to take it off your hands?"

"Don't be ridiculous," said Wolfowitz in a tone of transparent insincerity.

"Ponderous," repeated Green, tasting the ugly word in his mouth and feeling a frozen sliver of self-doubt in his stomach.

"You want my advice, forget it," said Wolfowitz. "Hell, you were writing bestsellers when these guys were screwing coeds."

"Yeah, maybe. Let me take another look, see if I can lighten it up a little."

"It might not be a bad idea," said Wolfowitz. He hung up and rubbed his hands together with genuine satisfaction. The old Mack Green wouldn't have worried about the opinion of a hundred editors.

It took six years, fourteen drafts and a hundred and ten cases of Jack Daniels for Mack to finish *Three to Get Ready,* and by that time both his manuscript and his personal life were a mess. He married—and quickly divorced—a bulemic fashion model named Sippy Downes who fleeced him in the settlement. To pay his bills he took on magazine assignments which he often failed to complete. At a small college in New Jersey he was laughed off the podium when he showed up drunk.

Wolfowitz followed the breakdown of Mack's private life with pleasure, but his real satisfaction came with the savage reception accorded *Three to Get Ready*. The *Times* review, written by Walter T. Horton, now a Gothic author himself, called it "an oddly tentative and flat work, full of uninteresting characters in dull situations. . . . A bitter disappointment for those of us who have been waiting anxiously for Green to return to form. If *Three to Get Ready* is any indication, it may be a long wait indeed."

With reviews like this, Wolfowitz didn't need to do much to ensure the commercial failure of *Three to Get Ready*. When the bookstores began returning copies, he summoned Tommy Russo.

"We've got a total fiasco on our hands," he said.

"I know it," said Tommy. "The good news is, Mack's working on something really special. He'll rebuild his career, I guarantee you."

"Not at Gothic, he won't," said Wolfowitz. "Floutie told me not to spend another cent on him. I'm sorry, Tommy, but he's finished here."

By this time Tommy Russo had learned a good deal about his profession. He knew, for example, that Wolfowitz, recently promoted to editor in chief, had a special relationship with Harlan Fassbinder and didn't take orders from Floutie. He knew that Gothic's decision to drop Mack would make it hard to find him another major publisher for decent money. And he knew it would be stupid to damage his own relationship with Stealth Wolfowitz by finding out too much about what really happened to Mack's last two novels.

"Jeez, I'm sorry about this," Tommy said to Mack over drinks at the Flying Tiger. "I don't care what the critics say, I still think it was a hell of a book."

"Yeah, well," said Mack, draining a bourbon. For once he seemed discouraged.

"You're having a bad run," said Tommy. "Your luck will change. Just keep writing, and when you've got something, let me know."

"I will," Mack promised, but he didn't. Instead he went to Ireland for ten months, spent most of his time in the taverns of Dublin, came back to New York and resumed his routine. From time to time he roused himself sufficiently to start on a new novel, but he never got past the first chapter. Once in a while he free-lanced a piece for *Sports Illustrated*. Mostly, though, he spent his time drinking and socializing and pretending, to himself and the rest of the world, that he was only resting until his next big project. When the literary ladies of the Midwest asked him why he wasn't working, he smiled his charming smile and said, "I'm just waiting for a great idea."

Wolfowitz followed the demise of Mack's career with a satisfaction tinged with sorrow. His campaign had been too easy and ended too soon; like many a successful general, he missed his vanquished enemy. Sometimes at night, lying next to a lightly snoring Louise, he put himself to sleep thinking of new ways to destroy Mack Green novels.

And then Tommy Russo had come along with the proposal for Mack's suicide book. Wolfowitz wasn't a religious man but he believed in fate, and he saw its hand in Mack's rejuvenation. He was being given one more shot, one last chance to even the score with the friend who had betrayed and humiliated him. He thought of old man Stanislaw and smiled. It was the time Wolfowitz had been waiting for—final payback time.

Eight

The first stop on Mack's suicide tour was the Flying Tiger. It wasn't yet noon and the place was empty except for a neighborhood alkie named Beth Ellen, who drank vodka martinis with her cat perched on her lap, and a bald, seedy-looking beer drinker in a cheap brown suit who sat staring at the change on the bar in front of him.

"Double Jack Daniels on the rocks," Mack said.

Otto looked at his watch. "Not a Bloody Mary?"

"This is a celebration," said Mack. "Can you keep a secret?"

"Can James Brown do the boogaloo?"

"Yeah." Mack laughed. "Okay, I just sold a new book to Stealth Wolfowitz. A fictional suicide diary."

"Great," said Otto. "Good for you."

"Now all I've got to do is write the thing. Listen, Otto, remember the other day, when I asked you what you'd do if you had a million bucks and a year to spend it?"

The bartender nodded.

"Well, supposing the reason you only had a year was because you were going to kill yourself at the end of it. What then?"

Otto frowned. "I wouldn't decide to kill myself," he said. "No way."

"Okay, let me put it this way way—what do you think I'd do?"

Otto shook his head. "I've been serving drinks to writers for a long time, Mack, and to tell you the truth, I never know what any of you might do. Remember Benson? He had a sex-change operation for Christ's sake, and wrote about that. To me that's worse than killing yourself any day."

"Benson was gay to start with."

"There's plenty of homos don't get their dick cut off," said Otto. "Anyway, my point is that you can't compare what I'd do with what you might. I've got a wife and two kids to think about. I'm happy."

"And I'm not?"

Otto shrugged. "You're in here socking away double bourbons in the middle of the morning and talking about suicide—"

"Fiction," said Mack. "A fictional diary."

"Shit, I wish somebody'd make me an offer like that," said the bald guy in the brown suit at the end of the bar. Otto glared at him and he quickly added, "I wasn't eavesdropping, I just heard."

"Okay, suppose somebody did. What would you do?" asked Mack.

"Buy me some pussy, that's what," said the guy in a country twang, Kentucky or Tennessee Mack guessed. He tentatively slid his glass and a loose pile of change in Mack's direction; close enough for him to see that the man's eyes were bloodshot and there was gray crud on his jacket. "Hell, you could prob'ly fuck Gina Lollobrigida for a million bucks. My name's Fred Mart, by the way."

Green shook the man's clammy hand. "Wouldn't you be afraid to go through with it?"

Mart shook his head, "Nossir. In the service I saw some guys die horrible, all shot up with their guts spilling out, just begging for one in the head. I said to myself right then, Fred, when the time comes, make it easy on yourself."

"Right," said Mack, encouragingly. "Make it easy. I see what you mean."

"Or let's say you've got a terminal disease, brain cancer, maybe. You ever been in a cancer ward? Shit, it'll make you want to vomit your damn heart out."

"Can't say that I have," said Mack, delighted by the ghoulish character. He reminded him of the tattooed man at the bar who had inspired *Bragging Rights*. Meeting Mart was a good omen; the gods of fiction were once again smiling on him.

"The thing I think about is, how would you do it?" Mart said in a far-off voice. "Shoot yourself? I read once that most guys use a gun. Most of your female suicides, they take pills. There's your difference."

"You could jump off a building," said Green. "Or cut your wrists in the bathtub."

"Jesus, Mack, this is sick," said Otto, looking disgusted.

"You know, a lot of people who cut their wrists don't die," said Mart, ignoring the interruption. He slid another seat closer, and his voice grew lower, confidential. "The mistake they make, see, is they cut crossways. How you do it is, you cut lengthwise. That way, the blood flows out nice and smooth." He ran his finger up the inside of his arm to demonstrate.

"Interesting," said Mack. He was concentrating hard, making certain he'd remember the details of the conversation. This guy was going in the novel, no question about it.

"I had a brother-in-law kill himself, that's how come I know so much about this. Know how he did it? He set in the car with the motor running and the garage door closed. My sister found him out there cold as a Popsicle. He wrote in his note that he did it for love." Mart laughed and Mack smelled his rancid breath. "He had a look in his eye, same as yours," he said.

"You're a freak," said Otto. "Why don't you go drink your beer someplace else."

"Take this," Mart said in an urgent whisper, handing Mack a dog-eared business card. "You decide to do it, call me, okay?"

"I'm not going to kill myself, I'm just writing a book about a guy who does."

Mart looked at Mack with feverish, disbelieving eyes. "Just call me," he said. "All's I want to do is watch."

Mack walked home from the Tiger feeling refreshed and reassured. He picked up a *Times* at the kiosk near his apartment and a coffee to go from the Greek on the corner, fished his mail out of the box and glanced at it in the elevator. As usual it consisted mostly of flyers for Chinese restaurants, utility bills and a warning from *Time* magazine that if he didn't renew his subscription they'd keep on warning him. He almost overlooked a plain white envelope at the bottom of the stack. It had a handwritten name on the upper left-hand corner which he didn't recognize, and a return address that he did: Oriole, Michigan. Mack couldn't imagine who might be writing to him from his hometown.

He let himself in the cramped apartment, plopped down on the tattered couch, ripped open the envelope and found a printed invitation: "The Class of 67 cordially invites YOU to attend our (can you believe it?!) 25th Reunion on Saturday, November 28th, Thanksgiving Day Weekend—at the Oriole Country Club. Featuring sixties rock, nineties nostalgia and lots of old friends. Please RSVP care of: Carla Meyerhoff (Stallings) by September 15 and don't forget to SAVE THE DATE!"

Mack sat staring at the invitation. It had been twenty years since he had been in Oriole, ten since he had been in contact with anyone there. And yet now, on the verge of setting out on his imaginary last year, he had received this invitation to come home. It was another omen—going home, he realized, was exactly what someone who was really going to kill himself might do.

Mack dialed Tommy Russo's number but got no answer. Feeling the need to share his excitement, he thumbed through his worn address book, but there was no one he wanted to talk to. Instead, he poured himself a tumbler of Jack Daniels, switched on a Yankees game, stretched out on the couch and let the voice of Phil Rizzuto lull him gently to sleep. Just before dropping off he briefly wondered why Tommy's answering machine hadn't picked up.

Nine

Tommy Russo's machine wasn't on because Herman Reggie had switched it off. That way, his colleague, a four-foot six-inch, two hundred-and-fifteen-pound midget named Afterbirth Anderson, could work undisturbed. The work consisted of hurling Tommy Russo all over his apartment while Herman watched.

Strictly speaking there was no reason for Herman Reggie to be there—he had seen the midget in action before and he had total confidence in his ability. But he appreciated artistry. Afterbirth would toss Tommy Russo around for exactly five minutes and, by the time he was through, Russo would be under the impression that he had narrowly escaped death. In fact, the session would leave him with little more than broken furniture, some fairly mild bruises and a severely damaged ego. Full-sized men found it humiliating to be kicked around by a midget, which is why Herman Reggie, who believed in psychology, employed Afterbirth. He had others—a woman karate expert from Salt Lake City, an old guy named Referee who smacked people with a cane, and a one-armed man with an extra-powerful grip who specialized in snapping people's fingers—but Afterbirth was his favorite collector. Aside from the blow to their male pride, many deadbeats, he had observed, had a real phobia about midgets. It was a prejudice Reggie deplored. He considered his clients' encounters with Afterbirth to be a lesson in tolerance as well as an effective form of debt collection.

Herman looked closely and saw that Tommy was finally ready for a serious conversation. "That will be enough," he told the midget in a suave, well-modulated tone. "Unless," he said to Russo, "you want to continue?"

"Fuck," mumbled Tommy through bleeding lips. His chest was heaving as he fell to the floor, retching on his white Berber-weave carpet. Afterbirth watched impassively, bouncing on his fat toes while Herman, porkpie hat still perched on his massive round head, clucked sympathetically.

"Would you like a glass of water?" he asked. "Afterbirth, give Mr. Russo some water, please."

"Piss on him, you mean?"

"No, just regular tap water. Unless there's some Perrier in the refrigerator. Do you have Perrier?"

"Fuck," Tommy groaned. He felt like he had a broken rib.

"I guess not," said Herman Reggie. "Well, if you change your mind, let me know. In the meantime, let's talk business. You owe me some money."

"There was no reason to do this," said Tommy resentfully. He waved at his apartment, where fifty thousand dollars' worth of interior decoration lay in ruins. "You know I'd have come up with it."

"Probably," Herman agreed softly, "but I'm trying to make a point. I want you to see that I'm an enigmatic man. For example, you don't know how old I am—you probably couldn't guess within a decade. You don't know if Reggie is my real name. For that matter, you don't know what ethnic group I hail from. That's very rare in my profession."

"Who the fuck cares," said Tommy, cautiously regaining his attitude.

"Ah, you'd be surprised," said Herman. "In the movies, for example, bookies always have an ethnic identity. Italians, no offense, are brutal. Jews are devious, Puerto Ricans are violent and so on."

"Yeah, so they use stereotypes in the movies, so what?"

"Let's take someone like you. You gamble, and if you come up short, you decide who to pay and who to stall, or maybe even stiff. Obviously you don't know most of the bookies personally; probably you've just spoken to them on the phone. Maybe you only know their names."

"So?" asked Tommy, fingering a painful lump on the side of his head, just below the scalp line.

"So you decide how to deal with a man based on ethnic stereotypes. But my clients don't know what to expect from me. What would you say I am? What nationality?"

"Who knows? A Polak, maybe?" said Russo, lulled into speculation by Reggie's conversational tone.

"Not at all." The huge bookmaker laughed. "There isn't a drop of Polish blood in my veins. Not that I'd be ashamed if there was, but I'm an American, plain and simple, and in this country, especially in my profession, that helps make me an enigma. Herman Reggie, Enigmatic American Bookmaker. It has a ring, don't you agree?"

"I guess," said Russo. His head was pounding but he was willing to go on talking as long as the alternative was Afterbirth.

"In other words, I'm a good citizen," said Reggie. "I don't discriminate. Anyone can bet with me, anyone can work for me—Italians, Mexicans, Irish, Jews, Danes—it doesn't matter a bit."

"They ought to give you a brotherhood award," said Tommy, massaging his ribs.

"No awards, thank you," said Reggie. "Just what I'm owed."

"I told you, I'll get it," said Tommy. "I'm working on a couple of things that will pay off next week."

Reggie shook his head. "Not soon enough. I want the money today, right now. Or else."

"Or else what?"

"Afterbirth," said Herman Reggie. The tiny wrestler hopped across the room and delivered a powerful elbow to Russo's abdomen, knocking the agent's wind out and sending him to the carpet, retching again. Reggie waited calmly until Russo was able to sit up. Then, in a mild voice, he said, "Or else you are going to be beaten to death by a midget."

Tommy took a deep breath and tried to regain his composure. "Look, Herman, this isn't the way things work. I owe you, I don't pay, you rough me up. I pay and you leave me alone. But you don't kill somebody over a gambling debt; you can't collect that way."

"That's logical," said Reggie in a pleasant tone, "but my business doesn't necessarily operate on logic. That's why I'm an enigma, so that my customers won't take me for granted. Sometimes I let a debt go on and on. Sometimes I collect the old-fashioned way. And sometimes I foreclose. You can never know when you bet with me. In fact, even I don't always know."

"You're talking about murder," said Tommy.

"Murder's a bad word," said Reggie. He turned to the midget who was peering out the window. "Cover your ears, Afterbirth," he commanded. The little wrestler dutifully put his hands over his cauliflower ears as Reggie continued in a stage whisper. "I've had people killed over bad debts. I've burned down their houses with their children inside. I can't even think of how many guys I've had maimed and crippled. Enigmatic's not the same as weak." He signaled to Afterbirth. "It's okay, you can take your hands down now," he said.

"You got any diet soda?" the midget asked. "Sprite, 7Up, something non-Cola?"

"In the refrigerator," said Tommy dully, his mind racing. He didn't really believe that Herman Reggie would kill him, but he didn't doubt that he would come close. The word ringing in his mind was "maimed."

"What can I do to make things right?" he asked.

"Like I say, pay up. If you don't have the cash right now, think of something else. But I'm not leaving without settling. Are you, Afterbirth?"

The midget shook his head without lowering his eyes from Russo.

"What kind of something would you take?"

"Well, in most cases—I'm letting you in on a professional secret now—in most cases what I do is, I take a piece of a man's business. I don't suppose you've got anything I could use?"

Tommy thought it over. He had spoken to Kleinhouse earlier that day and the author wasn't happy with Wolfowitz's offer. Eventually he'd come around, but it would take a while. The Hollywood deal was going slowly, too; he probably wouldn't see any money there until after the first of the year. At the moment he had only one sure thing.

"How about 10 percent of a new novel?" he asked.

"A new novel? Whose new novel?"

"Mack Green," said Russo. "The author of *The Oriole Kid*."

"Interesting proposition," said Reggie. "How much would you say it was worth? In your professional opinion."

"My cut of the publisher's advance comes to seventy-five hundred, but you'd also own 10 percent of everything else—paperback, movie and television, world rights. If the book takes off, it could be worth a hell of a lot more than eighteen thou."

"In other words, you want me to gamble," said the bookie. "Green hasn't had a bestseller in years. From what I hear, he's a dog."

"What, you're handicapping authors now?"

"I follow everything," said Reggie. "I was reading someplace that information is the most important single advantage in business. It's the reason why you're sitting here bleeding and not the other way around."

"Well, here's some information," said Russo. "Wolfowitz, the editor in chief at Gothic Books, happens to be one of Green's best friends. He's really behind the novel. And the book itself is a winner. Green's got a great idea."

"Tell me about it," said Reggie, leaning against the door frame. "Tell me about the great idea."

Talking quickly and, he hoped, convincingly, Russo explained the concept of *The Diary of a Dying Man.* He could see that Reggie was intrigued. "There's just one problem," said the bookie. "What if Green really kills himself and doesn't finish the book? Then I'm out the money."

"I've known Mack for years, he's not the type. This is strictly fiction. Whattya say? It's a gamble but, hey, you're a gambler."

"No, you're a gambler, I'm a financier," Reggie corrected him gently. "But I won't deny that I'm attracted. I've never owned a piece of an author before. All right, I'll take him. Draw up the paper—today—and I'll send Afterbirth by for it."

Russo breathed a sigh of relief. "I don't want Mack to know about this," he said.

"I won't tell if you don't," said Reggie. "Unless you give me a reason to."

"Okay, I'll have the papers ready by five," said Tommy.

"Good. Now that that's finished, I have another topic I want to discuss with you. I was wondering if you know someone at the Vatican, somebody on the inside."

"No," said Tommy, surprised. "Why?"

"The pope's not getting any younger," said Reggie. "A man with reliable information could make a lot of money when the time comes to elect a new one."

"Sorry," said Tommy tightly.

"You disapprove. Ah well, I can understand that, I suppose. Considering that you were once in the Church."

"I'm still in the Church, I'm just not a priest anymore."

"Whatever," said Reggie airly. "A man's religion is his private business, that's the American way. But if you do happen to hear something, I'd appreciate knowing who you like for pope. It would be worth money. In the meantime, we'll stick to the business at hand. Mack Green's contract makes us quits. If it isn't ready by five, Afterbirth will beat you up until you die. *Capiche?*"

"Yeah," said Tommy sourly, "*capiche.*"

"Good," said Herman. "In that case, I'll be running along. You go on handling Green like before if you want to. Just make sure I get what's coming to me."

"Thanks for the soda, Father," said Afterbirth, moving to the door behind the massive Reggie.

"You're welcome," said Tommy. "Drop in anytime."

"No need for sarcasm," said Reggie. He opened the door, paused briefly and then turned to Tommy. "When I said '*capiche*' before? That doesn't mean I'm Italian. It's a common word, something anyone might say. You knew that, right?"

"Right," said Tommy. "I knew that."

"Good," said Reggie with his most enigmatic expression. "I didn't want you to get the wrong idea."

Ten

Northwest Flight 108 landed in Detroit's Metro Airport just past noon, and Mack emerged from the gangway carrying a blue gym bag and a copy of *Rolling Stone*. He hadn't been in the airport for years, but it looked pretty much the same as it had when he left for New York, junior auto executives rushing to make flight connections and gleaming new American cars on display in the main hall. He ducked into the newsstand and inspected the book rack. There was a full selection of favorite son Elmore Leonard and, predictably, no Mack Green. Not even *The Oriole Kid* in paperback. As far as the public was concerned, he was a dead author.

At the Hertz counter, a young woman with dyed blond hair and a slight overbite handed him the keys to a late model LeBaron, preordered and charged to his Visa.

"Want a map?" she asked pertly.

"What makes you think I need one?"

"You look like a New Yorker."

"How can you tell?"

"In this job you get to know where people are from. You meet a lot of interesting types."

Mack ignored the opening. "Matter of fact, I'm from Oriole. I grew up there."

"No offense, but for Oriole you don't need a map, you need a bulletproof vest."

Mack smiled. In his early days in New York he had often entertained the crowd at the Flying Tiger with tales of his gritty hometown. But in truth, Oriole didn't scare him. During his long absence it had taken on a legendary quality; he no more feared its residents than he did his own characters.

"It can't be any more dangerous than Walter T. Horton," he said. The woman's puzzled expression reminded him that he was no longer on the Upper West Side. "It's sort of a writer's joke," he explained.

A keen look came over the woman's face. "I knew you were probably a writer or something like that," she said, extravagantly pleased with her powers of observation. "Are you famous? Have I seen any of your books?"

"You might have," said Mack, looking around conspiratorially and lowering his voice. "I'm Elmore Leonard."

"Your driver's license says Mack Green."

"I'm traveling incognito," Mack whispered, picking up the keys. "Keep it to yourself."

Mack claimed his luggage, found the black LeBaron in the Hertz lot and headed down I-94. He was out of the habit of driving—in New York he didn't own a car—and he tooled down the highway feeling as luxuriously free as a sixteen-year-old. He fiddled with the radio, found a Motown oldies station that fit his mood and began singing along with the Temptations, "You could have been anything that you wanted to and I can te-el, the way you do the things you do."

There was no familiar scenery along the highway, nothing particularly evocative, just fast-food restaurants, unremarkable housing developments and billboards advertising cheap motels. Mack headed north on I-94, until he turned off the freeway and saw a familiar sign: WELCOME TO ORIOLE, THE LITTLE GIANT; POP. 81,570.

The population hadn't changed much in Mack's absence, but from the looks of the east side the town had gone from scruffy to ramshackle. He knew all about the collapse of the auto industry, but he was still unprepared for the sheer physical decline it had wrought. Many of the tiny, dirty-white shingle houses he recalled from his boyhood now stood vacant and cannibalized. Others had broken-down porches and overgrown lawns where unkempt kids played among the weeds and debris.

Mack stopped at a red light on the corner of Monroe and Dixon and watched a group of defeated-looking men sharing a bottle in front of the Jive-5 party store. They huddled together under a billboard that pictured a giant black fist and the words: MINISTER ABIJAMIN MALIK TEACHES: AFFIRMATIVE ACTION—WHITE MAN'S DISTRACTION. SELF–RELIANCE MEANS BLACK DEFIANCE. JOIN ARCH AND START TO MARCH.

Mack was surprised to see Malik's name here; he thought he was a New York phenomenon. The sign seemed incongruous, even a little exotic for Oriole—the last time he had been on the corner of Monroe and Dixon, there had been a Wonder Bread billboard.

Downtown, which Mack recollected as a cheerful, bustling area with a mock-Corinthian county courthouse, fine stores and three tall office buildings, looked like it had been hit by a neutron bomb. The courthouse and the stores—Federals, Kresges, Gottleib's Fine Mens Wear—stood empty and abandoned. There were boards over the windows of the Oriole Hotel and steel bars on the doors of Golden's Department Store. A few dazed-looking people wandered through the streets, but they seemed more like survivors of some horrible disaster than downtown shoppers.

As he passed the State Bank Building, Mack simultaneously

remembered the phone number of his father's law office, and a conversation he had once had with Eddie Yew, a Korean freelance photographer who hung around the Flying Tiger drinking whiskey sours.

"How much you weigh when you twenty years old, Mack?" Eddie had asked him one day.

"One seventy-five."

"How much you weigh now?"

"One ninety, give or take."

"All the food you eat in twenty year, maybe one thousand pound of food. And you only gain fifteen. Where rest of food go?"

Green had shrugged and the Korean smiled broadly. "One thousand pound of food go right in you mouth and out you asshole."

It had been a sobering thought then, and it was now. How many bytes of information had his brain absorbed in the years since he had left Oriole? How much had gone straight out his asshole? And why did he still remember his father's number? "Proust, Proust, you're becoming a fucking Proust," Mack said to himself over the sound of Junior Walker and the All Stars.

Past downtown he took Bannister Avenue west, heading instinctively toward Nutmeg Village, his old neighborhood. He drove slowly, surveying the changes, and for the first time he began to feel a bittersweet nostalgia. The A&W, which had been his first Flying Tiger, was now an adult video rental shop. A new post office stood where his elementary school had been. Most of the little shops he remembered had vanished. But J. D. Murphy's Funeral Home, to which Buddy Packer had once obtained a key and sold illicit glimpses of the corpses for fifty cents a peek, was still there. He wondered where Buddy was now; probably dead, he figured, or in jail. His name wasn't in the phone book, Mack had checked from New York.

He passed Two Brothers Market, where the Kazonis boys didn't check IDs too carefully, and next to it, Vic Snipes's drugstore, where Vic, Oriole's Ping-Pong champion (how in the hell did he remember that?), had sold him Trojans with a manly wink and, after Green's father dropped dead, filled the prescriptions for Mack's mother's sleeping pills. Just past Vic's was the Oriole National Savings and Loan, where Mack had opened his first account. He was glad to see that the little bank hadn't succumbed to the S&L scandal.

The Bannister Theater was showing a Jodie Foster flick that had closed in New York eight months earlier. The summer Mack and Linda Birney fell in love they had gone to the Bannister almost every night; the little theater had a special nursery room for crying children that was unused after dark—except by them. He remembered the night the manager had found them, stoned and naked, lying on the carpet. Linda had looked up and said, "We're having a private moment here, do you mind?" Twenty-five years and a thousand women later, Mack still couldn't forget the cool, ironic sound of her voice, the fragrance of her long, silky hair, the taste of sex on her tongue, the contours of her willowy body.

Linda wasn't in Oriole anymore, either; he had no idea where she was, although over the years he had often searched for her by calling telephone information in probable locations—New York, LA, Miami—asking for a Linda Birney or a Linda Flanders. But she was gone, vanished like Oriole's downtown, the A&W, his old elementary school. Driving past the Bannister Theater, thinking about Linda, Mack's stomach ached.

At the corner of Berkley, he automatically turned left and the pain went away; there were too many other memories here. He cruised slowly down the street, effortlessly assigning a name to every house: Campanella, Graff, Walton, Rafferty, Moore, Valuchi, Hakenberger, Flite, Andersen with an *e*, Old Man Janowitz, who had a German shepherd that chewed tin cans, Mr. Chones, who drank and cried in his yard, Reverend Strickland, whose son, Terry, had been killed in Vietnam when Mack was a senior in high school. He hadn't seen any of these people in years, but he remembered them and the pointless details of their lives—the cabbage smell that hung in the air at the Raffertys, the day the Waltons got their first color television, the drama when Al Campanella left his wife and then came back. He wondered if any of his old neighbors carried around memories of him, but he doubted it. Small-town people with families to raise and jobs to go to each day probably wouldn't bother.

Mack stopped the car across from 52 Berkley and inspected the house with the expert eyes of a maintenance man. The black wrought-iron door knocker he had installed as a teenager was still in place. The shutters on the front windows, upstairs and down, that he and his father painted every second April, had a fresh white look. The ivy his mother had planted wound up the red brick on the side of the house.

There was no one on the street and only an occasional car passed by. Green sat in the LeBaron listening to Mary Wells sing "Two Lovers," and stared at his house, wondering who lived there now. In New York, the idea of starting his diary with a visit to his boyhood home had been a simple literary strategy, but now that he was here, he felt a curious shyness. He pictured being greeted at the door by his own sixteen-year-old self. "You're me?" the kid would say, disappointed.

"Jesus Christ," said Mack out loud, "I'm starting to crack up." He shut off the radio with a decisive jab, slipped out of the car and walked slowly across the street. On the front porch he hesitated, took a deep breath and rang the bell.

The door swung open almost immediately and Mack found himself face to face with a thin, coffee-colored woman. She seemed to be about sixty, although he had never been good at judging the ages of black people. She wore a flowered housedress and an expression that combined curiosity with caution. "Can I help you?" she asked.

"Hi. My name's Mack Green. I used to live here. A long time ago."

The woman smiled and nodded. "Uh-huh. I was watching you from the window, just sitting out there in your car. Now that I see you up close, I recognize you. Come on in, you must want to see the house."

Mack followed her into the small front hall. He let his gaze wander, feeling a little dizzy.

"Brings back memories, huh?" said the woman softly. "I'm Joyce McClain. My husband and I have been living here for, oh, ten, eleven years now. It's a fine house."

"My grandfather built it," said Mack. "Did you say you recognized me?"

"From your picture. On the jacket of *The Oriole Kid.*"

"Ah, that," said Mack.

"I liked it," she said in a low, soft voice with just a touch of a drawl, "and I liked *Light Years* even more. *The Oriole Kid* is my husband's favorite. He's read it probably half-a-dozen times. It's one of the few books he *has* read. Tell you the truth, the fact that you once lived here made him want to buy the house."

"How'd you know I lived here?" asked Mack, warmed by the woman's recognition. Praise for *Light Years* always made him feel especially good.

"The lady we bought the house from, Mrs. Polk, told us. It was a selling point I guess you'd call it—you know, the home of a famous novelist."

"My mother died in the upstairs bedroom," Mack blurted. "I'm sorry, I didn't mean to say that—"

"That's all right," said Mrs. McClain. "I'm not the kind of black woman's afraid of ghosts." Green couldn't judge if she was being ironic. "Why don't you just take a tour of the house?" she offered. "Then we'll have a cup of coffee and you can tell me what it was like growing up here."

"I really didn't mean to barge in on you. It was just a spur-of-the-moment thing."

Joyce McClain took him gently by the elbow and squeezed.

"This isn't an intrusion, it's a pleasure," she said. "Isn't every day we get a visit from a celebrity. You just take your time, I'll be in the kitchen."

Mack climbed the stairs to his old bedroom, which the McClains had converted into a guest room. Surprisingly, it hadn't changed much. There was still a desk under the window overlooking the street, bookshelves along the wall and a single bed in the far corner. The decor was different—a Watson lithograph hung on the wall where his Tiger pennant had been, a large Persian carpet covered the once-bare hardwood floor and an unused-looking stationary exercise bicycle dominated a corner of the room—but the place seemed much more familiar than Mack had supposed it would.

He sat gingerly on the narrow bed and let himself remember. When he was small his father had taught him a bedtime prayer in this room, and for years thereafter he had been unable to fall asleep without mumbling it like an incantation. Here, one unforgettable Saturday morning when he was nine he had turned on his Zenith clock radio and heard a sound so new and raw that it made him want to dance and cry and grow up all at the same time—it was the Chantels singing "Maybe." He had his first orgasm here, too, self-administered, thrilling and terrifying.

Mack lay back and put his hand on his crotch. He thought of Linda, and for a moment he was tempted to close the door and quickly masturbate. Then he heard the sound of voices downstairs—a sound that brought back boyhood afternoons when his father came home from the office and he could hear the reassuring murmur of his parents' conversation.

The thought of his parents melted his hard-on. Still, it was a great idea for the *Diary,* the hero beating off in his old room. He took out his notebook, quickly jotted down the thought and headed downstairs. He was ready for a cup of coffee, although what he really wanted was a drink at the Bannister Inn next to the firehouse.

". . . any more of that gumbo?" Mack heard a man say as he entered the kitchen, coughing to announce his presence.

Joyce McClain turned from the sink and smiled. "Mr. Green, this is my husband, John," she said, gesturing toward a tall, paunchy but powerfully built white man with grizzled silver hair, amused blue eyes and a large, hawklike nose, who was leaning against the refrigerator door.

McClain straightened and extended a giant hand. "Joyce told me you were here," he said. "I hope you're staying for dinner."

"I can't," said Mack.

"Other plans, eh? Meeting old friends?"

"Not really. But I just got into town and I haven't even checked into the hotel yet. Maybe another time."

"The hell with another time, check in later," said McClain with gruff heartiness. "Let's have a couple drinks and get acquainted. I guarantee you won't get a meal as good as Joyce's gumbo anywhere around here."

There was something immediately likable about the big man's direct, open manner. Mack had the feeling that he had seen him before, although he couldn't place him.

"Well—"

"Great," said McClain. He opened a well-stocked liquor cabinet and grinned. "Mack—okay if I call you Mack? And you call me John—"

"And me Joyce," said Mrs. McClain in her soft, low voice.

"—you're a bourbon drinker, right?" Without waiting for confirmation he splashed three fingers of Old Grandad into a glass.

"How did you know that?"

"Elementary, my dear Watson," said McClain.

"John's a retired police detective," said Joyce, pronouncing it *po-lice,* "and he's never gotten over it."

Now Mack knew where he had seen McClain.

"You don't read your own books," said McClain, pouring

himself a scotch and a Campari-and-soda for Joyce. "Bourbon's what 'The Kid' drinks."

"He's not me," said Mack. "None of my characters are."

"Yeah, right," said McClain. "You take it on the rocks, don't you?"

Mack laughed and nodded.

"You two fellas go in the other room and talk. I'll get the gumbo on the stove and join you," said Joyce.

The McClains' living room was decorated for comfort, like the set of a family sitcom. Mack's mother had had an artistic streak—he recollected Chinese prints, low-slung couches and lots of little Asian statuettes of bald figures with pot bellies in this room. But there were no statuettes now, just well-worn leather easy chairs, a soft sofa under the bay windows and some nondescript landscapes on the wall. Mack noticed ashes in the fireplace; when he was a boy they had never used it.

"Place changed much since your day?" asked McClain, who had been following his eyes.

"It seems pretty much the same. It's in good shape."

"They don't build 'em like this anymore," said McClain, slapping a wall. "Solid, made to last." He took a gulp of his drink. "You don't get back here often." It was a statement, not a question.

"How'd you know that? Another clue from *The Oriole Kid?*"

"Naw, just logic. We've been here eleven years now, and this is the first time you've come around to see the house. Besides, I figure if you'd been in town it would have been in the *News*. What brings you back after all this time?"

"Work, basically. I'm writing a book set in Oriole, or at least part of it is . . ."

"A book set here? Sounds exciting," said Joyce, wiping her hands on her apron as she entered the living room. She sat down next to her husband on the couch and he shifted his drink to take her hand. "You going to pull a Thomas Wolfe on us?"

"There's no astronauts around here," said McClain.

"That's Tom Wolfe," said Joyce.

"Whatever," said McClain, unruffled by the correction. "What I think you should do is a sequel to *The Oriole Kid*. Another baseball story."

"I believe *The Oriole Kid* was meant to be an American allegory of sports, sex and success, dear," said Joyce with affectionate irony, a bit of which, Mack realized, was aimed at him; those were the words from the blurb on the paperback edition of *The Oriole Kid*. He remembered them because he had written them himself.

"Allegory? Say it ain't so, Kid," said McClain.

"English teacher?" Mack asked Joyce.

"Joyce was principal over at Jackson Junior High until three years ago," McClain said proudly.

"I knew a kid whose mother was principal there, Derrick Milton. We played ball together."

"Derrick's my son," said Mrs. McClain. "He lives in California now. He's a computer programmer."

"He was a good guy," said Mack. "Good ballplayer, too. How's he doing?"

"He's doing just fine," said Joyce, glancing briefly at her husband.

"Derrick doesn't approve of his mother being married to a white guy," said John. "We don't see much of him."

Mack recalled that Derrick Milton had had a white girlfriend in high school, but he didn't mention it. He was amused to recognize his silence as an act of instinctive generational solidarity; never tell parents anything. "Derrick's father was a minister, wasn't he?" he said.

"My first husband," said Mrs. McClain. "He died in 1968."

Mack remembered the Reverend Booker T. Milton, a flamboyant preacher who wore expensive suits, drove a red Cadillac and sometimes delivered florid invocations at school events. "I'm sorry," he said.

"I'm not," said McClain, slipping his arm over his wife's shoulder. "Meaning no disrespect. You know how I met Joyce?"

Mack shook his head.

"I busted her," John said with a booming laugh. "Honest to God, at that big busing riot in 1970. She jumped an officer of the law and I had to take her in."

"That officer of the law was beating one of my students over the head with a club," said Joyce.

"I remember the first thing she ever said to me," McClain continued. "She said, 'Get your hands off me, you racist pig.' Romantic, huh?"

"It was bad enough getting arrested. I didn't know the punishment would be a life sentence," said Joyce dryly.

"In that case you and I have something in common," Mack said to her. "We've both been busted by your husband."

"I busted you? When? For what? I don't remember anything like that."

"The scene of the crime was Jerry's Liquor Mart. I was in high school and you caught me and a friend of mine, Buddy Packer, buying a bottle of peppermint schnapps with a phony ID."

"You were friends with Buddy Packer?"

"You know Buddy?"

"Yeah, I know him," said McClain with an expression Mack couldn't read.

"Back then you needed three pieces of proof to buy liquor," Mack said. "One day Buddy, ah, found this guy's wallet in the theater—"

"Lifted it, you mean," said McClain.

"—and it had a driver's license and a draft card in it. Buddy went down to Jacobson's Army-Navy and came back with a Red Cross card from World War II, granting safe passage across enemy lines. I remember it had stamped signatures—Roosevelt, Churchill, Stalin, Mussolini, even Hitler. Buddy typed in the name of the guy with the wallet and presto—three pieces of proof."

McClain smiled broadly. "It's starting to come back to me," he said.

"The next day we decided to try it out, over at Jerry's. Buddy sticks the schnapps on the checkout counter and the lady gives us this suspicious look and says, 'You boys got some ID?' Packer says, 'Hell yeah,' real confident, and drops the stuff on the counter. She looks at it and holds up the Red Cross card. 'According to your driver's license you were three years old when this card was issued,' she says. And Buddy, never missing a beat, says: 'Lady, we're talking wartime. They weren't taking no chances.' "

Joyce laughed, the loudest sound she had made all day.

"At which point," said Mack, "an off-duty policeman who was standing behind us put a hand on my shoulder and said"—he made his voice go gruff—" 'Boys, your asses are under arrest.' "

"And that was me," said McClain. "Hell yes, I remember it now."

"So then what happened?" asked Joyce. "I hope this isn't a story about po-lice brutality."

"Actually, he was pretty nice about it," Mack said. "He gave us a lecture and impounded the wallet. Nothing ever happened. I wonder where Buddy is these days?"

"He's around," said McClain, glancing at Joyce.

"His name's not in the book," said Mack. "You know how to find him?"

McClain shrugged. "If I had to," he said.

"I think the gumbo's just about ready," said Joyce, rising. "Mack, you probably want to wash up before supper; you know where it is. Dick Tracy here can give me a hand setting the table."

Dinner, from spinach salad to the homemade pecan pie, was as good as McClain had promised. Mack, famished, would have been embarrassed about eating so much if his appetite hadn't given Joyce such obvious pleasure. "No more, I can't," he groaned when she offered him a third helping of pecan pie. "God, I think this is the best meal I've ever had."

"I done married my wife for her cookin'," said McClain. "She the baddest soulfood specialiss in O–ree–O." Mack was startled— McClain's black accent and inflection, even the expression on his face, were uncannily accurate.

"John thinks he's Redd Foxx," said Joyce fondly. "Just ignore him when he gets like that. I do."

"You've got a good ear," Mack said.

"Spend twenty years working on the east side, you learn to talk like an eastsider."

"Why don't you sing 'Ole Man Ribbuh' for our guest, dear?" said Joyce.

"I only sings Motown," McClain said. "Anyway, I told you Joyce can cook."

"That's all I do these days, cook and keep house."

"Yeah, and volunteer three days a week at the daycare center. And direct the church choir. And play tennis every morning. Now she's thinking about running for city council." McClain leaned over and kissed his wife on the cheek. "She's really something, this woman."

"Do you have any kids?" Mack asked. "I mean, of your own? Together?"

McClain shook his head. "It's something I missed out on. I was married once before, but it didn't take. I always figured I'd get around to kids the next time. But then I met Joyce, and—"

"Forty-year-old women didn't have babies in those days," she said. "I already had a grown son. And, to be honest, I'm not sure I would have wanted to raise a mixed child in this town."

"Ah, well," said McClain. There was a long pause and then he asked, "How about you?"

"Nope," said Mack. "I was married once too, but I escaped. Not unscathed," he added, thinking of the settlement.

"Maybe you'll find a girl around here," said McClain. "Or

maybe that's the reason you came back. Returning to the scene of the crime."

"John, you leave this young man alone with your romantic po-liceman notions," said Joyce with mock severity.

"That's all right," Mack said. "It's been a while since I was cross-examined about girls in this room. Brings back old times."

"Everybody's got some girl in his old hometown," said McClain. "Tell me I'm wrong."

"As a matter of fact, you're right, in a way," said Mack. "There was a girl—"

"And?"

"And she didn't think I was good enough for her," Mack said lightly. "She married an all-American quarterback instead."

"No kidding?" said McClain. "Who?"

"Guy named Gregg Flanders."

"Gregg Flanders? From Vanderbilt? He won the Heisman Trophy. No wonder she didn't think you were good enough for her."

"Thanks. Anyway, it was a long time ago."

"She from around here?"

"West Tarryton."

"I know people over there," said McClain. "What's her name?"

"Linda Birney. I guess now it's Linda Flanders."

"Birney, Birney," mused McClain, searching his cop's memory. "Nope, doesn't ring any bells. You'd think I'd remember, a local girl marries a Heisman winner."

"Where is she now?" asked Joyce gently.

Mack shrugged. "Last I heard she was living in California."

"Well, it's her loss," said Joyce. "Are you fellas ready for some coffee?"

"Ah, would it be all right if I smoked?" asked Mack.

"How about a cee-gar?" said John. "I've got me some tasty Cubanos."

"John, you smoke those illegal stogies of yours in the basement," said Joyce. "I'll get the dishes cleared away and bring your coffee down."

McClain led Green to the wood-paneled basement rec room, where he produced two green coronas and a bottle of Hennessy. "Thought we might have us a postprandial libation," he said.

The two men sat puffing, chatting about the Pistons, who were still off their championship form, and the Tigers, McClain's special love, who he predicted would be in the thick of the pennant race next season. When Joyce joined them with coffee, Mack looked at his watch and saw it was past eleven.

"I didn't realize how late it was," he said. "I've got to get over to the hotel."

"Where you staying?" asked McClain.

"The Hilton. I hope they held my reservation."

"Forget the Hilton," said McClain. "Stay here tonight."

"Here?"

"Yeah, here, in your old room. Nobody's using it."

"I couldn't do that."

"Why not?" asked Joyce. "It might be fun for you. And it's no trouble at all."

"No, really . . . "

McClain laid a heavy hand on Green's arm. "It's a twenty-minute drive to the Hilton," he said, "and at the risk of sounding like a cop, you *have* had a few drinks."

Mack realized that McClain was right. He had forgotten he wasn't getting around by cab.

"John, maybe Mack would rather go to the hotel," said Joyce. "Why don't you run him over there and tomorrow we can arrange for him to come by for the car."

"No, I'd like to stay," Mack said, surprising himself. Suddenly he wanted very much to spend the night. In the morning he would justify it as an interesting experience to use in the *Diary*, but right now he was tired enough and drunk enough to admit that he felt an unaccustomed warmth and safety in this house, with these people.

"I'll go up and get your bed ready," said Joyce, already on her feet. "It's not your old bed, mind, but it's comfortable."

McClain grunted and rose. "Take Mack with you, honey. I'll lock up." He put an arm over Green's shoulder and squeezed. "By the way," he said. "Gregg Flanders? He never made it big in the pros. You did."

Eleven

Mack awoke to pale sunlight streaming through the windows and the aroma of bacon in the air. Feeling clearheaded and a little sheepish, he climbed into his clothes, washed up in the bathroom down the hall and then went downstairs to the kitchen. There he found McClain, dressed in a flannel shirt and khakis, sitting at the table eating scrambled eggs and reading *The Oriole News*.

" 'Morning, Big Mack," he said cheerfully. "How'd you sleep?"

"Slept great, but when I woke up I panicked. Thought I'd be late for school."

McClain laughed. "You forgot it's Sunday. Joyce's gone to church, but she left breakfast. There's coffee on the stove. Help yourself."

"Coffee's plenty," said Mack, pouring himself a cup. "I'm still stuffed from last night."

ZEV CHAFETS • 98

"Know what you mean," McClain said, patting his massive belly with satisfaction. He extracted a piece of paper from his shirt pocket and handed it to Mack. "Your friend Packer's phone number. He lives on Greenfield, other side of Melodie Highway."

"How'd you get the number? He's not in the book."

"Depends which book you're talking about," said McClain. "Mind if I ask you something?"

"Ask away," said Mack, sipping the steaming coffee.

"Packer. He owe you money or something?"

"Money? No, I told you last night, we're old friends. I haven't seen him for years. Is there something I should know about him?"

"Nothing you won't find out for yourself," said McClain. "Listen, what are your plans for today?"

"Get over to the hotel, check in. Then I thought maybe I'd take a drive around town, have a look. That's about it."

"I've got a better idea. The Pistons are at home against the Celtics and I happen to have a pal in security at the Palace who can get us great seats. You interested?"

"The last time I saw the Pistons they were playing at Cobo Hall."

"Then you should see the Palace, it's something else. Afterward we can stop by Joe Muer's, get us a lobster. And just to make you feel good, I'll let you pick up the check."

"Joe Muer's," said Mack. "I used to go there with my father."

"Then it'll be like old times," said McClain.

McClain was an enthusiastic host, ordering hot dogs and beer and expertly briefing Mack on the decline of the Pistons. But by the third quarter, with the home team trailing by eighteen, Mack began to sense that the ex-cop was sneaking glances at him. Finally he caught him in the act.

"What?" he asked.

"Nothing. I was just bored by this massacre," said McClain, not at all embarrassed. "Tell me something about this book of yours. You already have the story or are you just making it up as you go along?"

"Little of both," said Mack. He was bored with the game, too, but he didn't feel like discussing *The Diary of a Dying Man*. Ever since the *Light Years* debacle, he had a superstitious reluctance to talk about a work in progress.

"You going to write it in Oriole?"

"Depends," said Mack. "I'm not sure what I'm looking for yet."

"How long you figure on staying?"

"Couple weeks, at least. Maybe more."

McClain knitted his large brow and cleared his throat powerfully. "In that case I've got a proposition for you," he said. "Joyce and I had a talk after you went to bed last night. What we were thinking was, maybe you'd like to stay with us while you're in town. There's plenty of room, it's nice and quiet and nobody'd bother you. Most of the time we're not even home."

"I couldn't do that," said Green. "I mean, it's great of you, but—"

"You'd be a hell of a lot more comfortable than at the Hilton."

"I can't just move in with you because you happen to be living in the house I grew up in."

"Bull crap," boomed McClain jovially. "We wouldn't ask if we didn't mean it. This isn't New York, buster. People say what's on their minds around here. Especially me."

"You're tempting me," said Mack. If coming back to Oriole had been an inspired literary tactic, living in his old house with characters like John and Joyce McClain would be a gold mine. He had to admit, too, that he was flattered by McClain's obvious excitement—it had been a long time since he had been treated like a celebrity. And then there was the cozy feeling he had had falling asleep in his own room—he couldn't remember the last time he had felt so comfortably secure. "But I'm not a kid anymore."

"What's that mean?"

"I've got bad habits. You might not appreciate a houseguest who drinks and smokes and stays out late."

McClain grunted with amusement. "I ain't Father Flanagan," he said. "You want to drink, drink. You want to smoke, do it in your room with the window open or in the basement, same as me. As far as staying out late, you get a key, come and go whenever you feel like it. If you want to get laid, try a hotel."

"You've got this all figured out," said Mack. "How do you know I'm not an ax-murderer."

"The Oriole Kid? Besides, I used to be a cop, remember? I know something about people. Joyce does, too. Fact is, she's a lot smarter than me, but don't tell her I said that. Another thing I know is that you aren't going to be comfortable freeloading. A room at the Hilton costs ninety-two fifty a night, I checked. So I figured three hundred bucks a week, room and board, and you won't feel like a mooch. How's that sound?"

"Ah, so that's why you've been wining and dining me," said Mack, laughing. "You're in it for the money."

"Money my ass," snorted McClain. "You want to stay for free, fine, no problem. I was thinking about you, that's all."

"I was kidding," said Mack.

"Well, as long as you brought it up, I do happen to have an ulterior motive. The holidays are rough on Joyce now that Derrick X is boycotting her. For some strange reason she took a shine to you last night. It'd be good for her to have a young guy around the place."

"I liked her, too," said Mack. He paused. "Since you're being honest, I want you to know that the book I'm working on is going to be based on my experiences out here, which means you'll both probably wind up in it. Of course I wouldn't use your real names, but—"

"Why the hell not?" demanded McClain. "You could do a lot worse than me for a hero, I'll tell ya that right now. I've got some stories you wouldn't believe."

"Seriously, would it be a problem?"

"Depends on what you write, doesn't it?"

"I don't know yet," said Mack. "I'm just getting started."

"Would you let me see what you say about us? I don't give a damn about myself, but the stuff about Joyce?"

Mack paused, considering, and then slowly shook his head. "I never show anybody what I'm working on until it's finished," he said. "When I'm done, if there's something you really don't like, we can talk about it. But I can't promise that I'll change anything."

McClain let his gaze wander back to the court, saw a rookie guard throw a pass into the seats, winced and turned back to Mack. "Yeah, all right, it's a deal," he said, extending his hand. "That's the cop in me, snap judgments. Make a note of that, hotshot; you gonna write about Big John McClain, you got to start paying attention."

Twelve

The McClain household was an orderly place, dominated by routine and habit. Breakfast was served at 8:30. By 9:00, Joyce was already on her way to her various volunteer activities, while John headed to the Elks for a day of bowling, poker, pool and shooting the breeze. Joyce returned at 4:30 and began cooking; John got home by five. They chatted over cocktails (John, two large scotch-and-waters, Joyce, two weak Campari-and-sodas), then sat down to dinner, which Joyce called supper and which was never less than superb, at 6:00. Afterward they watched television in the living room. At 11:00, McClain rose and announced that he was going to lock up and by 11:15 they were in bed.

Weekends were equally predictable. Saturday mornings John did odd jobs around the house while Joyce prepared elaborate dishes to be defrosted during the week. In the afternoon they took a drive into the countryside and walked for an hour or so. Saturday nights, Mack was pretty sure, they made love. His room was just down the hall from theirs, and he overheard the sounds of their passion with the same slightly prurient fascination he had once derived from eavesdropping on his parents.

On Sunday mornings, Joyce attended a Holiness church on the east side. McClain, a lapsed Catholic, stayed home and read the papers. After lunch John watched sports on TV while Joyce took a nap. Supper was cold cuts. Sunday night they went to the movies, came home, went to bed and then began the cycle all over again the following day.

The McClains were relaxed hosts who let Mack know that he was welcome to join them when he chose and to keep to himself if he liked. Under their influence he adopted an uncharacteristically settled routine of his own. He slept late, drank his morning coffee alone and then spent days in his room, working on the *Diary*.

"How's it coming?" McClain asked at dinner one night, a week or so after Mack moved in.

"Not bad," said Mack happily; it had been years since he had written so confidently, so easily. "I've already got the first three chapters finished."

"That's exciting," said Joyce, passing him a platter of fried chicken.

"Probably a lot of stuff in there about me," said McClain, missing casual by an octave.

"Oh, I don't know, there might be a mention or two, I forget."

"How about a little peek? Just to make sure you're capturing the real me—"

"Nope," Mack said. "I'm not even showing it to my editor, and I promised him I would."

"Why not?" asked Joyce. "I mean, if you promised—"

"I once made the mistake of showing him an unfinished book and it threw me off for years. Besides, this isn't the kind of thing that benefits from other people's input. It's too personal."

"Well, you keep on keeping on, young man," said Joyce. "Detective McClain will restrain his curiosity. Won't you, dear?"

"Yes, dear," said McClain.

Joyce winked at Mack and he smiled. Lately he had begun to imagine himself as a teenager again, and the conceit was finding its way into the *Diary*—the hero as a suicidal middle-aged author improbably adopted by a pair of affectionate strangers.

"By the way, I'm going out tonight," he said.

"Hot date?" asked McClain, who had already wondered aloud several times in the past few days why a young guy like Mack would want to hang around the house when he could be out on the town.

"Not exactly. I'm meeting Buddy Packer. I called him this afternoon."

"Packer," McClain said, scowling. He seemed poised to add something more, but Joyce interrupted.

"You have a good time and don't pay John any mind; nobody appointed him social director around here."

"Packer's trouble," said McClain. "That's all I'm saying."

"That's the whole point," said Mack with a broad smile. "I'm looking for trouble."

When Mack had called Packer, earlier that day, a woman had answered with a three-syllable hello, like a telephone operator in an old-time movie.

"Hi," said Green, "is Buddy Packer there?"

"No, he is not," she said with wary formality.

Although it was a weekday, it had never occurred to Mack that Buddy might be at work. "Any idea when he'll be back? I'm an old friend of his, Mack Green? I'm here in town and I wanted to say hello."

"Mack Green? *The* Mack Green? Just a minute, I think he may have just come in." Mack heard her muffled voice and then Buddy Packer came on the line.

"Yeah?" he said in an expressionless tone.

"Yeah yourself. It's me, Mack."

"You gotta be shittin' me. Where the hell are you?"

"Fifty-two Berkley Street, top floor, corner room."

"What is this, some kind of time-warp thing, like on *Twilight Zone*?"

"Hey, you sound just like yourself," said Mack.

"Who'd you think I'd sound like, William F. Buckley? Come on, where are you?"

"Like I said, Oriole, at my folks' old place. It's a long story. I'll explain when I see you."

"How long you been in town?"

"A while. The guy I'm staying with, an ex-cop named McClain—he's the one who busted us that night with the Red Cross card, remember?—he got me your number."

"You're staying with John McClain?" Buddy's voice was flat, giving nothing away.

"Yeah. You know him?"

"We've had some dealings," said Packer. Mack waited, but Buddy didn't add an explanation. "Who answered the phone?" Mack asked.

"Name's Jean," said Packer.

"Your wife?"

"Nope. Squeeze. No big thing."

"Jesus, Packy, there's so much I want to catch up on. Can you get out, meet me someplace?"

"Yeah, I can get out," said Packer dryly. "Why don't you drop by my office tonight around nine. Seventy-six Larimore, off Monroe on the east side. Think you can find it?"

"Found tougher places," said Mack, lapsing into the terse rhythm of Buddy Packer's speech.

"Fine," said Packer, hanging up without saying good-bye.

Now, on the way over to Buddy's place, navigating instinctively through streets he hadn't driven since boyhood, Mack vividly recalled the last time he had heard from Packer. It had been almost ten years ago, when an unlabeled cassette had turned up in his mail in New York. Mack put it on and immediately recognized Buddy's fuck-you monotone.

"It's Monday morning, the sun is shining, the birds are shitting and I'm gunning my T-bird down the driveway," said Packer without preamble. This was followed by the sharp hiss of a joint being inhaled, twenty seconds of silence and the sound of exhaling. "I'm driving up the street to the corner and taking a left past the Texaco station. Now I'm heading east, driving in the right lane. On my right is a Burger King. Coming up is a Roy Fucking Rogers . . ."

The entire first side of the tape had gone that way, a travelogue in real time of Buddy Packer's trip to someplace. Mack had flipped the tape to find out what it was all about, heard the sound of another giant toke and then: "It's five o'clock and I'm heading home," followed by a forty-five-minute account of the drive back. There had been no explanation, but Mack had understood; Buddy was telling him that he was still alive and still cool which, for him, amounted to the same thing.

Their friendship had begun one Tuesday afternoon in the winter of Mack's junior year in high school, when Packer had accosted him at his locker. "I've been wondering about you, Green," he said in his flat, nasal voice.

"Wondering about me?" said Mack. Packer had never even spoken to him before. He was a dark legend, the leader of the Gamers, a collection of misfits not popular enough to be in a fraternity, not square enough to be in a car club and far too weird to belong to a conventional gang. Mack, an honors student, varsity basketball star and son of one of Oriole's best families, had long been fascinated by Packer; it had never occurred to him that the interest might be mutual.

"Yeah," said Packer. "Wondering if you're game. I think you might be."

"Game as the next guy," said Mack, at once flattered and intimidated.

"Let's find out," said Packer. "Meet me on your corner tomorrow morning at seven."

"Seven in the morning? What for?"

"I got a fo-ray coming up," said Packer, walking off in his odd, camellike slope.

At seven Mack had been on the corner, shivering in the cold January air, when Packer drove up in his red Impala. A Lucky Strike was clasped between his thin lips, and dark glasses hid his eyes. Mack climbed in the car, coughed away the smoke fumes and held on tight as Packer peeled rubber down Berkley Street.

They drove across town to an unfamiliar part of the north side, where Packer parked in front of a small storefront with Hebrew letters over the door.

"What's this?" Mack asked.

"A synagogue," said Packer. "For Jews."

"I didn't know you were Jewish."

"We both are," said Packer. "Just follow my lead."

Inside they found a small group of old men dressed in ill-fitting suits and skullcaps. "Here you are, boychik," one said to Packer. "We been waiting for you."

Buddy pushed Mack forward. "Meet Marvin Greenberg," he said. "He's the kid I told you about, just moved here from out of town."

Mack stood, blushing with confusion, while the old men inspected him with frank, bleary eyes. "You sure he's Jewish? He doesn't look Jewish," said one.

"100 percent kosher," said Packer. "I guarantee you."

The old man shrugged. "Okay, then we got a minyan." He and the others tossed fringed shawls over their shoulders and began winding little leather straps around their arms. Someone gave Mack a set of straps as well, but he just stood there, bewildered.

"You're sure he's Jewish?" asked the old man again.

"Yeah, but he's Reformed," said Buddy. "He doesn't know

how to put on tefillin. I'll give him a hand." He winked and began winding the leather straps around Mack's left arm.

The old men began chanting in odd, high-pitched Hebrew tones. Packer handed Mack a prayer book and winked again. "It'll be over in about twenty minutes," he whispered. "Just turn the pages backward and mumble."

When the prayers ended, the old men unwrapped themselves. One produced a bottle of cheap scotch and ten filmy shot glasses. They filled the glasses, yelled a Hebrew word that Mack assumed was a toast and tossed back the whiskey.

"These old guys are so out of it they don't even know there's a drinking age in America," Buddy whispered, draining his glass and taking a refill. "Drink up, Macky. It's on the Jews."

"Where'd you learn to do all that stuff?" asked Mack on the way back from the little synagogue. It was 7:30 in the morning and, for the first time in his life, he was buzzed.

"This Jewish kid I know taught me," said Packer. "They need ten guys to make the prayers official."

"Not ten Jewish guys?"

Packer shrugged. "They're not too picky," he said. "Anyway, I thought you'd enjoy starting off the day with a cocktail."

"You drove all the way over to the north side at this hour for a couple of shots of whiskey?"

"Yeah. And ten bucks each," said Packer, peeling off a bill and handing it to Mack.

That morning had been Mack's initiation into the world of Buddy Packer and his disciples: Brian Lifton, a clumsy boy Packer called "Ba-ba" because his father, a former high school football star, considered him the black sheep of the family; a dark-skinned, heavily muscled black kid named Roy Ray Johnson, who wore a beret, carried bongo drums and went around reciting Vachel Lindsay's poem "The Congo" as if it were his; and Chuck Mayes, a dirty-blond hillbilly from Arkansas with a movie star's profile and an 85 IQ.

Mack never became a full-fledged Gamer—he was too much a

part of the school establishment for that. But he had a craving for bizarre people and rebellious acts that Packer, who had X-ray eyes for human weakness, had spotted. Buddy granted him honorary membership in the gang and allowed him to participate in some of their less-dangerous scams and pranks—walking out of restaurants without paying, stealing golf clubs from the Oriole Country Club, making booze and grass runs into the far reaches of the east side ghetto. Later, when the action escalated and Buddy began dealing drugs and carrying a pistol, he sometimes warned Mack to stay away. Mack interpreted this as a form of respect; it never occurred to him that Packer didn't fully trust him. Even after he left Oriole for the University of Michigan and later for New York, Mack continued to think of himself as a Gamer, the way a staff officer in an elite combat unit might, in the course of time, come to remember himself as a genuine commando—

Shaking twenty years of memories from his head, Mack found the address on Larimore and parked his LeBaron on the dimly lit side street in front of a grimy, two-story brick building. The scruffy neighborhood didn't surprise him; he expected to find Buddy in an out-of-the-way, disreputable part of town.

The sour stench of sweat and disinfectant hit Mack as soon as he opened the door, and it grew stronger as he climbed the concrete stairs to the second floor. Before he reached the top, he heard the sounds of grunting and leather on flesh and realized that Buddy Packer's office was a fight gym.

The place was dim and smoky, and it took Mack a few seconds to adjust to the weak light. The first thing he saw was the practice ring, where two lightweights danced around each other while a brawny, chocolate-colored man in a boating cap hollered, "Mess it up in there, y'all, mess it up." Near the ring, a number of dark, shining bodies were punching heavy bags or skipping rope. Mack looked past them and saw Buddy Packer leaning against a wall.

The first thing that struck Mack was Packer's appearance. He had always been a weird-looking guy—six-foot six, at least, and not more than a hundred and fifty pounds, with wide, bony shoulders and a sunken chest. In the old days he had worn shades day and night, a cowboy hat indoors and out, and matching Ban-Lon-shirt-and-sock outfits. Now, although he was dressed in an expensively tailored dark suit, he looked even weirder. Strawlike brown hair, thin on top, hung over his collar, and round granny glasses of the type Green hadn't seen since the sixties sat on his small, pinched nose. Only his slouch and the cynical expression on his thin lips looked the same. With a stab of disloyalty it occurred to Mack that his old hero looked like the kind of geek who assassinates presidents and rock stars.

Packer saw Mack come in, but he didn't so much as nod. He waited, leaning against the wall, until Mack came to him. They shook hands and Packer examined him with the blunt stare of a pawnbroker appraising a watch. "You look good, Macky. What you been up to?"

"Oh, nothing special. A few books, a few laughs. Yourself?"

"Little of this, little of that. These days I'm a fight manager. Ever hear of Irish Willie Torres? That's him in the ring, over there." He signaled with his eyes at a mocha-colored Latino with a shock of black wavy hair.

"Can't say I have," said Green. "I don't get to the fights much."

"Tough little dude," said Packer. "He could be a main eventer with the right publicity—"

Suddenly Mack reached out and grabbed Packer, pulling the tall, skinny man to him in a tight bear hug. "Goddamn, it's good to see you, Packy."

Packer returned the hug for just a moment and then wiggled free. "Hey, be cool. This isn't a fucking bathhouse."

Abashed, Mack let his gaze wander around the room. "Any of these guys good?" he asked finally.

"Depends what you mean by good. Couple of them can take a punch. Irish Willie's got a future. And Mario di Vinci's a comer."

Mack looked more closely at the fighters; there wasn't a single white kid in the room. "Mario di Vinci?"

"That one over there," said Packer, pointing to an ebony welterweight of seventeen or so who was skipping rope with awkward little leaps. "Hey, Mario, come over here and meet a big-time writer."

The boy put down his rope with evident relief, loped over to Mack, extended a sweaty hand and smiled. He was missing a front tooth.

"Where you from, Mario?" Mack asked.

"Rome, Italy," said the kid with rehearsed alacrity. "My daddy's an I-talian. My mama be from around here."

"Good kid," said Packer, patting Mario on the ass and sending him back to his rope-skipping. "Like my own son. They're all good kids."

"You fool anyone with this routine?"

Packer ground his cigarette out with the heel of his shiny black boot. "Not trying to. The fight game today's like pro wrestling. Nobody gives a shit if one colored boy beats the crap out of another colored boy. You got to give the fans somebody to root for. So I got Irish Willie, Mario, Boom-boom Bernstein, Ivan Ivanovitch—practically the whole fucking UN. That way, when they fight, people say, 'He's a boogie, but he's our boogie.'"

"Why don't you just get some real Italians or Irish or whatever?"

"White kids can't fight," said Packer contemptuously. "Besides, quite a few of them have parents."

"So?"

"So how can I be like a father to my boys if their real dads come around wanting to check the contracts? Look, this is bullshit. Let's go someplace where we can get a drink."

"Sure. How about the Savoy?"

"The Savoy? They closed that dive years ago."

"Too bad," said Mack. "It was the only place I could beat the pinball."

"Yeah, by putting the machine on ashtrays." Packer laughed. "There's a place over on the north side called Stanley's. They serve decent food."

Mack could still taste Joyce McClain's fried chicken. "You eat, I'll drink," he said.

"No sweat," said Packer. "It's good to see you, Macky. You're right on time."

"On time for what?"

"To help me get out of this shithole," said Packer.

"Oh, yeah? How do I do that?"

Packer looked down at his old friend and gave him a dry smile. "Don't worry," he said. "I'm already working on it."

Thirteen

After supper McClain went down to the basement and smoked a cigar. Then he joined Joyce in front of the TV in the living room, went out to the kitchen for a beer, came back and began rereading the sports section of *The Oriole News* and humming to himself. "What's the matter?" Joyce asked.

"Nothing," McClain said. "What makes you think something's the matter?"

"All this jumping around and now you're humming 'It's a Grand Old Flag.'"

"I'm worried about Mack."

"Why, because he went out with his friend?"

"Buddy Packer," said McClain. "You know what he is."

"Mack's a big boy," said Joyce. "He'll survive an evening with a Bad Influence."

"You can laugh if you want to," said McClain, "but Mack's in trouble. You can't be a cop as long as I was and not sense it."

"Now you're going to tell me about your po-lice ESP," said Joyce.

"Well, there happens to be such a thing," said McClain. "Besides, you don't need ESP to see something's going on. I mean look, the guy hardly leaves the house—"

"First you're worried because he goes out and now—"

"That's not what I mean. How come he doesn't want anybody to know he's in town? Why doesn't he call up any of his old buddies, have 'em come over for a drink? Speaking of which, this morning there was another empty Jack Daniels bottle in the trash."

"He told you he likes to drink. A lot of writers do."

"And what about girls?" asked McClain.

"Girls?"

"Women, then. There aren't any. He hasn't been in touch with any old flames—"

"Old flames?" Joyce laughed.

"You know what I mean. I know he's not a faggot—"

"Nice word," said Joyce. "How in the world did I ever end up married to such a bigot?"

"Okay, gay, whatever. I mean, he was married, and he talked about that Linda Birney the other night. Maybe he's sterile, that could be the problem."

"Sterile? I think you mean impotent."

"Can't get it up, whatever the term is. Or maybe it's some kind of midlife crisis."

"Or maybe you just like butting into other people's business. Seriously, John, I want you to get out of this boy's face. There's nothing the matter with Mack except that maybe he's a little bit lonely—"

"Ah, so you agree with me that something's wrong?"

"There's no law against being lonely. You were, when we met. So was I. He'll be fine, just leave him be."

"Yeah," said McClain, "I guess. You wanna see *Murder, She Wrote* or can I dial?"

"I don't care," said Joyce. "Watch whatever you want, long as you stop humming that damn song."

They sat in front of the TV in silence for a while and then McClain said, "I wonder what he's writing?"

"He told you, a book about coming back to Oriole."

"I mean about us."

"He said he'll show it to you when it's finished."

"I was just curious," said McClain.

"You're never just anything," Joyce said. "You're always a whole lot of something. Don't go getting worked up about this book. I know Mack and it's going to be fine."

"You know Mack. Now who's got the ESP?"

"I don't need ESP, I got CPCS," said Joyce, taking her husband's hand.

"What the hell's that?"

"CPCS? Colored People's Common Sense," Joyce said.

Stanley's was a small steakhouse surrounded by a large parking lot full of late-model American gas-guzzlers. Its patrons were mostly beefy, red-faced businessmen in dark suits, accompanied by women young enough to be their secretaries. Dim red lanterns illuminated the booths, Barry Manilow filled the air and a sign over the cash register read: CASH ONLY. It was the sort of Mafia joint Mack had been in many times in New York, but never in Oriole.

"Nice, huh?" said Packer, slipping the wide-bodied host a twenty for the privilege of sitting in the center of the room surrounded by loud drunks. "Owned by a couple of friends of mine." He signaled for a waiter and asked for a tequila with lemon.

"Double bourbon on the rocks," said Mack, lighting a Winston.

"Well, at least you haven't turned into a health nut," said Packer approvingly.

"It's a funny thing," said Mack. "When we were kids we

drank and smoked to seem older. Now I don't quit because I don't want to feel like I'm getting old."

"You were always coming up with fake philosophical shit like that," said Packer.

"Ah, so you do remember me? Back at the gym I thought you were having a hard time figuring out who I was."

"I remember," said Packer. "I've thought about you over the years."

"Yeah, I noticed from all your calls and letters."

"You could have called yourself," said Packer.

"I didn't know where you were," said Mack. "You're not in the phone book."

"Every fucking bill collector in Michigan finds me, I figured you'd be smart enough to get my number if you wanted it."

They sipped their drinks in silence. "You ever see any of the old crowd?" Mack asked after a while.

"The old crowd? What crowd would that be, old bean?"

"Ba-ba, Roy Ray, Mayes—the Gamers."

"They're around," said Packer indifferently. "Ba-ba's a lawyer, J. Brian Lifton. He specializes in child abuse cases, if you can believe that."

"Where's Mayes?"

"Came back from 'Nam dumber than when he left. He was working as a security guard at the airport last I heard."

"What about Roy Ray?"

"You mean his Holiness, Minister Malik."

"Huh?"

"That's what he calls himself these days, Abijamin Fucking Malik. He's in New York, too; I'm surprised you haven't run into him."

"Roy Ray is Abijamin Malik? He's famous. Christ, my agent was bitching about some demonstration of his a few weeks ago."

"Your agent?" said Packer, arching an eyebrow and extending his pinky. "He any relation to your butler?"

"No, seriously. Malik is Roy Ray? I've seen his picture in the paper but I never recognized him."

"He probably doesn't even recognize himself. He's got a beard these days, and a fucked-up looking African hat," said Packer.

"Put that in a novel, nobody'd believe it," said Mack. "Roy Ray, militant minister."

"Minister my ass, he's a con artist," said Packer. "Doing good, too, I'll say that for him."

"You ever see him?"

"He's in town once in a while, we get together. In private. He doesn't like to be seen with white people. Says it's bad for his image."

"So much for the Gamers," said Mack wistfully. All these years he had imagined them together, under Buddy's imperious leadership, the way they had been when he left.

"What'd you think, I'd still be running around with my high school buddies, playing softball on the weekends? Life ain't a Beach Boys tune, Mack. Things change around here, just like in the big city." Packer pushed up his jacket sleeve, revealing a tattooed blue snake slithering through a heart on his thin forearm. "Ever seen one of these?"

"A tattoo? Yeah, I believe I have," Mack said. "Matter of fact, I got the idea for my first novel from a guy with tattoos. Lot of guys who work in the kitchens of Greek restaurants have them, too."

"Well this one ain't from Greektown, it's from Jackson."

"Jackson? Prison?"

Packer nodded and blew some smoke rings. "Yep."

"What were you doing in prison?"

"Some bullshit arson thing," said Packer.

"I'm surprised you got a license to manage fighters, with a record," Mack said.

"I didn't. Melvin Hudson, the guy in the boating hat, he's my partner. He was a guard in Jackson. Tell me something, you got any serious money?"

"What's serious money?"

"Say twenty-five thousand. For that you could buy a piece of one of my kids. You were always a sports fan. This would be like owning a big-league baseball team."

"No thanks," said Mack, signaling the waiter for refills. "I hear the fights are fixed."

"That's the whole point," said Packer. "Well, fuck it, I was just being sociable."

Mack could tell that Packer was angry, but he decided to let it ride; twenty-five thousand dollars was too much to invest in nostalgia. "Tell me something," he said. "Was it rough up there?"

"Up where?"

"In the joint."

"The joint? You sound like those fuckwits in high school who used to talk about 'the Nam.' Lemme tell you something, prison ain't glamorous, no matter what Norman Mailer thinks." He tossed down his tequila, wiped his thin lips with a napkin and grinned. "What's the matter, Macky, you surprised I know who Norman Mailer is? I read some of his books. I even read a couple of yours. Just to kill time, you know?"

"Mine and Mailer's."

"Yeah," said Packer. "His are better, but yours were okay, too. I liked the baseball one."

"Thanks. I'll tell Norman you're a fan, next time I bump into him."

"Yeah, do that," he said. They sat in silence again and then Packer said, "You gonna tell me what brings you back to town?"

"Business," said Mack. "I'm writing a book set here."

"In Oriole? Shakespeare couldn't write a book about this shithole."

"I don't know," said Mack. "We had some memorable times."

"Kid stuff," said Packer. "Small-time fun and games."

"You trying to tell me you sit around the house these days watching the tube? The great Buddy Packer grounded?"

"Well, I get out every once in a while," said Packer, flattered by Mack's image of him. "I still go on an occasional fo-ray."

"Next time, give me a call. This book I'm working on could use a few good Buddy Packer stories."

"Okay," said Packer. "Since you brought up favors, here's what I was thinking. How about a story on Irish Willie for *Sports Illustrated*?"

"What?"

"Aw shit, was I speaking in Latin again? I gotta quit that. I'll say it in English this time—how about writing up a story on Irish Willie Torres?"

"What kind of story?"

"Fuck if I know, you're the writer, I see your stuff in there from time to time. Something that'll help him get a title shot, make me some dough."

"Has he ever beaten anybody? Is he ranked?"

"If he was ranked I wouldn't need you, would I? It wouldn't be a favor."

"I'd like to help, but—"

"But," said Packer, dragging on his cigarette and looking at Mack through narrowed eyes. "But."

"Hey, it's not my magazine. Besides, I've got a book to work on. I didn't come out here to write articles."

"Yeah, well, call me in another twenty years," said Packer, raising a bony hand for the check. "Maybe you won't be so busy."

"Come on, man, I didn't mean it like that. Look, if it's that important to you, I'll get in touch with an editor I know, see if I can pitch him something. Maybe we can hang a story on fighters with strange names or something. But I can't promise."

"I don't accept promises anyway," said Packer, taking the check from the waiter and handing it directly to Mack. "I don't need some cutesy-pooh bullshit about nicknames, I need a piece says that Irish Willie deserves a shot at the title. He gets it, I'll give you ten thousand bucks. How's that?"

"I'll do my best," said Mack. He had no intention of calling

Sports Illustrated, but he didn't want to argue with Packer. He needed him too much for that.

It was just after eleven when they left Stanley's. On the way out to the car Mack turned to Packer. "You ever hear anything about Linda? Where she is, what she's doing?"

"What Linda?" asked Packer, although he knew exactly who Mack meant.

"Linda Birney."

"Linda Birney? Don't tell me you still got a thing for that stuck-up bitch."

"I haven't seen her in years," said Mack. "I was just wondering where she might be, that's all."

"Can't help you," said Packer. Just like you can't help me with twenty-five thousand, he thought to himself. He saw the disappointed look on Mack's face and made a mental note that, big-time author or not, Mack Green was still somebody he could lie to.

At eleven, Joyce went up to bed. McClain locked the front door, leaving the porch light on for Mack, and joined her. By 11:15 Joyce was asleep. At 11:20 McClain, dressed in pyjamas decorated with little brown bears, climbed gingerly out of bed and padded barefoot down the hall to Mack's empty room.

It took approximately forty seconds to jimmy the lock on the desk drawer where Mack kept his manuscript. McClain looked at the title page, *The Diary of a Dying Man,* felt a flutter in his large belly and began to read.

I decided to kill myself on my forty-fifth birthday. I could be cute and say that's the day I realized I was in the final stages of an incurable disease called life, but that's not what happened. The fact that I decided to pull the plug on my birthday was a coincidence, like the fact that it happens to be the anniversary of the Berlin airlift. Probably a few famous people were born that day as well, but I've never checked. I don't even know my sign, to tell you the truth; up until now, I've never believed in luck and now that I'm getting ready to die, I don't really need any.

No, what made me decide to do myself in (in what, I wonder; there's a lot of suicide terminology that doesn't make much sense) was a chance encounter on Columbus Avenue with a thief named Shit. Actually I think that's just his professional name.

McClain stood frozen, the manuscript in his hand, remembering Mack's story about his mugging in New York. "Holy Mother of God," he breathed to himself and turned the pages. When he saw his name he began reading again:

—Big John's the kind of guy I always wanted for a father when I was a kid. My dad was a lawyer, the type people called "dependable," but he wasn't much fun. I remember going up to his office as a kid, him looking around frantically for some way to amuse a ten-year-old. He wound up sending me to the dimestore with his secretary, Andrea. I've often wondered if he was banging her, but he died before I got a chance to have that kind of conversation with him. If there ever would have been such a time.

Big John wouldn't have had a problem entertaining a kid. He would have tossed me in his squad car and said, "Okay, hotshot, today your old man's going to take you out on the mean streets and show you how to maintain law and order." At least that's the way I picture it—

McClain nodded assent and read on for about twenty minutes. Then he carefully replaced the manuscript, relocked the drawer and went back to his bedroom. "Joyce," he said, shaking his wife's shoulder gently. "Joyce, wake up."

"What's the matter, baby?" she asked. "Are you feeling all right?"

"I'm all right," said McClain. "It's Mack. He's in worse trouble than I thought."

"What happened?" asked Joyce, her eyes widening with concern.

"It's not what's happened, it's what's going to happen."

"What do you mean, John? Stop talking in riddles."

"His book is a suicide diary."

"A what?"

"You heard me," said McClain. "He didn't come to Oriole to write a novel. He came home to kill himself."

Fourteen

On the flight back from Detroit, Wolfowitz eased off his loafers, sipped a Bloody Mary and took his time rereading the pages of *Diary of a Dying Man*. He was impressed. The concept was brilliant and the writing was vintage Mack—funny, touching and morbid. He wasn't surprised that a dolt like McClain had mistaken it for the real thing.

Thank God for McClain. Until his call, Wolfowitz had no idea where Mack was or what he was up to. Then, yesterday, Claire had buzzed him and said, "There's a man on the line who says he's a friend of Mack Green's and it's urgent that he talk to you—"

Wolfowitz signaled the stewardess for another Bloody Mary and idly hefted the purloined chapters of Mack's novel. He could see that the McClains were another Mack Green pickup, sidekicks like Tommy Russo, like himself, people for Mack to charm, to use and eventually to betray. This time, though, thanks to John McClain, it wasn't going to work out that way.

They had met that morning in the coffee shop of the Pontchartrain Hotel in downtown Detroit. "Thanks for flying out here on such short notice," McClain said.

"Mack's more than an author to me," said Wolfowitz. "He's a friend."

"I know. He's told me a lot about you."

"Some of it good I hope," said Wolfowitz, the hick expression coming easily to him; back in upstate New York, he had known a lot of dummies like McClain.

"I brought a copy of the diary," said the big ex-cop. He handed it to Wolfowitz gingerly, as if he were afraid the words might spill off the page onto the floor.

Wolfowitz raced through the first entries, making sure to furrow his brow and occasionally grunt with concern. "Thank God you called me," he said finally. "It looks like Dr. Ephron was right."

"Who's Dr. Ephron?"

"Mack's shrink. After you phoned yesterday I got in touch with him. Naturally he didn't want to say much—"

"Naturally," said McClain. "Those guys never want to talk for free."

"But between the lines he let me know that he's been expecting something like this. Apparently Mack's been sounding suicidal for months. Ephron wants to see these"—he tapped the papers in front of him—"and whatever else Mack writes from now on. Can you get it?"

"Long as he stays with us," said McClain. "Breaking into my own desk is a snap."

"Excellent," said Wolfowitz, smiling to convey admiration for the big man's professional skills. "Send me copies say, once a week, and I'll pass them on. That way Ephron can monitor Mack's state of mind."

"What happens if he, well, decides to go through with it?"

"Dr. Ephron said that Mack probably regards you as surrogate parents"—Wolfowitz shrugged to indicate his own inability to understand such abstruse psychiatric reasoning—"and that it isn't likely he'll do anything rash while he's with you."

"You ask me, what Mack needs is a good woman," said McClain. "He's lonely. It comes through on every page. I was like that until I met Joyce. You married?"

"Happily," said Wolfowitz. "Very happily. I won't be, though, if I miss my flight back to New York." He made a rueful, you-know-how-wives-are face and scooped Mack's pages into his briefcase. "Just keep sending me the pages and I'll stay in touch."

"This Ephron, you're sure he knows what he's doing? I mean, some of these shrinks—"

"Relax, John," said Wolfowitz, taking his elbow to convey manly intimacy. "Ephron's the best in his field. He won't let things get out of hand. Trust me on this, okay?"

"You know what they say about guys who say 'trust me,' " McClain said. Wolfowitz looked at him sharply and McClain grinned. "Hey, just kidding," he said, tapping the editor's briefcase. "I wouldn't be giving you this if I didn't trust you. If there's one thing I am, it's a judge of character."

The pilot announced the plane's descent into LaGuardia. Wolfowitz fastened his seatbelt and considered his next move. He took a small, leatherbound address book from his briefcase, checked under "H" and found what he was looking for: the phone number of Walter T. Horton.

Six months ago, Walter T. had come to him begging for help. He was HIV positive, had no health insurance and was desperate for money. "I'd even be willing to ghostwrite," he said.

Wolfowitz had nothing for him then, but he did now. Walter T. Horton was going to write a suicide diary of his own. Like Mack's, it would be the story of an author with a year to live who goes back to his hometown and moves into his old house. Its structure, plot, even some of its characters, would be strikingly similar to *The Diary of a Dying Man*. Only Horton's novel, published by a small house in which Wolfowitz was a very silent partner, would be on sale before Mack Green's diary was even due.

Naturally, Horton's extraordinary work, given force and drama by his personal circumstances, would get a lot of publicity. Wolfowitz would discover, to his horror, that Green had stolen the idea for *The Diary of a Dying Man* from another author—one suffering from AIDS, no less. Gothic would be forced to sue, the news would, of course, leak out—and Mack Green's career would be over; no publisher in America would ever touch one of his books again. As a bonus, the scandal would generate huge sales for Horton's novel.

Maybe, after all that, Mack might really commit suicide—there was a morbid core to *The Diary of a Dying Man* that encouraged Wolfowitz to hope. Or maybe he'd just spend the rest of his life as a drunken, dazed pariah. Either way, Dr. Ephron wouldn't be much help because there was no Dr. Ephron. Wolfowitz smiled, relishing the irony of inventing a fictional character to bring about the destruction of Mack Green. Maybe I should become an author myself, he thought, as the plane touched down on the runway.

Fifteen

Six weeks before Christmas, Herman Reggie made his annual trip to California. He stayed, as usual, with his cousin Jeff
Reggie and his family in Cheviot Hills. During the day he played
uncle, taking his two young nieces shopping, to the movies or out
to Venice to watch the roller skaters. Evenings he spent with Jeff
and his wife, Rosie, often in the company of other movie executives and producers. The only time Herman Reggie was alone was
when he was asleep in the guest bedroom, and even then he made
sure to keep the door open so that the sound of his snoring would
be audible throughout the house.

Herman's California routine was calculated to give the impression of a bachelor enjoying some time with relatives. In fact, he
came to LA for an alibi. The weeks between Thanksgiving and
Christmas were always a rough time in his business. People were
more reluctant than usual to part with their money, especially

when it was supposed to go for Johnny's new bike or Susie's new dollhouse. But a debt was a debt, and Herman Reggie wasn't Santa Claus. An unusual amount of coercion was needed during the holiday season, and sometimes accidents happened. It was a good time to be three thousand miles away from New York, surrounded by respectable citizens who could vouch for his whereabouts.

Still, Herman genuinely enjoyed the time he spent with his relatives. The little girls were well-behaved and Jeff and Rosie were old friends as well as family; they had all grown up together in the same Jersey neighborhood. For a while, years back, Herman and Rosie had been the couple, not Rosie and Jeff. Herman didn't hold it against her that she had chosen his cousin. Rosie was a smart handicapper, which he respected. Her choice had set her up for life in a big house with a pool and lemon trees in the yard, his-and-hers Porsches and a live-in couple from El Salvador to do the dirty work.

All this luxury had been provided by Jeff Reggie. At fifty-one he was two years younger than Herman, although the two cousins, with their bald, oval heads, pinched features and soft, pear-shaped bodies, looked enough alike to be brothers. Jeff was a successful and well-regarded producer of schlock movies—kick-boxing epics, made-for-TV tearjerkers about kids with fatal diseases, cheap sci-fi and the like—and he also did a flourishing side business in porno. He didn't need the money from the skin flicks, but he had never prepared himself for a life of virtue, and his unexpected respectability left him feeling somehow unfulfilled.

Herman understood this—his cousin was, after all, a Reggie—and it served as the basis for collaboration. From time to time, Jeff introduced Herman to high-rolling Hollywood customers. In return, Herman provided New York outlets for some of his cousin's raunchier porno movies. The deals weren't favors—each Reggie scrupulously took his percentage of the action—but there was a sense of family solidarity and trust to the transactions that Herman appreciated.

"I want your opinion about a property I own," he said to Jeff one evening as they sat, dressed in baggy wet bathing suits, sipping white-wine spritzers and snorting lines of coke by the side of the piano-shaped pool. "It's a book. I wonder if it's worth anything."

"A book? Since when do you need my advice about making book?"

"No, a real book, a novel. By an author named Mack Green. Ever heard of him?"

Jeff tilted his head and shut his eyes, trying to remember the name. "Yeah, Paramount bought a baseball story by him a while back," he said. "Nothing ever came of it as I recall. What do you mean, you own his book?"

"Not all of it, 10 percent. His agent owed me some money and I took his cut instead."

"No kidding? Who's the agent?"

"Fella by the name of Russo, in New York."

"Tommy Russo?"

"That's right, Tommy Russo. You know him?"

"Sure I know him. In this business, everybody knows everybody. You gotta be careful with this guy, Herm. He could be connected. Maf."

"Maf," scoffed Reggie. "The man's afraid of midgets."

Jeff looked at his cousin closely but said nothing—he had long ago stopped trying to understand Herman's enigmatic remarks.

"Anyway, I was wondering if maybe this book might not make a good movie," Herman continued. "And if so, how I go about selling it."

"What's it about?"

"I'll tell you the story," said Reggie. "See what you think." Slowly he recounted the plot as Russo had explained it to him in New York.

"Not bad," said Jeff. "It's what they call high concept. Guy decides to kill himself, one year to live, that's good. And author movies are hot these days. How's the book?"

"Green's still working on it," said Herman. "Russo says he's out in his hometown in Michigan."

"Nice touch," said Jeff. "Hero goes back to his hometown. Maybe he decides not to kill himself after all, the thing's got a happy ending. Happy endings are best."

"Well, they can change it around for the movies, no matter how he writes it," said Herman. "That's what they do, right?"

Jeff nodded. "Make it more commercial, yeah."

"So? What can I get for it?"

"Right now? Nothing. If it's a good story, maybe ten, twenty grand on an option. Of course a best-selling novel goes for seven figures. But that's a longshot."

"You're right there," said Herman. "Green's track record lately has been pisspoor."

The two men sat in silence for a while. Then Herman Reggie said, softly, "But what if he really did it?"

"What do you mean by that?"

"Well, supposing this suicide diary turned out to be real? Supposing he wrote it and then went ahead and killed himself?"

"Why would he do that?"

"I'm only asking what if," said Herman.

"A genuine snuff diary by a well-known author? With the right promo, it could be bigger than the Kennedy assassination. Bestseller, movie, TV series, it might be worth fifty million. Hell, these days the sky's the limit."

"I could retire."

"Keep dreaming," Jeff said.

"That's my right as an American." There was another silence and then Herman turned to his cousin and said, "Would you be interested?"

"Like I told you, it depends on how the book does. I don't buy unpublished novels."

"What about if it comes with a corpse? Would that interest you?"

"Herm, this is heavy stuff—"

"Look," said Herman, lowering his voice, "here's how I see it. Green's writing the diary one way or the other. The only question is, will he be alive or dead when it's finished? You care if Mack Green lives?"

"I've never even met Mack Green," said Jeff.

"I rest my case," said Herman. "If you saw in the paper that Mack Green dropped dead tomorrow, you wouldn't even bother reading his obituary. Am I right?"

"Yeah, but he's not going to drop dead."

"Yes he is," said Herman. "For that kind of money, he's going to kill himself, guaranteed."

"Okay, I'll ask again. What's in it for him?"

"That's not the question," said Herman. "The question is, what's in it for you? Half of fifty million bucks is the answer."

"Why half?" asked Jeff.

"Because I'd be in for the other half," said Herman. "Plus my 10 percent agent's fee. But the flick, the TV, anything else, we'd go down the middle. Green delivers the book, I deliver the body and you take care of the show biz."

"They have capital punishment in California," said Jeff. It was a statement of fact, not an objection.

"Michigan doesn't. Besides, that's only for murder. Green's going to commit suicide."

Jeff Reggie rose laboriously from his deckchair, walked around the pool gulping large lungfuls of lemon-scented air and then returned to his seat, lowering his large behind into the pool of water he had left. "Okay, yeah. If this's all I need to know, I'm interested," he said.

"Good. Set us up a production company, something that can't be traced directly to the name of Reggie. Get a front man. Can you do it?"

"No problem. I got a Jew lawyer could set up a phony country if he had to."

"You and your damn ethnic stereotypes," Herman said. "What difference does it make if the lawyer's a Jewish-American?"

"None, none," replied Jeff impatiently. "Forget I mentioned it."

"Okay. I'll sell you the film rights, television, the whole package for, say, a hundred thousand dollars. That sound about right?"

"For an unfinished Mack Green novel? It's outrageous."

"Good, that means it'll motivate him to finish quickly. From what I understand he's a quitter."

"Why not wait until he's dead?"

"Because I need his signature on the contracts, otherwise we could get tied up in all kinds of probate problems. Oh, and make the offer through Tommy Russo. I don't want anybody knowing I'm connected to this."

"Except Tommy. He'll know."

"I'll deal with Tommy."

"You've really thought this through, haven't you?" said Jeff with admiration. "Tell me, how's Green going to kill himself?"

"Does it matter?" asked Herman. "I mean, as far as the movie's concerned?"

"Not really," said Jeff. "I'm just curious."

"Don't worry about it, then," said Herman, draining the last of his spritzer and daintily wiping a speck of coke from one nostril with the back of his plump, liver-spotted hand. "He's a writer. He'll be creative."

Sixteen

Mack sat at his desk watching the cold autumn drizzle run down the window, remembering the last time he made love to Linda Birney, here in this room, more than twenty years before. It had been raining then, too, a warm, sexy summer rain. He could see himself lying naked next to her, eyes closed, running his hands over her soft skin, and he felt a great surge of tenderness for the young man on the bed, which was interrupted by the jangling of the telephone.

"Hey, Macky, what's happening?" Buddy Packer's salutation hadn't changed since high school.

"I'm what's happening," Mack replied automatically, annoyed that his reverie had been interrupted.

"No, as a matter of fact *I'm* what's happening," said Packer. "And I'm happening in about half an hour. You still game for a little fo-ray?"

Mack glanced at the clock on his desk. "Can't it wait till after dinner?"

"This is an afternoon fo-ray situation," said Buddy. "Something you might appreciate."

"Well—"

"I'll pick you up at three-thirty. You got a dark suit?"

"Yeah. Is this a formal occasion?"

"Not exactly," said Buddy. "More like a humanitarian type deal."

Mack hung up, lay down on the bed, closed his eyes and thought about the last time he had spoken to Linda. He had been a junior at the University of Michigan, she was a freshman at Vanderbilt. Even after all these years he could recall every word of their conversation.

The subject had been Christmas vacation. Linda said she wouldn't be able to get back to Michigan to spend it with Mack, as they had planned.

"If you can't get away, I'll come down there," he said. All semester they had been meeting in the middle, in Covington, Kentucky, where they spent long weekends in a motel. Nashville was a serious drive, especially in the snow, but Mack didn't care. He was twenty years old and in love.

"I don't think so," said Linda. "I've got a lot to do."

"Come on, this isn't your parents you're talking to. How busy could you be?"

"Busy," said Linda tightly.

"Jesus, Linnie, what's going on down there? Are you seeing somebody else?" Until that moment the thought had never crossed his mind, but as soon as the words were out of his mouth, he knew they were true.

Her silence confirmed it. For twenty seconds, the only sound on the line was two people breathing.

"Who is he?" said Mack.

"Mackinac, I'm sorry," she said in her throaty voice. "I really am. It just happened."

"Who is he?" Mack screamed softly into the phone; he was calling from a booth in the lobby of the Student Union.

"Just a boy. A football player."

"A football player? What kind of football player? What position?"

"What difference does it make?"

"It makes a difference," said Mack. "I want to know, is he a great big hairy linebacker? Or a skinny little pass receiver? Or maybe it's one of those muscle-bound linemen with no neck—"

"Don't piss me off, Mackinac," Linda said. "I feel bad enough already."

"What fucking position does he play?" Suddenly it was the most important question in the world, because it kept him from asking what he dreaded to find out—if she was lost to him.

He heard her sigh. "He's a quarterback."

"Not Gregg Flanders?"

"Yes, as a matter of fact. How did you know?"

Green felt a wave of angry misery wash over him. "He's an All-American, Linnie."

"Mack—"

"Jesus, I can't believe you went off to college and fell in love with a quarterback. It sounds like some movie from the forties. What next? You going out for the cheerleading squad?"

"If I feel like it," she said coolly.

"Linnie, I'm sorry. Listen, let's get married. I'll be down there in eighteen hours and we can go to Nevada—"

"I don't want to spend Christmas break with you, how can we get married? I don't love you anymore. I wish I did but I can't help it, I don't."

"So, you want to just be friends, is that it?"

"No," said Linda. "I want us not to be in touch."

"Okay, no problem," said Mack. "If that's the way you feel." He heard the phone click, and then he put the receiver against his forehead and began to cry. He cried until a fat kid began tapping on the glass booth with a quarter. He gave the kid the finger and went home.

Mack opened his eyes and sighed. It would make a great scene for the *Diary;* the hero, laying quietly in his old room, longing for a girl he had loved years ago. He sighed again, climbed out of bed, sat down at the keyboard and began to write, working steadily until he heard Buddy's horn. He quickly slipped into his suit and went outside, where he found Packer slouched in the driver's seat of his T-Bird, smoking a joint and listening to a Patsy Cline song on the radio.

"I was right in the middle of a great erotic scene," Mack said, taking a hit off the joint. "This better be good."

"It will be," said Packer. He was in high good spirits. "What's it like, making up stories about pussy? Do you have to be horny to do it, or does it get you horny as you go along?"

"You should know." Mack laughed. "You've been making them up long enough."

Packer let the jibe pass. "Tell me something—you ever written about lawyers?"

Mack nodded. "A couple of times. Why?"

"Irish Willie's got a little legal problem and seeing as how you've got the gift of tongues, I thought you might be able to help him out."

"You want me to impersonate a lawyer?"

"No big thing," said Buddy. "I'll fill you in on the way."

They drove out the north side, past the abandoned auto plants and boarded-up stores into the green, damp, semirural countryside, Buddy talking all the way. After twenty minutes or so, Packer pulled into a small subdivision of ratty-looking wood shacks no bigger than double-wide house trailers. "This looks like it," he said, parking his car in the weedy grass in front of one of the shanties. "Remember now, you're a lawyer. Act snooty."

Packer knocked on the door and waited. After a minute, it opened and a thin man of about forty with a nasty-looking scar on his deeply sunburned neck stood glaring at them.

"If this is about the electric, I sent in the money," he said. The ripe aroma of marijuana and rotting garbage wafted past him onto the tiny concrete porch.

"No, it's about your daughter, Ivy," said Packer. "My name's Buddy Packer, Willie Torres's manager. And this is my attorney, Mr. Green."

The man's eyes narrowed and the scar on his neck seemed to throb. "You tell that little Spanish-speaking nigger to stay the hell away from Ivy or I'll cut his fuckin' cock off with a butcher knife."

"I'm sorry you feel that way," said Mack smoothly. "From what Mister Packer tells me, he's a good lad."

"Good lad my ass," said the man, stepping back inside. "I got nothin' more to say to you, mister."

"Wait," said Packer, catching the door with his foot. "I'd ask to come in, but it stinks. What I drove all this way for was to tell you that Ivy's pregnant."

The man stood speechless with fury. "Congratulations, Mr. Twilley, you're going to be a grandfather," said Mack.

"That little fucker's going to jail," said Twilley in a rage-choked voice. "Ivy's not but fifteen years old. That's underage."

"Yes, but she's a very mature young woman," Mack said, in an urbane tone that made Packer glance at him with approval. "Due to your upbringing, I'm sure."

"This is my property and you're trespassing," said Twilley. "Get your ass out of here. Right now."

"You see, the thing is, Willie and Ivy were hoping to get married," said Mack, unperturbed. "And since, as you just pointed out, she's underage, she needs your consent."

"Soon as you leave, I'm goin' down to the police station, fill out a warrant against your nigger," Twilley said to Packer.

Mack coughed. "I was afraid you'd say that," he said. "You see, Ivy mentioned something about, well, a sexual relationship between the two of you, and I—"

"Sexual relationship? Are you saying that I fucked my own daughter?"

"I don't blame you," said Packer blandly. "Hell, I'd probably do the same in your position; Ivy's a real fine piece of ass. But daughter-fucking happens to be illegal in the state of Michigan, isn't that so, counselor?"

"Yes, indeed," said Mack. "Not to mention incest, sodomy, contributing to the delinquency of a minor, sexual harassment and abuse, statutory rape, ah, violation of fiduciary responsibility—"

"How much time is he looking at, Mr. Green?" asked Packer.

"Perhaps ten years," said Mack. "Maybe more."

"I got nothing to worry about," said Twilley uncertainly. "You got no proof."

"Ah, but I'm afraid that under the prevailing writ of mandamus and the Dred Scott Decision, the court will be predisposed to accept your daughter's deposition as, ah, empirically conclusive," said Mack. He looked at Packer out of the corner of his eye and saw that he was fighting hard against a snicker.

"I ain't got money for no lawyers," said Twilley, in a low, defeated tone that Mack imagined he had used often. Packer took a piece of paper and a pen from his inside jacket pocket and handed them to the man. "Sign this, Mr. Twilley, and there won't be any problems."

Twilley looked at the document suspiciously. "Is it legal?" he asked.

"Perfectly legal," said Mack.

"Well, in that case, fuck it." He took the pen and scrawled his name. "I got other daughters," he said.

"That was quite a fo-ray," said Mack over drinks at Stanley's, where he and Packer had gone to celebrate their legal triumph. "Did what's-her-name, Ivy, really tell you her old man was screwing her?"

"She didn't need to. I know these 'necks out here. It was an educated guess."

"You're unbelievable," said Mack, shaking his head.

"You weren't bad either. The fucking Dred Scott Decision. Where'd you come up with that one?"

Mack shrugged modestly and Packer slapped him on the back. "You know something, Macky? You turned out all right. I thought you might have gone a little uptown on me, but you and me, we make a good team. I think you should reconsider about going into business with me."

"Going into business?"

"That offer I made you about a piece of Irish Willie still goes."

"No thanks," said Mack. "I'll stick to being his lawyer."

"Yeah, well, fuck it," said Packer. "I've got other possibilities. Too bad Willie didn't knock up a rich girl, I could have got the dough from her family."

"Were you born this way or did you have to work at it?"

Packer laughed. "Just comes natural. Now let me ask you something—are you horny by any chance?"

"As a matter of fact I am," said Mack. He was—thinking about Linda that afternoon had made him want a woman—but even if he hadn't been he never would have admitted it to Packer. "Why, you pimping on the side?"

"Not exactly. This thing is, Jean's hot to meet you—she read one of your books at the junior college. It's required reading in some course she took on Michigan writers."

"I'm required reading?"

"Yeah, like fucking *Hiawatha*. Anyway, she's got this friend, Debbie. I figured I could get her to make it a foursome."

"I'd have to call Joyce, tell her I'm not coming back for supper."

"Goddamn, Macky, you already had one fucked-up childhood out here, wasn't that enough? Why don't you move into a hotel like a grown-up?"

"I like it where I am," said Green. "What's she look like? Debbie?"

"She's a fox. Works as a model at Hudson's out in West Tarryton. Dumber than dogshit, but who cares? Anyway, I figure if you have to spend a night listening to Jean tell you all about what a big man you are at the junior college, the least I can do is get you laid."

"Sure," said Mack. "Give her a call."

The two women arrived an hour later. Jean was a dark-rooted blond with large breasts and a resigned attitude; just the kind of convenient girlfriend Mack expected Buddy to have. Debbie looked like a young Faye Dunaway, with long brown hair, high cheekbones and full, pouty lips. Mack got excited just watching her saunter across the room.

"It's a real honor to meet you, Mack," said Jean. "I've never met an author before." The words had a stiff, rehearsed sound.

"I have," said Debbie brightly. "This girl I work with at Hudson's? Sherrie Lyle? She wrote *Firm Thighs in Fifty Minutes*? They sell it in the supermarket."

"Mack's a novelist," said Jean, showing him that she appreciated the difference.

"Well, Sherrie's book did real well," Debbie bubbled. "She said they sold, um, three hundred thousand. Does that sound right?"

"Probably," said Mack, mentally calculating the royalties, which, he guessed, came to roughly five times more than he had earned on his last two novels.

"We call her Jane," said Debbie. "After Jane Fonda."

"I forgot to bring my copy of *The Oriole Kid*," said Jean. "I wanted you to autograph it for me."

"Next time," said Mack, looking at Debbie out of the corner of his eye, hoping she'd be impressed. He didn't feel like working too hard.

"Some of my favorite books are when people write about their hobbies," said Debbie, who didn't seem to care if Mack autographed novels or not. "Like—" She paused, trying to think of one, and then smiled. "Well, you know. Do you have any hobbies, Mack?"

"He does impersonations," said Packer.

"I play the mouth organ," said Debbie. "My dad taught me. He says that the mouth organ's the hardest instrument in the world to play. Know why?"

"Ah, no," said Mack, avoiding Buddy Packer's eyes. "Why?"

"Because you can't see the holes!" She took a small silver-plated harmonica from her purse, rapped it once on her palm and played a few bars of "For the Longest Time." "See what I mean?"

"Yeah, I do," said Green, making a mental note to record this conversation; Debbie didn't know it, but she had just become a character in the *Diary*. "How about another drink?"

"I'll have a boilermaker, hold the beer chaser," she said. "I'm watching my weight."

"I'm watching it too," said Mack, signaling for the waitress.

Three drinks later, Debbie suddenly stood and straightened her dress. "I've got to go home now," she said. "We're shooting swimsuits tomorrow at seven."

"I'll walk you to your car," Mack said.

In the parking lot, next to her white Corvette, Debbie faced Mack and put her arms loosely around his neck. "You're fun," she said. "Not stuck up like I was afraid you'd be."

Out of instinct Mack pulled her to him, but her soapy scent made him slightly queasy. He flashed again on Linda, and felt himself spring erect. Debbie felt it, too, squirmed against him for a moment and then pulled back.

"I really have to get up early," she said. "But don't feel bad, you're not missing out. I never make it with a guy on the first date, no matter how much I like him. Only tramps do it on numero uno."

"Yeah, I don't do it on the first date, either," said Mack.

"You don't?" said Debbie, her eyes widening. "Oh, you're just kidding." She pinched Mack's cheek and slid into the driver's seat. "Give me a call over the weekend. I don't have any rules about numero dos."

"Dos?"

"Yeah, like the beer," she said, pleased with her witticism. "Will you call me?"

"Sure," said Mack. "Absolute. Like the vodka."

Mack went inside and rejoined Packer and Jean. "Struck out, eh?," Buddy said with a nasty grin.

"Nah, we did it in the parking lot," said Mack.

"Debbie doesn't sleep around on the first date," Jean said.

Mack nodded. "She mentioned that."

"Only tramps do it on the first date," said Jean loyally.

"What does that make you then?" asked Packer.

"That's different," said Jean, flushing. "I meant with a stranger. I already knew who you were."

Packer looked at his watch. "I've got someplace to be," he said. "Drink up and I'll drop you both off."

"You going to see that African friend of yours?" Jean said, losing a little of her genteel manner.

"He's not an African, he's just got an African name," said Packer.

"Everybody you know's got some kind of weird name," said Jean. "Present company excepted," she added, smiling at Mack.

"Roy Ray?" Mack asked Packer.

"Yeah, he's in town."

"I'd love to see him. Can I come along?"

"He doesn't socialize with white people."

"I don't want to take him to the prom, I just want to say hello. Besides, who are you, Kunte Kinte?"

"This is business."

"It's business for me, too," said Mack. "Something I could use, maybe."

Packer thought for a moment and then nodded. "Yeah, okay," he said. "Maybe we can both get something out of it."

• • •

Packer dropped Jean at home and then drove through downtown Oriole to a small wooden church only a few blocks from his gym. As they pulled up, a uniformed chauffeur was languidly wiping the dust from a Rolls-Royce Silver Cloud. "This is it," said Packer, parking behind the Rolls. "Check out the royal chariot."

Packer led Mack into the building, which smelled of incense and wax, through a long hallway into a large, shelf-lined room filled with exotic-looking merchandise—colorful robes, red-tassled fezzes, wooden masks and African artifacts. There were also books on sale, all written by Abijamin Malik, and cassettes of his recorded sermons. Off the room was a small office where a staid woman in a white robe and turban sat typing at a computer. She greeted Packer with an African salutation and a smile. "You can go right in," she said. "Minister Malik is expecting you."

"You wait here," Packer told Mack. He entered the room without knocking. There, behind a brilliantly polished rosewood desk, sat a large, ebony-colored man wearing a flowing silk robe and a fez.

"You're late," he said.

"I've got a surprise for you," said Packer. "A mystery guest."

Malik scowled. "This is a private meeting."

"It'll just take a minute." Packer leaned out the open doorway and signaled for Mack to join them.

Mack walked into the room with a broad grin on his face. "Hey, Roy Ray," he said.

Malik's face lit up in a broad smile. He rose, extended both hands in a gesture of welcome and took Mack by the shoulders. They stood for a moment, beaming at each other, and then Malik took Mack's right hand and stroked the palm with two fingers. Mack recoiled slightly and Malik gave a deep, full-throated laugh. "That's our special greeting," he said. "It means you're among friends. What on earth are you doing in Oriole?"

"Working on a book," said Mack. "I'm an author."

"I know," said Malik, the slow, formal cadence he lent to the words sounding like it was borrowed from James Earl Jones.

"When Buddy told me who you were, I couldn't believe it," said Mack. "Is it all right if I call you Roy Ray?" Malik nodded. "I mean, I've been reading about you, I see your signs all over the place and I had no idea it was you. ARCH. I don't even know what it stands for."

"The African Racial Church of Holiness," said Roy Ray. "ARCH. Incorporated." Mack thought he detected a slight twitch at the corners of the minister's mouth. "We've got ninety-one congregations across the country. The mother church is in Harlem."

"And you're the head? Of all of them?"

"He owns them," said Packer.

"You own ninety-one churches?"

"Only God owns the church. I merely collect His rent."

"From the looks of that Rolls out front, you must be collecting heavy duty," said Mack.

" 'The earth is the Lord's and the fullness thereof,' " intoned Malik. "Can I offer you gentlemen some refreshment?"

"I could use a drink," said Mack. "This is amazing."

"We don't indulge in alcoholic beverages," said Malik with heavy dignity. "Alcoholic beverage, white man's leverage. Perhaps you'd care for a glass of African carrot juice. We manufacture it ourselves. It's called Archade."

"It's Kool-Aid," said Packer. "They just change the label. I'd skip it if I were you."

Malik ignored the remark. "We should get together some time in New York," he said, handing Mack a gold-embossed business card. "Call me when you get back to the city."

"Sure," said Mack. "I'd like to hear you preach some time."

"I'm afraid not," said Malik. "Our services are racially exclusive. My people need to be free to express their true selves, especially in church. Bring a white man around and black folks start acting like they're on *The Cosby Show*."

Mack shrugged. "Maybe. But I've been living with a mixed couple—you remember Derrick Milton? His mother married an Irish ex-cop named John McClain—and I'd say it looks like a pretty good relationship."

"Race-mixing leads to race-nixing," said Malik with doctrinal finality.

"You really believe that?"

"It's one of the four pillars of my Church," he said. "Racial purity, daily prayer, tithing and economic justice. We're the Church that takes the 'boy' out of boycott."

"And puts the black in blackmail," said Packer. "Lookit, Roy Ray, we've got to talk. Mack, you wait in the other room, okay?"

Mack sat in the outer office leafing through an ARCH publication he found on the coffee table. He was reading an article about the Nigerian origins of the British royal family when the door to Malik's private office opened and Packer emerged, a sullen look on his face. He gestured to Mack to follow, and walked out of the church with long, angry strides.

"Problems?" Mack asked.

"Fucking asshole," snapped Packer.

"What happened?"

"He was going to take a piece of Irish Willie, but he backed out. Says it would be bad for his image if it gets out he's doing business with a white man."

"It probably would," said Mack. He wondered if the piece of Irish Willie Roy Ray had turned down was the same one Packer had offered him, and how many pieces the fighter had been divided into already.

"He was shucking and jiving," said Packer, "trying to get a bigger slice. Imagine, him trying to bullshit me. Jesus, Macky, it's not fucking fair. I'm scrambling around for a measly twenty-five thousand bucks and His Holiness in there's running a five-million-a-year con."

"Maybe it's not a con."

Packer shot Mack a sharp look. "Are you kidding? It's a scam, pure and simple. Roy Ray's a Gamer. The man's a master fucking humbug, just like the rest of us."

"The rest of us? You including me?"

"Anybody earns his living making up stories is a bullshit artist," said Packer. "I mean that as a compliment."

"I'm sure you do," said Mack. "So, you don't think he really hates white people?"

"Naw," said Packer, cupping his hands against the wind as he lit a Lucky. "Why should he? He's making a fucking fortune off 'em. Whips up the natives, gets them to boycott some company and then sells 'em out to whitey. Shit, I should have been born black. I'd be a fucking trillionaire by now."

"Yeah, a tough break," said Mack, amused and a little surprised. He had never heard Packer feel sorry for himself like this before.

"Listen, Macky, I know you've got twenty-five thousand bucks. You don't want to invest, loan it to me. I'll pay it back with interest in two, three months."

"Sorry," said Mack. "I can manage a couple thousand if you need it—"

"Fuck a couple thousand," said Packer, walking toward his T-Bird. Suddenly he turned to Mack and thrust a bony finger into his chest. "What about the article?"

"What article?"

"The one you said you'd do on Irish Willie for *Sports Illustrated*. You forget?"

"I didn't forget," lied Mack. "I pitched it to an editor and he said he'd get back to me on it."

"Yeah, get back to you," said Packer. "Everybody's bullshitting me today." He unlocked the car with an angry twist of the key, climbed into the driver's seat and turned the ignition. Mack stood on the curb, waiting for him to open the door on the passenger side. Packer cracked the window an inch or two and said, "You and Roy Ray were made for each other, you know that? You're a couple of ungrateful front-runners."

"Come on, Packy, open up," said Mack, trying the locked door.

Packer peered at him through his granny glasses and put the car into gear. "Walk home, front-runner," he said and peeled out, leaving Mack alone on the curb.

"Hey, come back here," he called out. Roy Ray's chauffeur turned and stared at him for a moment and then went back to wiping dust off the Silver Cloud. Mack headed up the block, right past the blue Mitsubishi parked farther down the street. There was a man sitting in the car, but Mack was too mad to notice. Even if he had, it wouldn't have mattered. He had never seen Arlen Nashua in his life.

Seventeen

Douglas Floutie liked to think of Gothic Books as a publishing house with rich traditions; and none, in his view, was richer than the annual Thanksgiving party. It was held on the Tuesday before the holiday, and its guest list included editors, authors, literary agents and other members of what Floutie referred to as "our creative family." Refreshments were, inflexibly, sherry, rum punch and Stilton cheese; entertainment consisted of an oration-length greeting by Floutie; and attendance, at least for the Gothic editorial staff, was mandatory.

Wolfowitz didn't usually enjoy social gatherings, but he eagerly anticipated each Thanksgiving reception. It gave him an annual opportunity to witness several hundred of the most influential people in American publishing squirm as Douglas Floutie made an ass of himself—thereby buttressing the generally held opinion that credit for Gothic's prosperity belonged to its editor in chief rather than to its pompous publisher.

This year Wolfowitz was in an especially good mood. Earlier that day Horton had agreed to write his own version of *Diary of a Dying Man,* based on the outline Wolfowitz had prepared—an outline culled from the chapters McClain had been sending him. "Of course this isn't my usual way of working," Horton said, "but these aren't usual circumstances, I'm afraid."

"I'm afraid not," Wolfowitz agreed. Eventually Horton would realize that the book he had written had been based on Mack Green's novelized diary, but it didn't matter. He owned Walter T. Horton. "Listen, take good care of yourself," he said.

"Why, thank you, Arthur," said Horton, smiling wanly.

Wolfowitz didn't return the smile. "I want the book finished on time," he said. "Make sure it is."

It had been a good morning's work, thought Wolfowitz as he scanned the crowd, catching sight of Louise talking animatedly to several of the younger editors. He felt no pangs of jealousy or suspicion: Louise was still a beautiful woman, but time had dampened her appetite for sexual adventure. What she hungered for now was fame and professional esteem. Since *Village Idiots,* she had written (and Gothic had published) five novels and two volumes of short stories. The books all sold well, and the Gothic PR people saw to it that she got more than her share of talk-show appearances and interviews. The Thanksgiving party, where Louise could see influential critics and editors sucking up to her husband, served as a useful reminder of how crucial he had been, and still was, to her ambitions.

"Surveying your empire, Arthur? Or just counting the house?"

"Hello, Dorothy," said Wolfowitz. He didn't bother smiling or opening his hands in his usual gesture of warmth; Dorothy Ravitsky had long since decoded his ersatz body language and was annoyingly immune to it.

"Brad Knox told me you're enthusiastic about his idea for promoting *The Big Book of Smiths,*" she said.

"A brilliant gimmick," said Wolfowitz. "One that I might not have thought of, but—"

"Jesus, Arthur, a launch party in Smith City, Kansas?"

"The exact geographical center of the United States," said Wolfowitz in a fair imitation of Bradley Knox's pedantic tone.

"Why are you doing this to him?"

"I'm just rewarding staff initiative," said Wolfowitz blandly. "Besides, Bradley has the confidence of our esteemed publisher."

"What's the matter, Arthur, has Louise been making eyes at him? Is that what this is all about?"

Wolfowitz regarded her coldly. "You know what, Dorothy? You can be a real bitch sometimes."

"And occasionally you aren't a prick," said Dorothy, walking away. "That makes us both unpredictable."

Wolfowitz watched her leave. Suddenly he felt a hand on his elbow, turned and saw Douglas Floutie and his father-in-law, old man Fassbinder. Floutie was dressed in tweedy Ivy League fashion, his salt-and-pepper hair carefully tousled, a pair of reading glasses dangling carelessly from a cord around his neck. The getup was intended to convey donnish understatement, but to Wolfowitz's eye it made Floutie look like a road-company Mr. Chips.

Fassbinder was a different matter. Like masters who come to resemble their pets, he had acquired the wattled neck and beaky features of the poultry he slaughtered by the millions. There was also something roosterish in the mean indignation he radiated. He made no effort to hide his contempt for his son-in-law, especially from Wolfowitz.

Fassbinder gave the editor in chief's elbow a squeeze just short of a pinch and fixed him with a nearsighted stare. "We gonna make any money this year?" he demanded. It was a rhetorical question; the old man knew Gothic's earnings to the penny.

"That's what we're in business for," said Wolfowitz.

"Thank God somebody around here knows that," Fassbinder snorted. "I just asked Floutie what kind of year we're having and he started telling me about Pulitzer Prizes and National Book Awards."

"Prizes translate into prestige, and in publishing prestige is a very valuable intangible," said Floutie defensively.

"Prizes are chickenshit," squawked Fassbinder, whose conversation leaned heavily on the imagery of the poultry business. "The only prize that matters is what's under the little line at the bottom. Am I right or wrong on that, Wolfowitz?"

"You're going to like this year's numbers," said Wolfowitz smoothly.

"No thanks to Floutie here. Poems give him goosebumps, but he don't care about the number under that little line. Well, why should he? It's my money, after all. Ain't that so, Floutie?"

"I don't believe that this is the most auspicious time for a financial discussion," said Floutie with a forced smile.

"I got a poem for ya," Fassbinder said. The old man cleared his throat and began to declaim in a loud voice: " 'Oh, her lips were pink like a rooster's dink and her hair was chicken-shit brown. Her titties flopped loose like the nuts of a goose and she come from a hot-shit town.' " He stopped abruptly, glared at Floutie, who had reddened at his father-in-law's vulgarity, and grinned. "Wanna hear the rest?"

"Not particularly."

"Too bad," said Fassbinder, and resumed reciting: " 'I fucked her once and I fucked her twice and I fucked her once too often. I broke the mainspring in her ass and sent her to her coffin.' Now, that's poetry. Know who wrote it?"

Floutie shook his head; Wolfowitz looked on, enjoying the encounter enormously.

"Neither do I," said the old man. "Don't matter, either, 'cause you can't sell it. Nobody buys poems or little books about sensitive bull dykes in London or Christ knows what all. The public wants adventure, gossip books, how-to-do-its. That's what sells."

"You ought to write a book yourself," said Wolfowitz, snapping his fingers to signal a brainstorm. "Practical advice from a hardheaded tycoon. It could be a bestseller. Good advertising for the poultry business, too."

"Not a bad idea," said Fassbinder. "Hell, if Iacocca and Perot can do it, why not me? I've even got a title. *How to Lay the Golden Egg.* Whaddya think of that one?"

"By Harlan Fassbinder, the Prince of Poultry. I love it," said Wolfowitz, glancing at Floutie. "If you're serious I'll get somebody to work with you on it, do the technical stuff."

"Like what?"

"Oh, just the writing," said Wolfowitz.

"Sure, why not? Maybe we'll get Floutie here to do the scribbling. Save some money that way."

The publisher flushed and glared at Wolfowitz. "I think we'll find another ghostwriter, if you don't mind," he said. "I have a few other duties—"

"Duties my ass," said Fassbinder. "Your duty is to keep my daughter smiling and not fuck up while I go on laying golden eggs. Ain't that so, Wolfowitz?"

"You'll have to excuse me," said Floutie, in a voice choked with anger. "I have guests to attend to."

"Go, go," said Fassbinder, waving a veiny hand. "Go mingle, professor. Me and Wolfowitz got things to talk about."

Floutie organized his features into a semblance of a smile. "Happy Thanksgiving, Harlan. Arthur," he said, walking off into the crowd.

"Think I was too hard on the boy?" asked Fassbinder with a malicious grin. "Think I hurt Douggie's feelings?"

"I wouldn't presume to say, sir," said Wolfowitz, imitating the publisher's rounded diction.

"Goddamnit, you're a pisser, Wolfowitz." Fassbinder laughed. "Are you serious about that book or were you just pulling Floutie's wee-wee?"

"Little of both," said Wolfowitz. "Frankly, I think writing a book would be a waste of your time. Even a bestseller would be chicken feed by your standards."

"Chicken feed, eh? You're sounding more like a poultry man every day. You ever get sick of fooling around with authors and such, you come down to Little Rock and make some real money. Eventually somebody's got to take over, and it sure as hell ain't gonna be Floutie."

"It's an interesting idea," said Wolfowitz noncommittally.

"Well, think on it," said Fassbinder. "There's a lot of satisfaction in the poultry business. Hell's bells, they call Thanksgiving Turkey Day, don't they? You never heard of a holiday called Book Day. See my point?"

"Must give you a lot of pleasure, knowing how many Americans are eating birds you slaughtered," said Wolfowitz dryly.

"Pleasure don't begin to cover it," said the old man, his eyes glinting and his nostrils flaring with pride. "This kind of power makes a man feel like fucking Joe Stalin."

Fassbinder walked away, chortling audibly. Wolfowitz turned to look for Louise and bumped into Tommy Russo, who extended a pudgy hand. "Congratulations," he said.

"Congratulations?" For a moment he thought Tommy had overheard Fassbinder's offer about the poultry business.

"To all of us. On Mack's novel."

"What about it?"

"Andy Ligget called me this morning. He offered me a hundred thou for the movie rights."

"Who the hell's Andy Ligget?"

"An indie out in California. I've sold him a couple of things before."

"How the hell did he know about the *Diary*? The book's only half finished. From what Mack tells me," he added quickly.

"Yeah, well, I got the word around," Russo lied. "That's what I get paid for. Anyway, it looks like we've got a winner."

"You do," said Wolfowitz. "We don't own a piece of the movie rights, you know that. You're the one who should be happy."

"I am happy," Russo lied again. When Ligget had called, Tommy had immediately understood that Herman Reggie was behind the deal; it would be the bookie, not he, who collected the commission. Still, he certainly wasn't going to tell Wolfowitz that. He didn't want it getting back to Mack that he was being represented by a gangster—a gangster with heavy Hollywood connections, evidently. Probably Ligget was paying back a gambling debt, too, Russo thought, giving Reggie a double-dip on what should have been his project. If word of the arrangement ever leaked out, Tommy knew he'd be the laughingstock of the entertainment industry.

"How's Mack taking it?" Wolfowitz asked.

"He doesn't know yet. I called out there earlier, but he wasn't home. I can't wait to tell him, though—he's gonna go crazy."

"That's for sure," said Wolfowitz. "Are they paying up front?"

"The whole amount. Those Hollywood guys throw money around like dirt."

"Wonder what he's going to do with it?"

Russo shrugged. "You know how Mack is with money. He'll probably blow it."

"Well, like you said, he deserves some success after all these years," said Wolfowitz. With any luck, Green would wind up not only humiliated and discredited, but in debt to a Hollywood studio that would certainly sue him when his plagiarism was discovered. The thought made him chuckle. "You know what this proves?" he asked.

Russo shook his head. "What?"

"That sometimes good things really do happen to good people."

Eighteen

When Mack came down to breakfast the next morning, he found McClain sitting in the kitchen. "It's past ten," he said. "What'd they do, close the Elks?"

"I'm going out to the mall today," said McClain. "Buy Joyce a Christmas present."

"Little early for that, isn't it?"

"I like to shop early, before all the good merchandise gets snapped up," said McClain. "How about coming along for the ride? I could use a second opinion."

"Well—"

"Good. Drink your coffee and let's get going. We finish early, I'll have time for a few lanes this afternoon."

They drove out to Four Corners, a huge, confusing warren of upscale shops and chain boutiques in West Tarryton. McClain hummed "It's a Grand Old Flag" over and over as he led Mack through the labyrinth, going in and out of jewelry stores and clothing shops, examining dozens of potential gifts and rejecting them all.

"Jesus, buy something. We're running out of stores," said Mack.

"What's the matter, hotshot, you getting tired?"

"Aren't you?"

McClain consulted his watch. "It's 11:45," he said.

"So?"

"Time for a bite to eat. Go over to the food court, get us some refreshments and I'll save a table."

Mack went to one of the counters, picked up two large plastic cups of beer and two slices of pizza, and brought them over to the round metal table McClain was guarding. "Budweiser all right?" he asked.

"King of beers," said McClain, taking a swig. "So, hotshot, how's your love life?"

"What?"

"You heard me. It's a simple question. What's the matter, you embarrassed to admit you're not making any headway with the local chicks?"

"Hey, just last night I had drinks with a model who plays the harmonica and does it on the second date." Mack laughed.

McClain snorted. "You know how many ditzy beauty queens I went out with in my life? Before I met Joyce?"

"Is it an odd or even number?"

"My fair share, wise guy. More than my fair share, ask any-body. It was fun, too, until I found the real thing." He shot Mack a look of such bald significance that he laughed out loud.

"Is this when we discuss the birds and the bees? 'Cause if it is, I want to take some notes."

"I'm talking love here, not sex. Something you don't know diddly-squat about."

"And you do?"

"Goddamn right," said McClain. "The Queen of Sheba comes along, you'd still want something better."

"So I'm choosy, so what?"

"Here's so what: see that cotton-candy stand over there?" Green followed McClain's finger with his eyes and nodded. "Okay, now look to your left, the Ward's sign?" Mack nodded again. "Good. There's about thirty feet between them, right?"

"About that."

"Okay, that's your field of vision, Ward's and the booth. Don't look beyond them in either direction."

Mack swung around in his seat, positioning himself for an unobstructed view. "Now what?"

"Now I'm going to teach you a game. What you do is, start counting the women who walk by. Look 'em over good because you have to choose one of the next ten females to spend the rest of your life with."

"I don't get it," said Mack.

"When I was about your age a guy I know, Maury Steiner, he's dead now, heart attack right in the middle of a bowling tournament, he taught me this game. Called it the Game of Life. Just look at the women as they pass by, and when you see the one you want, say *stop*. Then go on counting until you get to ten. That way you see what you missed."

"What if I don't want any of them?"

"In that case you wind up with number ten," said McClain. He gestured to a gangly teenager in a Tigers' cap who skipped by holding the hand of a pimply boy. "There's number one."

"Hey, she's just a kid, she doesn't count," Mack protested.

McClain shook his head decisively. "All females with jugs count," he said.

"Is that what it says in the official rule book? Jugs?"

"Just concentrate, hotshot. The next Mrs. Green could be by any time."

A tall, well-built woman in her late twenties walked past pushing a baby stroller. Mack examined her closely. She had curly dark hair and a full, rounded figure, but her complexion was spotted and she wore a vacant expression. He was tempted, but decided to wait for something better. "Pass," he said.

"She looked pretty good to me," said McClain.

"I've got eight more to go," said Mack, enjoying himself.

"Six," said McClain, pointing in the direction of two very fat women who looked like sisters. "Unless you're into plush uphol-stery."

"No thanks," said Mack. In quick succession he vetoed a mannish woman whose gigantic breasts swung loose in a white T-shirt, a pale teenager eating an ice-cream bar and an old lady shuffling along in a walker. Then there was a break in the crowd; for almost a minute no one came along.

"Three more to go," said McClain. "The tension mounts." Mack was surprised to find that he actually did feel tense. He took a slug of beer and waited.

"Here's number eight," said McClain, nodding in the direction of a thirtyish woman in a flowered skirt. She had slumped shoulders and unkempt hair the color of mud, but she was smiling to herself and there was something pleasant about her regular features. Once more Mack was tempted but he finally shook his head. "Naw, let's go for broke," he said.

Number nine and number ten passed together, a stout woman in her fifties with white hair, walking arm in arm with an elderly lady who appeared to be her mother.

"There she is," McClain crowed. "The future Mrs. Mack Green."

Mack laughed. "Well, at least I didn't get the one with the walker. Not a bad game, Big John. Maybe I'll use it in the book."

"Use it in your life, hotshot," said McClain. He took a swig of Bud, belched for punctuation and surreptitiously peeked at his watch. "Okay, you ready to try it again?"

"Why me? It's your turn."

"I already said *stop* when I met Joyce. You're the one looking for Miss Right."

"No offense, but I don't think I'm going to find her walking around the Four Corners mall."

"You never know," McClain said. He nodded toward a buxom woman in a housedress who crossed their field of vision. "There's number one."

"No thanks," said Mack. "Okay, one more round." He swiveled in his chair for a better view and quickly rejected three more shoppers. "Not much of a selection here. Maybe we should try—"

"Try what?" asked McClain.

Mack seized his arm. "John, do you see that woman over there, in front of the record store?"

"The blond with the long legs? She's a knockout," said McClain.

"She looks just like Linda Birney."

"Is that right?" said McClain, but Mack didn't hear him; he was concentrating on the woman, who was about fifty feet away, looking into the window of the record store. "Maybe it's her."

"Huh?"

"I said, maybe it's her," McClain repeated.

"Couldn't be," said Mack. "She's too young."

The woman turned from the display window and began walking slowly toward the food court. She moved like Linda, head up and cocked slightly to the side, her stride, even in high heels, unhurried and easy. As she came closer Mack fought the impulse to jump up and rush over to her. He made himself remember all the times he had felt foolish after mistaking women in the street in New York for Linda.

"She's coming this way," said McClain. "What number you on?"

"Number?" Mack felt his excitement grow with every step the woman took. She didn't look quite so young now, early thirties maybe—Linda could look that young. She wore an expensive black silk business suit that revealed the shape of her hips. Linda had been thinner, willowy, but she had been a girl then; this woman had the kind of body Linda's body could have become. And then, when she was no more than fifteen feet away, she paused, looked over in the general direction of the food court and grinned her unmistakable, lopsided, sexy-pirate grin.

Mack grabbed McClain's arm. "That's her!" he whispered. "That's Linda! What do I do now?"

"Go over and say hello," said McClain. "Unless you want to keep waiting, see if someone better comes by."

"What if she doesn't remember me?"

"She'll remember you," McClain said, pushing him to his feet. The glee on his face told Mack that this was not a guess.

"You set this up," he said, accusingly.

"Quit stalling," said McClain. "Go get her."

Mack rose, gave McClain's arm a squeeze and walked toward Linda. McClain watched as he approached her, saw her face light up and smiled when she pulled Mack into her arms for a long embrace. The hell with Dr. Sigmund Ephron, he thought; Dr. Big John McClain had come up with the right medicine. It hadn't been easy finding Linda Birney, but seeing them together, standing close and talking intensely, their arms still wrapped loosely around one another, McClain felt an overwhelming sense that now everything would be all right with Mack. He couldn't wait to get home and tell Joyce all about it.

At a nearby table, a middle-aged man in a gray cardigan watched the scene, too. He didn't know why McClain was blowing his nose, didn't know who the woman was or why Mack Green was kissing her in the middle of the mall. He didn't particularly care, either, although he'd find out if he was asked to. For that matter, he didn't know why he had been asked to keep an eye on Green. It was just a job, and if the boss didn't want him involved in the big picture, that didn't bother him. Arlen Nashua had long since come to terms with the undeniable fact that he was not a big-picture kind of guy.

Nineteen

"What if I had just bumped into you on the street?" Mack asked Linda. "Would you have recognized me?" They were together at the Markham Inn, having dinner in a quiet corner of the room. In high school, the Markham had been considered an elegant place, Oriole's answer to the Four Seasons, with a real continental chef from Quebec and candles on the tables. Linda had smiled when he suggested it tonight and now he knew why—it seemed like a pavilion in Disneyland: The Midwest Fake French Food and Corny Atmosphere pavilion. Mack didn't care, though; he was barely aware of his surroundings.

"You were my first love," said Linda, in a tone somewhere between sincerity and self-mockery. "Girls don't forget their first love."

"Yeah, right," muttered Mack, afraid to take her seriously.

"Tell me about you, Mackinac. About your glamorous life."

"Glamorous? I guess if you look at it from the outside, my life does seem glamorous, doesn't it?"

"You've developed a little New York accent, you know? Maybe not an accent exactly, but a way of talking. I used to hear it a lot in LA. It's not how I remember you sounding."

"You remember me that well? The way I talked?"

"I should. You talked enough," she said, giving him her crooked smile.

"You should have married me," Mack blurted. The thought had been running through his mind all evening.

"Maybe," she replied. "I've wondered about it over the years."

"You have?" She nodded and looked at him evenly; he noticed the flecks of gray in her dark-green eyes. "Then why didn't you? We were perfect for each other."

"Nobody's perfect for anybody, especially at that age," she said. "Besides, I thought I could do better." She saw the hurt expression on his face and put her hand on his. "I was eighteen years old, Mack. And I didn't trust you."

"Why not? I never lied to you. It's a unique distinction, by the way."

"That's why, that kind of comment. You were always saying things like that, making yourself sound so distant and cynical. I suppose it was your way of trying to act grown-up—Jesus, do you realize we were just about my son Teddy's age?—but I didn't know how to handle it. And you didn't believe in love."

"I was in love with you."

"You said love was just a literary device."

"And you believed me? Shit, I didn't mean 90 percent of what I used to say back then." He paused and grinned. "These days it's around 65."

Linda laughed. "You want to scare me all over again?"

"You don't look like you scare so easily."

"Maybe a little easier than you think. But yeah, not so much. Not anymore."

"What happened, Linnie. After that day on the phone?"

"The story of my life?"

"The highlights. What about Flanders?"

"Gregg and I got divorced twelve, no thirteen years ago. He busted up his knees, the Rams cut him and he cut me. It was a bad season, you could say."

"Were you in love with him?"

"Not at the end, no. But I liked him all right. He was good about my going to law school while Teddy was small—"

"How old is he now? Teddy?"

"Nineteen. He's a sophomore at Columbia."

"Not a football player?"

"No, not a football player," said Linda.

"Okay, so you and Flanders split up. Then what?"

"I stayed in LA. By that time I was with a firm that did entertainment law and I was making very big money, three hundred dollars an hour—"

"You must be a good lawyer," said Mack.

"Damn good," Linda said. "And I enjoyed it, the entertainment scene. It was fun. That's how I met my second husband. Roger Chadwick?"

"Should I know the name?"

"I guess not, although if you lived out there you probably would. He's a producer, not one of the biggest, but fairly well known."

"How long did that last?"

"A couple years. More than a couple, really. Four, I guess. And then we broke up and I came back here."

"Why?"

"The short answer is that my father died and left me a lot of money. When I came home to work out the details of the estate, one of the lawyers told me about Liberty Records, which was for sale. It seemed like a good opportunity, so I decided to stay."

"And what's the long answer?"

Linda extracted a Kent from her purse, lit it with a gold Ronson, took a long drag and exhaled with her eyes closed. "The long answer is I didn't like the way I was living out there. Roger was into drugs in a big way, and I got into it, too. Coke mostly, but we did everything. And when he got high, he liked to play games."

"What kind of games?"

"Sex games, mostly, California style. He used to invite a dozen or so of his closest friends, get naked in the Jacuzzi and then see who did what to whom."

"If you hated it, why did you go along?" asked Mack. He was trying to sound sympathetic, but he had an erection.

"I didn't hate it, I loved it," Linda said in a flat voice. "It got to be the only thing I did love, really; getting wrecked and going crazy and then coming down so I could get wrecked and crazy again. The funny part is, it seemed natural. I mean, that's the way we were raised, isn't it? You and I were smoking dope and dropping acid and screwing when I was a junior in high school.

"Then one day I came home from shopping and I found Roger in bed with Teddy and a woman. Know who she was?"

Mack swallowed hard and shook his head. "Who?"

"Teddy's guidance counselor," she said. "Honest to God. The three of them were stoned, and she was tied to the bedposts, sort of wriggling around. I just stood there staring, and Roger—I can't believe I'm telling you this—Roger smiled this dopey smile and said, 'Hop in, honey.' "

"How old was Teddy?"

"Fifteen. He had this dreamy, stoned look on his face and he said, 'Come on, Linda, it's cool.' "

"Holy shit."

"Yeah," she said, taking another long drag on the Kent. "You want to hear the rest? The worst part?"

Mack nodded.

"I was tempted. Just for a second, you know? It was like, okay, this is where things have been heading, let's get it on. All those years I'd been living like there was no such thing as right and wrong. We got high in front of Teddy, we never made any effort to hide what we were doing. It was just another lifestyle, like belonging to a country club or a church. For just that split second I thought, 'All right, this is where you step over the line, go all the way.' "

"And then?"

"And then I vomited. All over the guidance teacher, who didn't seem to mind at all. I slapped Teddy so hard he noticed, dragged him, buck naked, out of bed and pushed him out of the room. I don't really remember what happened after that, just a lot of screaming and breaking things and Roger lying there saying, 'Chill, baby, it's no big thing.' If I had had a gun I would have shot him, and myself, too."

"Jesus, Linnie," said Mack.

"Yeah, Jesus. Anyway, I took Teddy and checked into the Beverly Hills Hotel. For the next few weeks I just sort of lay around trying to figure out how the hell my life had turned out this way. 'You're Linda Birney,' I kept saying to myself, as if that meant something. I guess I was detoxing, too, although I didn't admit it at the time. God only knows what Teddy thought."

"You never discussed it with him?"

"I was too ashamed. I wanted to believe that he was too young to understand what a whore his mother was."

"And then what?"

"And then, luckily, my father died. I guess I shouldn't put it that way, but it's true. I mean, we weren't especially close, and he'd been sick—he died of cancer. Anyway, I saw a chance to get out of LA, move to someplace normal, get myself back."

"You should have called me—"

"And said what? 'Hi, Mack, this is the girl who dumped you in college, how about fixing everything for me, just for old times' sake?' I told you I've thought about you a lot, especially since coming back here, but I never considered getting in touch with you. That was over."

Green noted the past tense. The story shocked him, but it excited him, too; he had to admit that he wondered what it would be like to be with Linda in a room full of naked strangers. He lit a Winston and looked around the darkened restaurant, trying to figure out a way to ask what he wanted to know.

"So, what's your life like now?" he said finally. "Have you Seen the Light?"

"I'm not a nun, if that's what you're asking. Maybe I wanted to be at one point, but I don't have the temperament for it. I'm damn careful, though, I can tell you that. And I don't do drugs anymore. Do you?"

"Just this," said Green, holding up his glass. "Maybe smoke a joint now and then."

"Well, a joint . . . "

"I guess there's not much action in Oriole, anyway," said Green.

"There's action everywhere," said Linda. She took a sip of water.

"You seeing anyone now?"

"Not really. This is going to sound terrible, but most of the men I meet here are too square for me. I hate the life I lived in California, but the thing is, I lived it. It's like a secret; once you know it you can't unknow it. God, I'm sick of hearing myself talk. Tell me about you, Mack. What kind of book are you writing?"

"I'm not sure," said Mack. "It keeps changing on me."

"Well, whatever it is, it brought you back here. I'm glad."

"Me too. Especially now. This feels like a dream."

"What kind of dream?" asked Linda in a soft voice.

"Well, an erotic one," Mack said.

Linda gave him a direct look. "Do you want to seduce me, Mackinac?"

"It's crossed my mind."

"Then consider me seduced," she said. "Have you got somewhere we can go?"

"How about your place?"

She shook her head. "No. Teddy's home for fall break."

"Okay, what about the Hilton? There's one around here, if I recall."

"All right," she said.

Mack laughed. "You know, I've been fantasizing about you for twenty-five years. Linda Birney, the unattainable dream. And now it's happening. I feel like pinching myself."

"Let's go to the hotel and I'll do it for you," said Linda in a low voice.

"Easy as that?"

"Yeah," she said, stubbing out her cigarette. "Easy as that."

Twenty

Wolfowitz met Conlon at his office, a small suite of rooms in a gray commercial building west of Herald Square. It was the kind of office an old-time movie private eye would have, grungy and disreputable, not unlike the man whose name was on the door. Wolfowitz appreciated the investigator's unabashed authenticity. Over the years he had published a number of mysteries by ex-cops and private investigators who looked as wholesome and healthy as forest rangers. Nobody would ever mistake Conlon, with his pot belly, blue-veined nose and heavily Brylcreemed pompadour, for a forest ranger.

Years ago, Wolfowitz had told Conlon that he wouldn't be needing pictures of Mack and Louise, and he had never used him to snoop on his wife again. But he had been impressed with the investigator's discreet professionalism and had employed him ever since on sensitive cases. Conlon had looked into the backgrounds of potential libel litigants, engaged in industrial espionage against other publishing houses and tracked down writers who had gone AWOL with their advance money. This time, he had a report on Mack Green's movie deal.

There were things about the Hollywood offer that had bothered Wolfowitz from the start. For one, Tommy Russo seemed almost unhappy about it. Even more puzzling, he didn't understand why anyone would buy a Mack Green novel sight unseen, for six figures. He had asked Conlon to look into it, and now the detective was ready to give him some answers.

"The first thing is, this guy Ligget's a front," said Conlon, coming right to the point. He knew, after all this time, that Wolfowitz was not a man interested in pleasantries.

"A front for who?"

"Guy named Jeff Reggie," said Conlon. "He's a producer out there, does a lot of porno crap and some regular B movies." He squinted at his typewritten notes. "I could give you some titles if you want. I've got 'em right here."

"Later," said Wolfowitz. "Unless it's important."

Conlon shook his head. "What's important, looks like, is that Jeff Reggie's cousin is Herman Reggie. That's interesting."

"Why? Who's Herman Reggie?"

"He's a bookie," said Conlon. "Very big time. Also, he does enforcement for other bookies. You wouldn't like him."

"And he's connected to this?"

"Yep," said Conlon, consulting his notes again. "He owns a part of the deal. It's a payment for a bad gambling debt."

"Mack's not a gambler. He doesn't even play cards."

"No, but his agent does. Tommy Russo. He bet with Herman, he lost to Herman and he paid up by giving his share of the book, which is entitled *The Diary of a Dying Man,* to Herman."

"I know the name of the book," said Wolfowitz impatiently; the one drawback in dealing with Conlon was his plodding thoroughness. "How do you know he gave the book to Reggie?"

Conlon fixed the editor in chief with a mysterious stare. "Mr. Wolfowitz, I can't reveal that information," he said. In fact, Conlon knew because Jeff Reggie had told Ligget, who had told Conlon's associate in California. The reason Ligget had been so forthcoming was that Conlon's associate was a moonlighting LA narcotics detective who threatened to bust him for dealing cocaine if he didn't talk. These transactions were almost always easier than the client imagined, which was why Conlon liked to keep his professional secrets to himself.

"Okay, so Reggie owns 10 percent of the book," said Wolfowitz. "That still doesn't explain why his cousin bought the movie rights."

"They think it's going to make a lot of money," said Conlon. "Ligget says his cut, just for fronting the deal, could be half a million bucks."

"Half a million dollars?" Wolfowitz repeated, scratching his head. For once the gesture was real; he was genuinely baffled.

Conlon shrugged. "I'm not a movie critic, but they think a story like this, the author offs himself and leaves a book about it as a suicide note, is a big deal."

"Offs himself? They're crazy, Green's not going to kill himself, he's just writing a novel about someone who does. It's fiction."

"Whatever," Conlon said noncommittally. It occurred to Wolfowitz that the ex-cop, with his little notebooks and written reports, probably hadn't forgotten that he had once caught Mack Green sleeping with his wife.

"I wonder where they got the idea that Green was going to kill himself?" Wolfowitz mused. "Wait, did the name McClain come up?"

"McClain?" said Conlon, scanning his report. "Nope, no McClain. Who's he?"

"Nobody," said Wolfowitz. "It was just a thought." Suddenly he felt a shiver of apprehension. Mack's book, whatever Reggie had in mind, would be worthless once Horton's suicide novel appeared. And if the bookie found out that Wolfowitz had ruined his investment, there could be trouble. "Tell me something. This guy Reggie—would you say he was dangerous?"

"Which one?"

"Either one, but I meant the bookmaker."

"Jeff Reggie's a pussy," said Conlon. "Herman?" He raised his eyebrows. "There's better people to owe money to."

"No, I mean in general. If somebody cost him a lot of money, say, do you think he might do something violent?"

"That would be speculation on my part," said Conlon.

"We're not in court," said Wolfowitz impatiently. "Speculate. What do you think?"

"What I think is that Herman Reggie wouldn't gamble a hundred bucks, let alone a hundred thousand, unless he knew it was a sure thing."

"You mean Green killing himself?"

"I didn't say that," Conlon said, looking directly into Wolfowitz's cold gray eyes. "I just said that if Reggie thinks he can make that kind of dough on a book by a dead writer, and he's shelling out a hundred grand of his own money for a book by a dead writer, you're gonna wind up with a book and a dead writer."

Wolfowitz was silent for a long moment as he digested Conlon's analysis. "It would have to be suicide, though," he said finally. "Or at least look like suicide. Could he do that?"

Conlon grunted as he shifted his weight off his hemorrhoids. "Make it look like a suicide?" he said. "Hell, there's ways to make it look like he croaked from the bubonic plague."

Twenty-one

"God, you're magic," said Mack, running his hands lightly over Linda's bare back. They were in bed at the Hilton, a bed they had barely left for two days.

Linda rolled over on her side and ruffled Mack's hair. "That's what you keep saying," she said.

"It's the way I feel."

"Yeah, but I think I'm entitled to better dialogue."

"If I were an electrician would you expect me to rewire your house?"

"Damn straight," said Linda, kissing him lightly on the lips. "That's better, by the way. Most guys would have said, 'If I were an electrician, I'd turn you on.' 'Rewire the house' is original."

"Glad you like it," said Mack. "Do most guys say the same things in bed?"

"Sure," said Linda. "At least in the beginning."

"Is that what this is? A beginning?"

"Why don't you answer some questions for a change?"

"For instance?"

"For instance, what do women say to you in bed?"

Mack flashed on the long, dreary line of literary ladies from the Big Ten states. "They say, 'Why haven't you published a novel in so long?' "

"Good question," said Linda. "Why haven't you?"

"I've been waiting for a really great idea," said Mack.

"That's the official answer," said Linda. "Now, tell me the real one."

"What makes you think that isn't it?"

"Because I'm not a moron. Look, Mackinac, I told you about my life and I told you the truth, every sordid, shitty, scary detail. You asked and I answered. Now it's your turn."

"Ah, Linnie," Mack sighed, "I don't know what the real story is myself. One day my books stopped selling, the critics turned on me and I guess I lost my nerve. I couldn't work anymore."

"Writer's block," said Linda.

"People think it's some kind of a romantic affliction," said Mack, "but it's not, it's like having insomnia. You know how the more you want to sleep the harder it gets, and the harder it gets the more frustrated you are? That's writer's block. You get up in the morning and you say, 'It's ten, I'll start at noon.' At noon you say, 'I might as well get some lunch first.' At two you decide that there's no point in starting so late, you'll get to work tomorrow. Tomorrow comes, it's Wednesday, you decide to wait until Monday, get a fresh start with the new week. On Monday you look at the calendar, see it's the twenty-fourth, and say to yourself, 'I'll begin on the first of the month.' And every single time you know you're lying, that you won't start in an hour, or tomorrow, or next month, because when you sit down to write, nothing comes out. You start to hate yourself for lying, and feel sorry for yourself because you know you're not lying on purpose, you just can't help it because you can't force yourself to be smarter or funnier or more interesting than you are. And you start to feel desperate."

"It sounds awful," said Linda.

"Yeah," said Mack. "It is." In all the years of failure he had never admitted to anyone how scared and miserable he was. He had misgivings about telling Linda, too; he didn't think she was the kind of woman who liked losers. But now that he was talking, he felt a compulsion to continue. "You remember my dad, right? He used to tell me, 'Life's what you say it is.' That's what I did, I said 'Everything's all right.' I said it to other people and I said it to myself, and in the meantime I kept drinking and laughing and racing around, trying to drown or placate or outrun whatever it was that was keeping me from writing."

"I notice you haven't said anything about women," Linda said.

"There was a time, just after *The Oriole Kid* was published and everything was great that I think I was ready for a real relationship."

"You were what, thirty?"

"Yeah, about that. I hate to admit it but it took me that long to get over you."

"You're kidding."

"Every time I was on TV, I used to think, 'I wonder if Linnie is watching.' Sometimes, when the phone rang, I thought it might be you, calling to say you'd seen me or read one of my books and you wanted to come back to me."

"And what did you say to me?" Linda asked softly. "Did you take me back?"

"I gave you a hard time first, though," said Mack, grinning to lighten the mood of what was becoming a dangerous conversation.

Linda sensed it, too. "You got over me, though," she reminded him. "When *The Oriole Kid* was published."

"More or less. Anyway, I married a fashion model, which is probably as close as I could come to a quarterback—"

"You're not blaming me for that?"

"I'm not blaming you for anything. I'm just explaining what happened. I got married, I got divorced, there were no kids, it was like breaking up with a girlfriend. Then things started to come apart with my books, I got all blocked up and—" He paused, surprised at his own insight; he had never quite put things together this way.

"And?" Linda prompted.

"I guess I felt like a cripple," said Mack. "Women who saw it were too painful to be with, and women who didn't were too stupid to be with. One-night stands were easier."

"Poor Mack." Linda rubbed her hand across his shoulders.

"See what I mean?"

"That's not pity, that's empathy, you jerk," said Linda.

"I was kidding," said Mack. "You wanted dialogue, I gave you dialogue. Anyway, things are different now. I'm not a cripple any more, I'm writing again." He leaned over and kissed Linda on the neck. "And I've got you."

"Not yet you don't," she said pulling away gently.

"Hey, all I meant was—"

"That now you're okay, you get the girl and a happy ending? This isn't a novel, Mack, it's not that neat. I'm here, too."

"I thought this meant something to you," said Mack, certain now that his candor had been a mistake.

"It's great fun. But I told you the other night, I haven't been sitting around thinking about you all these years and I didn't know you were, either."

"Great fun," Mack repeated.

"Sure, you're a good-looking guy, still got all your teeth, not bad in the sack. Healthy, I hope—"

"That's all this is to you, huh? Recreational sex? Nostalgia?"

"I didn't know until ten minutes ago that it was supposed to be something more. What are you saying to me, Mackinac, that you love me?"

"Yes, goddamnit, I do. I've been in love with you just about my whole life."

"At the risk of being banal, there's a difference between being in love and loving someone. But let that go for a second. Are you proposing to me? Do you want to get married?"

"It's crossed my mind," said Mack defensively.

"Going in which direction?"

"Come on, Linnie, it's only been a few days—"

"Relax, Mackinac, I'm not trying to trap you. You're making my point, that it's too soon to know what might happen between us. You've told me something I didn't know, tonight, that maybe you'd like to have this turn into something serious. Okay, maybe it will. Let's take it a step at a time, see how it goes."

Mack lay back and closed his eyes. For a second, when Linda had mentioned marriage, he had felt a surge of panic. Slowing things down wasn't such a bad idea. "So, what do we do now?" he asked. "Go steady?"

"That sounds all right," said Linda. "Maybe I can get on *Oprah:* Middle-aged Women who go Steady with their High School Boyfriends."

"I think I saw that one," said Mack. "Writer's block and day-time TV go together. Speaking of high school, will you be my date for the reunion?"

"What reunion?"

"My class. It's Saturday night."

"I think I'll pass. Sitting around listening to stories about Tuffy Frankling throwing water balloons at Mrs. Staley and how many beers Jerry Campbell drank after the Midland game isn't my idea of fun."

"Come on, Linnie, I went with you to your senior prom. You owe me one."

"Yeah, I suppose I do," she said. "You were so cute in your white tuxedo. Yeah, okay, it's a date."

"Great," said Mack. "We'll have fun, don't worry. I'll even buy you a corsage. Afterward we can go out for breakfast at the Pancake House. Remember?"

"Middle-aged Women who go to Class Reunions with Their Senior Prom Dates," intoned Linda. She leaned over, kissed Mack gently on the lips and lay back on the pillows. "I must be out of my mind."

Twenty-two

The sign outside the main gate of the Oriole Country Club read: WELCOME, ORIOLE CENTRAL HIGH CLASS OF 67. HAPPY TWENTY-FIFTH. Mack parked in the lot and walked hand in hand with Linda to the clubhouse, a graystone relic built in the flush days of the 1940s by war-rich auto executives. At the registration table, a pie-faced, heavily made-up woman smiled at them vaguely. Mack recognized her immediately—Karen Browning, a studious, uninteresting girl who had sat in the front row of his Spanish class for two years. It amazed him that he remembered her so easily—he even recalled a green argyle-plaid skirt she used to wear—while she obviously had no idea who he was.

"Hi, I'm Mack Green," he said.

Karen's eyes widened, and she reached into her purse for a pair of designer glasses. "Mack Green," she bubbled. "I'm Karen Duff. Karen Browning? I'm sure you don't remember but we were in the same history class."

Green didn't correct her. "You know Linda Birney? She's an infiltrator from the Class of sixty-nine."

"Everybody knew Linda," said Browning.

"I'm not sure I like the way that sounds," Linda said with a smile.

"Don't confuse me," Karen said, writing out name tags for them. "I'm confused enough tonight." She lowered her voice to a conspiratorial giggle. "And I'm stoned, too. Isn't that wild?"

In the ballroom, decorated with Oriole Central High blue and white balloons and streamers, people sat at large round tables, drinking and chatting. On the dance floor, couples moved to the Motown music of a band composed of elderly black men in white tuxedos and a young woman singer dressed in red. When they walked in the band was playing "Dancing in the Streets." Within eight bars Mack felt a heavy hand on his shoulder, turned and found himself looking into the tanned, vacant face of Randy Jamison, the class president.

"Unbelievable," Jamison boomed. "The great Mack Green in person. Accompanied by the queen, Linda Birney. What an unexpected honor." There was scotch on his breath and malice in his voice as he pumped Mack's hand in a strenuous salesman's grip. "Recognize me, or are you too famous to remember old friends?"

"Too famous," Linda deadpanned. Mack squeezed her hand in appreciation. "Hello, Randy," he said. He let his gaze wander around the room. "Great decorations."

"You've never been to a reunion before," said Jamison.

"I live in New York."

"Freddy Kinsella lives in Honolulu, and he comes every year. Freddy's one of the biggest dental surgeons in Hawaii."

"All the way from Honolulu," said Mack, trying to edge away.

"Damn straight," said Jamison emphatically. He shot Mack a resentful look. "You're not the only success story in the class of sixty-seven. Not by a long shot."

The band shifted into "Two Lovers." "Our song," Linda said to Randy, leading Mack toward the dance floor.

"Since when is this our song?" asked Mack, holding her in a tight high-school embrace as they swayed to the music.

"Ooh, I'm so confused," said Linda, mimicking Karen Duff. "I guess this was my song with Freddy Kinsella, the world-famous dental practitioner."

"One of the thousands who knew you in high school," Mack said, laughing. He held her even closer. "I feel like we're in a bubble together, you know what I mean? Like everybody else is a prop, and we're the only real people—"

"Mack! Mack Green!" a man called from behind him.

"Pop," said Linda.

"Pop?"

"The sound of the bubble," she said, looking over his shoulder. "It's what's-his-name, Jerry Campbell."

Mack spun Linda around and saw Campbell bearing down on him with a wide grin and comically outstretched arms.

"Mack! Linda! We saw you guys come in. I've been deputized to bring you over to the table. Everybody wants to see you. The gang's all here—Tuffy, Len, Billy Dartmouth—"

Mack looked at Linda who shrugged almost imperceptibly. "Great," he said, without enthusiasm, and followed Campbell through the crowd.

At the table the men boisterously shook Mack's hand and kissed Linda on the cheek, while the wives, none of whom Mack knew, regarded them both with frank interest. "They've been telling Mack-and-Linda stories since you walked in the door," said Amy Dartmouth.

"They were the Liz and Richard of Oriole Central High," said Campbell.

"The who and who?" asked Amy. She was young, no older than thirty, and she was wearing a low-cut dress. She saw Mack sneaking a look and winked. Linda saw it too, and when she caught Amy's eye she winked back at her, making the younger woman blush.

Mack and Linda sat down at the round table. "It's good to see you guys," he said.

"There have been rumors around town of Mack Green sightings, but we didn't take them seriously," said Billy Dartmouth. "I guess they were true."

"I've been keeping a low profile," said Mack. "Trying to get some work done." Sitting here surrounded by old friends, with Linda at his side, he felt a warm glow of connectedness and belonging. "Billy, I should know this, but what do you do?"

"I'm a lawyer. Mellman, Saperstein, Dartmouth and Levine. I'm Dartmouth. We do personal injury, mostly."

"You should see his ads on TV," said Campbell. "He's the Crazy Eddie of litigation—his prices are *in-sane*." Everybody laughed.

"I'm not complaining," said Dartmouth. "I'm not in Len's league, but I make a pretty fair living."

"What league is Len in?"

"The big leagues," said Dartmouth. "He owns Angelo, Mickey and Bruce."

"What's that, a gay takeout service?" asked Mack. Linda snickered, the others looked blank.

"Barbers," said Leonard. "A chain. It's an idea I came up with a few years ago in Chicago. I was at a sales convention and I went into the hotel barbershop for a trim. The barber was this terrific Italian named Angelo, real old-world, handlebar mustache, smelled of rose water, hummed Vivaldi, right out of *The Godfather*."

"You're lucky he didn't cut your throat," said Linda sweetly.

"Nah, he was a nice old guy," Leonard said. "So was the barber in the next chair, this wisecracking Irish type named Mickey. And next to him was another barber, Bruce, a kid with long hair who talked a blue streak about movies and rock stars and what concerts were coming to town. But what was great about it was the banter between the three of them—they had a real routine, joking with one another, involving the customers. I was sitting there, getting my hair cut and having the time of my life."

Len paused and looked around; it was obviously a story he enjoyed recounting. "And then it came to me. Why not get three barbers, give each of them a character, and set them up here? So I went out and found myself an Angelo, a Mickey and a Bruce and started a shop in West Tarryton."

"It sounded nuts to me at first," said Campbell. "But it worked. To put it mildly."

"We've got twenty-three shops now in Michigan, Ohio and Indiana," Leonard said. "You can walk into any one and get your hair cut by an Angelo, a Mickey or a Bruce."

"Where do you find them? The barbers?" asked Mack.

"Easy," said Leonard. "We've set up our own training college. There's even a drama coach."

"Unbelievable," said Mack.

Jerry Campbell raised his gin and tonic. "To the entrepreneurial spirit," he toasted.

"To the class of sixty-seven," said Tuffy.

"To the ladies' room," said Linda, rising. "Mack, when I get back you better be ready to dance."

They watched her wind her way through the crowd. "God, it's great to see you two together," said Campbell. "Just like old times."

"She's got quite a sense of humor," said Amy Dartmouth.

"Quite a body, too," said Billy Dartmouth.

"Here's a toast. To old loves," said Tuffy Franklin, raising his glass again.

"And good bodies," added Dartmouth, slurring his words.

"And loose shoes and a warm place to shit," said a flat, sardonic voice from behind Mack. He looked up and saw Buddy Packer towering over him. The others stared coldly; no one said hello.

"What are you doing here?" asked Mack. They hadn't spoken since Packer had left him stranded in front of Roy Ray's church.

"Displaying my school spirit," said Packer. "Let's go over to the bar, get a drink."

"So you can apologize for ditching me?"

"Yeah, okay," said Packer. "You pissed me off is all."

"I had that much figured out," said Mack. "Fuck it, I'm in too good a mood to hold a grudge. I'm in love, Packy. Linda and I are back together."

"In love, eh? That's great. Seriously, I want to talk to you about something."

"Not right now," said Mack. "Linda wants to dance. She'll be back from the ladies' room in a minute."

"I only need a minute," said Packer. "Come on."

Reluctantly, Mack rose and accompanied Packer to the bar. He ordered a bourbon, and kept a close eye on the table, watching for Linda.

"I see you're hobnobbing with the cream of Oriole society," Buddy said.

"I'm just catching up," said Mack. "I was friends with those guys in school."

"Right, I forgot," said Buddy. "Your respectable side. I can catch you up in twenty seconds. Leonard's a glorified hairdresser. Dartmouth's the front man for a bunch of Jew-boy shysters. Campbell sells life insurance to little old ladies and that cocksucker Franklin is the judge who sent me to Jackson. They all have two-and-a-half kids, screw each others' wives and brush after every meal. What else you want to know?"

"I didn't know Tuffy Franklin was a judge."

"Fuck him," said Packer decisively. "The other day, you said you could let me have a few thousand bucks, remember?"

Mack nodded.

"I need ten, can you swing that?"

"Ten's a lot of money."

"What's the matter, Macky, you don't trust me? I'll get it back to you in a week, guaranteed. With fucking interest if you want."

"You knew Linda was in town," said Mack suddenly, realizing it for the first time. "Didn't you?"

Packer shrugged. "Must have slipped my mind."

"Bullshit. Why didn't you say something when I asked you?"

"Tell you the truth, I thought it would be better for you if you didn't get mixed up with her," said Packer. "She's a cunt."

"Everybody's a cunt to you," said Mack. "Roy Ray. John McClain. Tuffy Franklin. Linda—"

"Yeah, I've got a real bad attitude. I'll work on it. What about the money?"

"When we were kids I thought you were the coolest guy I ever met," said Mack, looking at his old friend with professional detachment. "What the hell happened to you?"

"Like I told you that night at Stanley's, I grew up," said Packer. "Are you going to loan me the ten or not?"

"Uh-uh," said Mack, shaking his head. "I can let you have two, if it helps."

Packer peered down at Mack through his granny glasses. "Save your money," he said. "I don't need a fucking handout."

"I'm sorry," said Mack.

"Yeah, you are," said Packer, his thin lips forming a nasty sneer. "You're a sorry motherfucking cunt."

Packer stalked out of the ballroom, stopped in the men's room, where he did six quick lines of coke and stepped outside into the clear, cold Michigan night. He was pissed at himself for mishandling Mack—not telling him about Linda had been a stupid mistake—but it was too late to do anything about that now. As he walked through the quiet parking lot he recognized Mack's rented black LeBaron. On an impulse he stopped, reared his leg back and kicked a good-sized dent into the right front door with his cowboy boot. Then he went over to his T-Bird, removed a six-inch knife from the glove compartment and walked back to the LeBaron. He took a quick look around, saw that no one was watching, and gouged a heart into the paint on the left front door. Under it he scratched the words, "Mack and Linda Forever." He walked around the side and added "Pussy Wagon" in big letters on the other door. Then, in a frenzy of angry creativity, he slashed all four tires. There, he thought, let Green explain that to the fucking Rent-a-Car people.

Packer went back to his own car, lit a joint and peeled out of the lot. A row away, sitting in his blue Mitsubishi, Arlen Nashua watched him drive off. He wasn't sure, but he had a feeling that he had found what Herman Reggie was looking for.

Twenty-three

Long before it became a familiar term in pop psychology, Herman Reggie considered himself a people person. He was in a business founded on understanding human nature and it was this that gave him his greatest satisfaction. There were other bookies who thought only of odds and numbers, who boiled everything down to a mechanical conjuring of sums, but Reggie pitied their soulless arithmetic. He cared about his clients, rejoiced with the winners and, if they paid up, sympathized with the losers. And so, the first time he had heard the phrase, on a radio talk show, he had recognized himself and thought: "That's what I am. I'm a people person."

Over the years, Reggie had established and cultivated a vast army of friends and associates around the country. In virtually every city and many small towns he knew someone who would be happy to do him a favor—lay off bets, collect a bad debt, provide inside information, arrange the outcome of a sporting event, all the little things that meant prosperity in his business. Arlen Nashua was one of those people.

Like many of Herman's friends in the Midwest, Nashua had worked for a labor union. He had also served five years in Marquette for committing mayhem in the line of duty. Nashua had a bad case of emphysema and was semiretired, but Herman respected his industry and his judgment. For that reason he had given him the Mack Green assignment, and Nashua hadn't let him down.

"Tell me a little more about Packer," he said to Nashua. It was the day before Christmas and they were at a corner table at the Anchor Bar in downtown Detroit. "Is he smart?"

"Not as smart as he thinks he is, but yeah, he's no dummy."

"Can he keep his mouth shut?"

"He's got a good reputation," said Nashua. "I checked him out with a couple guys he did time with. They say nice things about him."

"And you say he needs money?"

"He's been trying to scrounge dough all over," said Nashua. "I think that might have something to do with his fight with Green, but I'm not sure."

"Know what he needs it for?"

Nashua coughed and shrugged at the same time. "I could probably find out, you want me to."

"It's not important," said Reggie. "Tell me, is there anything he wouldn't do? Anything that might scare him?"

"I don't think so," said Nashua. "If you want to be a little more specific, maybe it would help."

"It's not that I don't trust you," said Reggie. "Not that at all. You've done a terrific job."

"Thanks," wheezed Nashua.

"You've shown that a good man with a disability can accomplish anything," Reggie said.

"Thanks," Nashua repeated. Sometimes he wasn't sure if Herman was putting him on or not.

"Tell me, is Packer a family man?"

"I wouldn't put it that way, no."

"In that case I'd like to invite him to Christmas lunch at Carl's Chop House," said Reggie. "Give him a call for me, will you? Tell him I'm a promoter who wants to talk about booking some of his fighters."

"Sure," said Nashua. "By the way, what does it matter if he has a family?"

"I wouldn't want to take him away from his kids on Christmas," said Reggie. "A man with a family should spend national holidays at home."

As Christmas approached, the normal routine of the McClain household gave way to a burst of holiday preparations. John bought a large tree and decorated it himself with popcorn balls and little angels. He put a wreath on the door, hung stockings over the mantel and spent an entire day draping the front porch with colored lights. When Mack offered to help, he rebuffed him with jovial brusqueness. "You want to decorate the place, bring Linda for dinner on Christmas Eve," he said. "The rest of this stuff I can do myself."

Linda was delighted by the invitation, especially when she heard that Joyce had been cooking for three days. She arrived for dinner with a bottle of Pinot Noir, Acacia 1984, and a stack of CDs from the store. "Everybody except Henry Kissinger's got a Christmas album out this year," she said.

"We'll put these on after supper," said Joyce, kissing Linda on the cheek.

"But we've got our own Christmas sounds," McClain protested, looking to his wife for confirmation.

"John thinks if he doesn't play the same songs every year, Santa won't find him," said Joyce.

"What music do you have?" Mack laughed. "Bing Crosby and Gene Autry?"

"Charles Brown and Chuck Berry," McClain said in his east side dialect. "They the baddest Christmas singers they is."

"All right, Superfly," Joyce said affectionately, "when you're ready for supper, it's ready for you."

Joyce said grace, while Mack and Linda held hands under the table and McClain fidgeted in his seat, staring at the turkey. When Joyce murmured "Amen," he was already on his feet, carving knife in hand.

"You must have had a lot of Christmas dinners in this room," Joyce said to Mack.

"My mother always cooked a goose and my father made a toast. 'God bless us every one!' It was pretty corny."

"That's from *A Christmas Carol,*" said McClain. "It was a hell of a movie, right up there with *Dial M for Murder* and *Rocky III.*"

"Lord God Jesus, why did you send me this man?" Joyce said, laughing.

"Because he knew you had been a good little girl," said McClain.

"That's Santa Claus, not Jesus," said Mack.

"Same thing," said McClain.

"John, I will not have you blaspheming in this house, especially not on Christmas Eve," said Joyce.

"You're the one said Lord God Jesus," said McClain. "Where I grew up, that was taking the name of the Lord in vain."

"Where did you grow up?" asked Linda.

"Right here in Oriole, on the north side."

"You know, the first time I ever went to the north side, it was to a synagogue. With Buddy Packer, if you can believe that."

"Let's not spoil dinner by talking about him," said Joyce.

"Amen to that," said Linda.

"I never thought I'd say this, but I feel sorry for him," said Mack.

"Sorry my ass," snorted McClain. "He's scum. You know he was in prison?"

Mack nodded. "He told me, yeah. Something to do with arson."

"You make it sound like a bonfire," said McClain. "A man died in that fire."

"John, it's Christmas," said Joyce.

"He had a club out on Monroe," said McClain, undeterred. "A real dive. Called it Packer's Airport Lounge for some stupid reason, although there wasn't an airport within twenty miles."

"You've got to know his sense of humor," said Mack.

"I don't have to know a damn thing about him," said McClain. "I know too much already."

"What about the arson?" asked Linda.

"I'm coming to that. He ran the place with his wife—"

"Buddy was married?" said Mack. "He never told me that."

"Yeah, to a trailer-park hookerette named DeeDee Hunter. She had a kid named Donnie when she was about fifteen. By the time she married Packer, Donnie was nine or ten, around there. The kid was a real standout, too, even in this town. Half the burglaries on the north side were him."

"When he was nine years old?" asked Mack.

"Naw, when he got older. The thing is, the kid worshiped Packer, that's how screwed up he was. The only thing he really wanted was for Packer to adopt him, which naturally he refused to do. He wouldn't even let the kid call him Dad, just Buddy.

"Then, one day Packer calls little Donnie in and says, 'How would you like to be my son?' 'Course the kid gets all excited, Buddy Packer's gonna be his daddy. 'Well,' says Packer, 'if you want me to adopt you, you've got to prove your love.'

" 'What do you want me to do?' the kid asks. Know what Packer told him?"

Mack shook his head.

"Burn down the nightclub."

"What for? The insurance?" asked Mack.

"Yeah," said McClain. "He did it, too, only he burned down

more than he planned on. He caught a whole block and an old guy died of smoke inhalation."

"How do you know so much about it?" asked Mack.

"Because I'm the one who arrested him," said McClain. "It was my case."

"You? That's quite a coincidence."

"It's a small town, hotshot," said McClain.

After dinner they went back to the living room. McClain lit a fire, poured a round of Hennessy VSOP and raised his glass. "God bless us every one!" he said, looking at Mack.

"I'm going to answer that they way I used to answer my father," said Mack.

"How's that?" asked Joyce.

Mack rose from the couch, reached out his hand for Linda's and gently pulled her to her feet. Then he shook hands with McClain and kissed Joyce on the cheek. "Merry Christmas," he said, grinning, "dinner was delicious, and I've got to go over to Linda Birney's house now."

When they were gone, McClain went up to Mack's room, jimmied open the lock on his desk and returned to the living room with a stack of pages. "Just listen to this," he said. He cleared his throat and began reading aloud:

> "It's been a long time since I came three times in one night, and I was feeling pretty good about it. 'You make me feel like my old self,' I said.
>
> "L. flashed me her crooked grin and said, 'You're better than your old self. You may have lost a little off the ole fastball, but your slow stuff is terrific—'

"Looks like the Oriole Kid is back in championship form," chortled McClain.

"I don't think you should be reading that out loud," said Joyce. "It's not meant for us."

"Are you kidding? If it wasn't for us, none of this would be happening. Listen to what he wrote about you today:

> 'Joy's hurting because her son isn't coming home for Christmas, but you'd never know it. She's such a strong woman. When things go wrong for her she just says, "I'm blessed anyway," and she sounds like she means it. My own mother spent the last ten years of her life stoned on sleeping pills and vodka because she couldn't face life without my dad, and I guess some of my own need to put liquor between me and reality comes from watching her do it. Lately, though, I've been thinking about how blessed I am—what a weird thought—maybe even as weird as having a sixty-five-year-old black woman schoolteacher as a role model—'

"How's that sound?" said McClain happily. "Is Mack out of the woods or what?" He set the pages down on the coffee table and put his arm around his wife. "Joy," he said. "That's a good name for you. Maybe I'll call you that from now on."

"And what am I supposed to call you? Big John?"

"No, baby," said McClain, kissing her exuberantly on the lips. "From now on, you can call me Doctor Feelgood."

Wolfowitz sat alone in his study, listening to Louise and the maid fussing over last-minute arrangements for Christmas lunch. In a few minutes Josh and his young wife Steffie would arrive; he had just enough time to give himself a little Christmas cheer. He opened his safe, took out the list of options he had drawn up after receiving Conlon's report and privately contemplated Mack Green's demise.

The list, written on yellow legal paper in Wolfowitz's precise script, was headed "Contingencies." A list followed:

> 1—Warn Mack that Reggie is after him. Pluses: a) None. Minuses: a) Reggie's plan would fail; b) Reggie might break my legs.

2—Cut a deal with Reggie. Pluses: a) Maybe I could talk Reggie into giving me a part of the movie money in return for silence or cooperation; b) Personal satisfaction in taking part in the operation. Minuses: a) Reggie would know about me and Mack, giving him leverage over me; b) Reggie might break my legs.

3—Do nothing. Pluses: a) If Reggie succeeds, the Diary will be a bestseller and Mack will be dead; b) If Reggie fails, I can activate the Horton book. Minuses: None.

As much as Wolfowitz regretted being relegated to passivity, there was no denying that logic dictated plan three. Even from a business standpoint, letting Reggie go ahead made sense. Mack's pages, which continued to arrive on schedule, were terrific; much better than Walter Horton's version, which he had delivered earlier that week. There had been a small scene when Wolfowitz had informed Horton that his book was being held and that he would receive no money unless it was actually published. Walter T. had pleaded, cajoled and eventually stormed out cursing, but Wolfowitz didn't care. At this point the Horton diary was insurance, nothing more. If something went wrong with Reggie's plan, Horton would get his money; if not—well, that was his problem. Nobody had told him to go out and get AIDS.

Wolfowitz heard the front door open and the sound of loud, cheerful voices in the hall. It wouldn't be long now, he reflected; Mack's novel was almost finished. He carefully replaced his options list in the safe, glanced briefly at the photo of Louise on his desk and felt a brief, sharp pang of emptiness. The renewal of his vendetta had given him a sense of purpose and satisfaction he hadn't known for years; losing Mack permanently would leave a void. As he left the room to greet his guests, Arthur Wolfowitz wondered, a bit sadly, what he would have to celebrate next Christmas.

"How about the book?" Tommy Russo asked Joey Byrne. Like Russo, Bryne was an ex-priest. Every year they met at Antonelli's for Christmas lunch, and every year Tommy began their meal with the same question.

"I'm still working on it," said Byrne with a wide grin. He was a heavyset redhead around Tommy's age, with a broad boyish face set off by flaming ginger eyebrows that rose halfway up his forehead when he was amused. The pretense that he was writing a novel—writing anything, in fact—amused him greatly, especially since it enabled Tommy to write off their lunch as a business expense.

"Well, keep at it," Russo said, returning the grin. "What else you up to?"

"Still coaching," said Joey. "We're fourteen and one right now. What'd you, stop following sports?"

"I don't usually bet junior high," said Russo. "Why don't you get a high school team, a junior college maybe? We could both make some money."

"Gambling's your vice, not mine," said Byrne. They both knew what Byrne's vice was—and that it was the reason he liked coaching thirteen-year-old boys.

"Well," said Tommy, raising his glass, "Merry Christmas, Father Joseph."

"Merry Christmas to you, Father Tomas," said Byrne, sipping his wine. "How you feeling this year?"

It was another ritual question; Christmas was hard on ex-priests. Byrne and Russo were not close friends, not really friends at all. They met only once a year, on Christmas Day, to share a meal and a mood that others couldn't understand. And, although neither one had ever actually articulated it, to act as each other's confessors, one spoiled priest to another.

"Not bad," said Tommy. All morning he had been planning to tell Joey about his sellout of Mack Green and what he suspected might be happening. Now that they were here, though, he found it hard to talk about. It wasn't that he was afraid—he had absolute confidence in Joey's discretion. It was more a superstitious feeling that putting his suspicions into words would make them real.

"That's it? Not bad?" asked Joey after a moment.

"Well, you know, middle age. I drink too much, I curse, I screw hoo-ers. And in my business, you have to cut a few corners—"

"That's true of most businesses," said Joey, leaving Tommy plenty of room.

"I guess. But there's this one situation. You remember Mack Green? I've mentioned him to you before."

"Sure," said Joey. "What about him?"

"Well, he's got this book I'm representing and—shit, that's my phone," said Tommy, removing the ringing cellular phone from his jacket pocket. "Who the hell calls on Christmas Day at lunchtime?" He hit the "on" button and said: "Russo."

"Russo?"

"Yeah, I just said that." Tommy snapped. "Who's this?"

"Otto Kelly, at the Flying Tiger."

"Kelly?" he said, immediately alert; Otto Kelly had never called him before in his life. "What's the matter?"

"You know a writer named Walter Horton?"

"Walter T," said Russo. "What about him?"

"He's in here right now, sitting at the bar drunk. Came in that way. Says Artie Wolfowitz screwed him on a new book he was writing."

"So what?" said Tommy. "He's not my client."

"No, but Mack is," said Otto. "You happen to have his number out in Michigan?"

"No," lied Russo. "What's this got to do with Mack?"

"I'm not sure," Otto said, "but I think you better get over here and talk to Horton. Sounds to me like there's two authors writing the same book."

"I'll be over in a little while," said Tommy. He clicked off the phone and put it back in his pocket.

"Problem?" asked Joey Byrne.

"Only if I make it one," said Russo. All the years he had refrained from warning Mack about Wolfowitz, he had consoled himself with the excuse that, at worst, it was no more than a sin of omission. But if he went to the Tiger, learned what Wolfowitz was up to, he would have to call Mack or be guilty of a sin of commission. The word rattled in his brain. A 10 percent commission, right off the top. That's what all his dealings with Wolfowitz amounted to: sins of commission.

"Are you going to? Make it a problem?" asked Byrne.

Russo shrugged and rose to his feet. "Listen, Jerry, something's come up. You stay and finish your lunch."

"On Christmas? Can't it wait?"

"Nah," said Tommy. "Believe it or not, I gotta go hear a confession."

Buddy Packer arrived at Carl's ten minutes early and found Herman Reggie in the bar. He walked up behind him, tapped him on the shoulder with a bony finger and said, "I believe you're waiting for me."

"How'd you know me?" asked Reggie.

"Your name's come up from time to time," said Packer in his sardonic monotone. "Somebody in the joint once told me you've got a head like an Easter egg."

Reggie nodded at the justice of the description. "Let's get a table," he said. "I want to talk to you about something."

"Not fighters," said Packer, making it a flat statement.

"No, not fighters," Reggie agreed.

They ordered drinks and T-bones, Packer sitting in silence while Reggie kidded with the waitress. Then, over lunch, they felt each other out, gossiping about fixed fights, well-known scams and mutual acquaintances. It was professional chatter, an effort to establish common ground, accomplished with a light, noncommittal touch. Reggie noted approvingly that Packer was cagey, getting more information than he gave. By the time coffee arrived he had decided to take the conversation one step further.

"How would you feel about doing a job for me?" he asked.

"I'm self-employed," said Packer.

"This would be a freelance thing, a one-timer."

"Are you getting ready to tell me what it is?" asked Packer. When Reggie nodded, Packer leaned forward, reached a long arm across the table, opened the first three buttons of Reggie's shirt and ran a hand across his fleshy chest. "Okay, go ahead," he said.

"You're a cautious man," Reggie said. "I like that. Let me start with a hypothetical question. Is there anything you wouldn't do for twenty-five thousand dollars?"

"Jesus," said Packer, "you get me all the way down here on Christmas to insult me?"

"I didn't intend to insult you, not at all," said Reggie. "I told you it was hypothetical."

"Yeah, well that doesn't make it any better. Let's say I asked you, hypothetically, if you'd suck my dick for twenty-five grand. Wouldn't you be insulted?"

"You're right and I apologize," said Reggie. "Would you be willing to kill a man for twenty-five thousand?"

Packer peered at the bookie through his granny glasses and slowly shook his head.

"Even if there was no chance of getting caught?"

"You know there's no such thing as that," said Packer.

"Fair enough. When you say no, do you mean no in principle or no for twenty-five thousand?"

"I don't see any principle here," said Packer.

"All right then, what would it take?"

"Depends on who the guy is, how hard it would be. Plus I'd want to know why you came to me. Contracts aren't my line of work."

"I'll answer the last question first. I need somebody from Oriole and I heard good things about you."

"There's guys in Oriole would off somebody for twenty-five *hundred*," said Packer.

"I need someone smart," said Reggie. "A local man but not

one of the usual suspects. This won't be hard, but it could be a little tricky. Should I go on?"

Packer nodded. "Who's the guy?"

"I can't tell you that until I know we have a deal," said Reggie. "He's a regular fella, nobody with connections. In fact, I don't think he's even got any family. And he won't be suspecting anything."

"Why do you want him dead?"

"Uh-uh," said Reggie, shaking his head. "It doesn't matter, so don't worry about it."

"If you say so," said Packer, sipping his coffee.

"You still haven't told me your price," said Reggie.

Packer swallowed hard, his Adam's apple bobbing in his bony throat. "Fifty thousand, cash," he said. "Half up front."

"That's a lot of money," said Reggie. "Way out of line."

Packer shrugged his thin shoulders. "For a fulltime hitman, maybe. But I told you, I don't usually do this kind of work. I might not even like it."

"But you'd do it? For fifty?"

Packer nodded. "Who's the guy?"

"If I tell you, that's it, you're in," said Reggie. "Agreed?"

"Agreed."

"And one more thing. I don't mind giving you money up front, but if something goes wrong, I'd be back. You know that."

"Yeah, I know that."

"So we've got a deal?"

"Yeah, we do. If you ever get around to telling me who's the guy."

"His name's Mack Green. He's an author. Know him?"

"Yeah," said Packer, struggling to maintain his poker face. "I went to high school with him."

"Is that a problem?"

"Not for me," said Packer. He lifted his cup and took another sip of hot coffee. "I graduated high school a long time ago."

• • •

Buddy drove back to Oriole with twenty-five thousand dollars in cash and something new to think about. When Mack had turned up in Oriole, Packer had sensed it was his chance to get out of the sticks and into the big time. The thing was, he hadn't figured on killing anybody to get there.

Idly, he wondered why Herman Reggie wanted Green dead. The fact that a big-time bookie like Reggie was interested in Mack made Buddy feel a new respect for his old friend. Fifty thousand was a lot of money for a hit; Mack, he figured, must have done something pretty special to command that kind of fee.

Of course it might not be fifty. Reggie could be thinking that he'd get him to do the job and then stiff him for the other half, or maybe even take back the up-front money—the contract-killing business was an unregulated industry. He was pretty sure that Reggie hadn't been straight with him, pretending not to know that he and Mack were old friends, or that there was bad blood between them now.

If Herman hadn't been straight before, he might not be again. On the other hand, Buddy had a few options of his own. The twenty-five thousand he already had would be enough to buy Irish Willie a shot at the title. Not the real title—maybe one of the off-brand boxing federations, but a win would put Willie on TV and bring in a very tidy sum. Or he could go for the fifty, buy the fight and bet the other twenty-five on Willie losing. He might even get a bonus from Reggie for alerting him to the tank job. It was like one of those TV game shows where you had to decide if you wanted to double your prize or quit while you were ahead. The only difference was, if you made the wrong choice on TV, all you lost was a trip to Hawaii.

Packer lit a joint and filled his lungs with smoke. Despite his dilemma he felt good, better than he had in years. He had a sense of optimism he recalled from his younger days, the time before he went up to Jackson. He had cash money, he could make a move, do something for himself for a change. And he had something else, too, even more important than money: the elated high that came from knowing he was still his old self, Buddy fucking Packer, a Gamer ready for a dangerous, fuck-the-consequences, good old-fashioned fo-ray.

Twenty-four

On New Year's Eve, Mack took Linda roller-skating at the Huron Rink, and then for chili dogs at Buster's. He put ten dollars' worth of Motown on the jukebox, came back to the booth where Linda was devouring a foot-long and sang along with Smokey, " 'My mama tole me, you better shop around.' "

"She should have told you to use a napkin," said Linda, affectionately wiping mustard off his chin.

Mack let his gaze wander around Buster's, which was full of high school kids and college students on winter break. "Brings back memories," he said.

"Nothing brings them back," said Linda. "Jesus, I feel like a faculty supervisor in here."

"Anybody ever tell you you're an unsentimental broad?" said Mack with a smile.

"As a matter of fact, yes. Anybody ever tell you you're corny? Roller-skating and Buster's."

"Our first date."

"I remember," she said, taking his hand.

"Don't you think we've been going steady long enough?"

"You mean you want to break up? Date other people? Make sure we're right for each other?"

"You know what I mean," said Mack. "Let's get married for a change."

"I don't think so," said Linda gently. Mack waited for the punchline, but there was none. "That's it?" he said finally. "Just, I don't think so?"

"Let's leave things the way they are," she said.

"Come on, Linnie, this is a serious proposal."

"And this is a serious refusal."

"Because you don't love me?"

"No, I love you. I'm even in love with you. The problem is, I don't trust you."

"What's that supposed to mean?"

"Let me ask you a question. Have you been writing about us? In the novel you won't show me?"

"Sure," said Mack. "Not literally, but the basic story, yeah. Nobody will recognize you, if that's what you mean. Any objections?"

"I object to being used."

"Used? For what?"

"For research, drama, whatever you want to call it. What happens when the Mack Green character meets the high school heartthrob character after twenty years. Isn't that how it's going to read?"

"Okay, I'm an author, shoot me," said Mack. "I use reality to create fiction."

"I'm not sure what's real to you and what isn't," said Linda, idly pushing her fries around the plate. "I don't think you know yourself. Everything's a plot to you, everybody's a character."

"That's not—"

"You said yourself you're staying with the McClains because it's a great situation—"

"Yes, but I genuinely—"

"Let me finish, I'm telling you something and I want you to hear it. Remember you told me about that kid mugging you in New York? You thought it was such a great story, but all I could think was, here's a guy whose life is in danger and he sees it as a scene in a novel. You don't get more detached from reality than that."

"It was a momentary thing," said Mack. "A fluke."

"No it wasn't," said Linda. "You talk about your life like a saga. You're the Oriole Kid. You call your editor Stealth, your agent is Father Tommy, McClain's Big John. Nobody's a person, everyone's a character. And so am I. I'm Linda Birney, the Beautiful Blond Who Broke the Oriole Kid's Heart."

"You're the one who's being dramatic," Mack said. "Sure I see the world in terms of stories, that's what writers do. But it doesn't mean I'm, what did you call it? Detached from reality."

"Really? Just now, when I told you I wouldn't marry you, didn't you, in some part of your mind, think about how you would use it in the novel?"

"That's ridiculous—"

"You should see the look on your face," said Linda.

"You're scaring me, Linnie. I don't want to lose you again. I mean that."

"Okay. Stay in Oriole, get a real job and I'll marry you."

"Maybe you want me to have my nose done while I'm at it," said Mack.

"Those are my conditions. Take 'em or leave 'em."

"You're serious? You want me to live in Oriole?"

"Why not? You grew up here. Where did you think we'd live?"

"In New York."

"And what would I do there? Besides cooking and cleaning, that is?"

"You could be a lawyer. Or open another record store—"

"In other words, change my life for you. Why shouldn't you change yours for me?"

"I don't belong in Oriole," said Mack. "I'm a New York guy. What would I do here?"

"Go to work for the *News*," said Linda. "Teach writing at the university. There are plenty of things."

"You want me to write for *The Oriole News*? Linnie, I'm a major novelist. Okay, I've had a bad run, but when this book comes out, I'm going to be back where I belong."

"That's fine," said Linda. "But you'll be there without me."

"I'm asking you to give up a record store, you're asking me to give up my life," said Mack. "It's not reasonable."

"I know that," Linda said, taking a last sip of her root beer and signaling the waitress for the check.

"I can't do it," said Mack. "No matter how much you mean to me."

"I know that, too."

"Well, if you know so goddamned much, what else do you know?" said Mack, suddenly furious.

"I know I love you," she said quietly.

"Jesus, I can't believe it. I'm getting dumped by you again."

"Nobody's dumping you, Mackinac. You want me, you got me. But me, not some fictional character. And the real me lives here now."

"So if I say no, it's all over?"

"Hey, you're the one who brought up marriage, remember? I'm happy the way things are."

"You really are cold-blooded."

"What I am is grown-up. And if you want to be with me, you're going to have to grow up, too."

Twenty-five

Mack came home and retreated to his room, working and drinking more or less continuously for three days. He emerged only to get another bottle or to fix himself an occasional sandwich. McClain cornered him on one of his excursions to the refrigerator.

"I haven't seen Linda lately," he observed.

"If you miss her, give her a call," said Mack morosely.

"Lovers' quarrel? Hey, it happens, hotshot. You know how many times me and Joyce broke up and got back together?"

"I forget," said Mack.

"You can't just sit around here and mope."

"As it happens, I'm working. But if you want me to leave, I'll leave."

"Sorry I brought it up," said McClain.

He waited until Mack went back upstairs before going to look for Joyce. "Mack's all bent out of shape over Linda," he told her. "We've got to do something."

"Like what?"

"I think maybe I better go over there, have a talk with her."

"You stay out of their business, John," she said. "They don't need any of your po-lice psychology."

"In that case, you go," he said. "Talk woman to her. Come on, Joyce, I'm worried again. Either you go or I do."

"I'll go," Joyce said. She didn't want to alarm her husband, but she was worried about Mack, too.

After supper she drove out to Linda's place in West Tarryton. It was already dark and she felt uneasy; she didn't like driving around all-white neighborhoods alone at night. The cops in West Tarryton had a habit of pulling over black drivers and hassling them. "Next time that happens, tell 'em you're married to me," John had instructed her, but she refused to do that. Instead she informed them that she had a constitutional right to drive on any damn street she wanted and took their badge numbers. It didn't do any good, but it made her feel a little less helpless.

The porch light was on when Joyce pulled into the driveway, and Linda appeared in the doorway while she was walking up the front steps.

"Sorry to barge in like this," said Joyce, handing her coat to Linda. "It was either me or a visit from Cupid McClain."

"How is old Cupid?"

"Worried about Mack. Actually, I am too."

"How come nobody ever worries about me?" asked Linda with a smile.

"Well, it's different," said Joyce. "You know."

"Know what?"

"He was doing so well with you and now John's afraid he might get back to where he was."

"I'm not sure I get it."

"His old frame of mind," said Joyce. "The suicide thing."

Linda stared at her for a long moment. "What suicide thing?"

Now it was Joyce's turn to stare. "You mean John never told

you?" She shook her head. "Linda, when Mack came to town, he was thinking about committing suicide."

"No he wasn't," said Linda.

"Yes he was. He was keeping a suicide diary," said Joyce. "He's still keeping it."

"It's a novel," said Linda. "Fiction."

"Honey, I'm sorry, but it's no novel. I've seen it."

"He showed it to you?"

"John went snooping around his room one night and found it in a desk drawer."

"And you've been worried Mack was going to kill himself? In your house? Poor Joyce."

"Listen to me, now. John talked to Mack's editor. This isn't any novel."

"He talked to Wolfowitz?"

"Arthur Wolfowitz, yes."

"And he said it wasn't a novel?"

Joyce nodded. "He consulted with Mack's psychiatrist, who says Mack was suicidal before he left New York. That's why John's so concerned now. The psychiatrist says that since you two got together there's been a real improvement."

"How would he know? Mack's been here the whole time."

"John's been sending him pages from the diary," Joyce said.

"Behind Mack's back? He's been sending Mack's book to a shrink in New York?"

"To Wolfowitz," said Joyce. "He's the go-between."

"Oh, no."

"What?"

"John's been had," said Linda. "Mack promised to send pages to Wolfowitz, but he didn't, he's got some kind of phobia about it. He told me about the novel, but he wouldn't even show it to me. Obviously this was Wolfowitz's way of getting his hands on it. When John called, he saw his chance and he took it."

"He knew all along that Mack wasn't going to kill himself?"

Linda nodded. "He must have."

"Then why would he go to all that trouble just to see a manuscript he was going to get anyway?"

"Beats me," said Linda. "Curiosity, maybe. Or one of those testosterone things. Mack thinks they're great friends, but from what he's told me about Wolfowitz, he sounds like a creep."

"Oh, my," said Joyce. "We've made a mess, looks like."

Linda nodded. "When you found the diary, why didn't you just confront Mack with it?"

"John didn't want him to know he'd been going through his things. And he was afraid, if he mentioned it, he'd scare Mack off."

"I guess that's why he didn't tell me, either," said Linda. "He was afraid it would scare me off, too."

"I'm sorry," said Joyce. "If I'd have known, I would have told you myself. It never occurred to me that he hadn't."

"Men," said Linda.

"Men," agreed Joyce. "Well, so what do we do?"

"You better tell Mack now," said Linda. "He's got a right to know."

"I can't," said Joyce. "John would rather kill himself than have him find out."

"You think he'll care? Reality never upsets Mack. He'll probably put the whole episode in the novel."

"You may be right about that, but it would make John feel like a fool."

"Well, you must admit—"

"Hold it, now," said Joyce. "John's no fool. He may act foolish now and again, but he's a smart man and he's proud. It's hard enough for him being retired like he is. I won't have him humiliated."

"I'm sorry," said Linda, taken aback by Joyce's fierce reaction. "I like John, you know that. He did what he thought was best."

"It's all right," said Joyce, softening. "Being married to a man like John can make you protective. Mack's a lot like him in some ways. You'll see what I mean."

"What makes you think I'm going to marry Mack?"

Joyce narrowed her eyes in mock anger. "Don't even try that stuff on me, girlfriend. Like my mama used to say, I been where you been and you gettin' to where I am."

"Well, don't tell Mack, for God's sake." Linda laughed. "I hate New York."

"I'm not going to say a word, and neither are you. About the Wolfowitz thing, either. Not to Mack and not to John. This is going to be our secret."

"All right," said Linda. "I guess it can't do any harm."

Twenty-six

McClain stood, hands on his hips, glaring with frustrated disbelief at a seven–ten split. It was only a morning practice game at the Elks but he had been working on a possible two–twenty, and now he wouldn't get it. He cursed loudly and kicked the ball-return rack.

"Take the frame over, nobody's looking," said a voice from behind him. McClain recognized Buddy Packer's snide monotone even before he turned and saw him smirking through his granny glasses.

"It's members only in here," said McClain.

"The Oriole House of Lords," said Packer looking around the scruffy bowling alley, deserted at this hour except for McClain and a fat man in a soiled, short-sleeved white shirt who was stacking bags of potato chips at the snack bar. "Very exclusive."

"What do you want, Packer?"

Buddy stared at McClain with steady deliberation as he fired up a Lucky, took a deep drag and exhaled through his thin, hard lips. "Came to say good-bye," he said. "I'm on my way out of town."

McClain went to the rack and picked up his ball. "That's a damn shame," he said, looking down the lane at the mocking gap between the seven pin and the ten.

"Could be a while before I get back," said Packer. "I might even miss Mack's funeral."

McClain lowered the black bowling ball and replaced it in the rack. Slowly he walked over to Packer. "What funeral?" he asked in his cop's voice.

"There's a contract out on him. Buy me a bag of chips and I'll tell you about it."

"What?"

"I said, 'Buy me some chips.' " He gestured toward the refreshment stand. "And a Coke."

"What are you, nuts?"

"Naw, just hungry. I want a little hospitality, McClain. All those years I let you and your cop buddies booze on the cuff, I figure you can spring for a snack. This is your club, after all."

McClain looked up into Packer's hard brown eyes and saw he was serious. "You want barbecue or regular?"

"Jesus, regular. This is breakfast."

McClain returned to find Buddy sitting at the scorer's table. "You got a pretty good game going here," he said sociably, pointing to the score sheet.

McClain handed him the chips and the Coke and sat down next to him. "What about Mack?"

"A guy wants him dead."

"What guy?"

"Bookie named Herman Reggie. You know the name?"

McClain nodded. "I've heard of him. What makes you think he wants Mack dead?"

"I don't think, I know. He gave me twenty-five thousand bucks to make him that way."

"Wait a minute," said McClain, his professional sense of order taking control. "Run this down for me a step at a time. What's the motive?"

"Beats me," said Packer. "He didn't say and I didn't ask."

"You're not a hitman, you're a fucking bunko artist. Why you?"

Packer shrugged. "I guess he wanted somebody with a little finesse."

"So he offered you the job?"

"I took it, too," said Packer easily. "The twenty-five's up-front money. I get another twenty-five after."

"Why would he give you so much up front?"

"I talked him into it," said Packer. "Besides, he said if I stiffed him, he'd be back. He would, too, no doubt about it. That's why I'm splitting."

McClain thought about that for a while. "A big-time bookie from New York comes around and hands you twenty-five thousand dollars. You con him because you're a fucking thief—"

"What do you want me to do, off Mack?" asked Packer indignantly.

"What'd I do, hurt your feelings? Scamming Reggie's got nothing to do with your so-called friendship with Mack. We both know you don't have the balls to kill anybody. Okay, I see why you took the money and I see why you're running. What I don't see is how come you're telling me about it."

"Because I want to come back," said Packer. "And I can't until you take care of Reggie."

"Why would I do that?"

Packer took another deep drag on the cigarette. "The way I see it, if Reggie's willing to shell out fifty grand to hit Mack, he's got a fucking great reason. Which means he'll try again. And you're not going to let that happen."

"You got a lot of confidence in me," said McClain.

"I know you, just like you know me," said Packer. "You're not exactly Sherlock Holmes in the brain department, but this is your town, you got the home-court advantage here. And you got motivation."

"What motivation?"

"You're queer for Mack."

McClain stared at Packer. "What did you say?" he asked in a menacing tone.

"Hey, be cool, I'm not calling you a cocksucker," said Packer with a nasty smile. "Not that it didn't cross my mind when you asked him to move in. But I've been watching the two of you; the way I figure it, you've got a daddy hard-on for him. He's the son you never had because of your dinky little sperm count."

"There's nothing wrong with my sperm count," said McClain.

"Have it your way. All I'm saying is, I understand this shit. I have paternal feelings myself—"

"Don't compare me to you, asswipe."

"Fuck it," said Buddy, rising. McClain stood, too, annoyed that he had to look up at the giant Packer. "I came by to give you some information and you got it. The hit's supposed to be soon, Reggie said he'd get back to me on the time. And it's supposed to look like a suicide." He walked over to the ball rack, hit the reset button and watched as the metal bar descended and knocked the seven and ten pins on their sides. "Get Reggie first and you save your boy," he said, walking past McClain. "Otherwise, Mack's a fucking gutter ball."

McClain found Mack in his room listening to a "Best of the Contours" CD and leafing through *Sports Illustrated*. A glass of bourbon and half-melted ice sat on the desk and a Winston burned in the ashtray.

"Hard at work, I see," said McClain.

"Contemplation is part of the writer's craft," Mack replied with an off-center smile. "Want a belt?"

"No thanks, I think I better stay sober. I had a visit this morning, over at the Elks. From Buddy Packer."

"Since when are you and Buddy on speaking terms?"

"It wasn't a friendly chat. He came by to tell me that somebody offered him fifty thousand dollars to kill you."

"What for, to impress Jody Foster?"

"I'm not kidding," said McClain, looking at Mack steadily. "That's what he said."

"He was probably wrecked," said Mack. "Don't tell me you took him seriously?"

"You think I can't tell when a guy's stoned? He was serious, all right."

Mack laughed. "Who'd pay fifty thousand dollars to kill me? Who'd want to kill me at all?"

"A bookie named Herman Reggie."

"Never heard of him," said Mack. "Why would he want to have me killed?"

"Packer doesn't know."

"But he agreed to do it anyway? Come on."

"Packer's ripping Reggie off," said McClain. "He's on his way out of town with the money."

"Why did he tell you about it?"

"He figures if Reggie's willing to pay him, he'll try again. I stop him, Packer keeps the dough."

"He probably just drove by the Elks, saw your car and decided to mess with you. He's got a demented sense of humor."

"It's no joke," said McClain stubbornly. "I want you to take a look at this." He handed Mack a plain manila folder that contained a thick sheaf of papers and photographs.

"What is it?"

"A copy of Herman Reggie's FBI file. See if you recognize anybody."

Mack opened the folder and leafed through it. He stared for a while at Reggie's picture and shook his head. "Weird-looking guy, isn't he? I'd remember a face like this."

"How about the others?" said McClain. "Reggie's associates."

Mack scanned the photos and shrugged. "Looks like the Addams family." He turned a page and suddenly brightened. "Hey, here's Afterbirth Anderson."

"You know him?"

"No, but I recognize him. I did a piece for *Sports Illustrated*, maybe ten years ago, on the demise of midget wrestling. I saw films of a bunch of his matches."

"You didn't happen to slime him in the article?"

"I don't think I even mentioned him. He was more of an opponent."

"Well, he's working for Reggie now. As an enforcer and collector."

"For guys who come up a little short," said Mack. "By the way, how did you get this file?"

"I bought it at Doubleday," said McClain. "Listen, have you still got that pistol you took off the mugger in New York?"

"Yeah, I do."

"I don't suppose it's registered."

"I doubt it. He didn't look like the NRA type."

"Okay, Bret Damon in the detective bureau will fix the paperwork for you and arrange some target practice. From now on I want you to carry it and I want to know where you are at all times. And if you get any telephone calls from strangers, let me—"

"Hey, wait a minute," said Mack. "I'm not going on Red Alert because of a practical joke."

"I'm gonna have to insist," said McClain stiffly.

"And I'm gonna have to say no," replied Mack. "I'm a big boy, John. I'll make my own decisions."

"There's more than just you involved," said McClain. "Somebody tries to hit you while you're here, it could be dangerous for Joyce."

Mack thought about that while he lit a cigarette. "In that case, if you're really worried about this nonsense, I'll move out," he said.

"That's not what I'm saying at all," protested McClain. "I want you to stay. But you've got to let me protect you."

"Nope," said Mack, finishing his drink and pouring another. "I've imposed on you long enough as it is. We both know I can't stay forever. I'll check into the Hilton until I'm ready to go back to New York."

"Wait a minute," said McClain. He pulled a ring of keys from his pocket, detached one and handed it to Mack. "I've got a condo over on Newbery. It's free, it's quiet and it's yours for as long as you need it."

Mack looked at the key. "Don't tell me you're leading a double life."

"Naw, nothing like that, hotshot," said McClain. "I had it before I met Joyce and I held on to it as a rental place. Right now it happens to be vacant."

"Okay, thanks," said Mack, taking the key. "I'll be happy to pay you rent, whatever the going price is."

"Forget the rent, just do me one favor," said McClain.

"Sure, what?"

"Somebody comes by to shoot you, go outside. I got new carpeting."

Joyce received the news of Mack's departure with a rare flash of anger. "The boy's in trouble and you just put him out," she said accusingly. "That's not like you, John."

"Come on, honey, that's not the way it was," McClain said.

"Well, you better explain how it was, then, because that's sure how it sounds."

"I did it for his own good. He's got to take this seriously, but he won't. He acted like it was a big joke."

"That's just his way of trying to control reality," said Joyce. "It's a good thing you po-lice got fingerprints and lie detectors or you'd never figure out a damn thing."

"I may not be a deep thinker, but I know a threat when I see one, and if Mack won't face it, he's better off at the condo. There's half a dozen cops living in the complex I can get to keep an eye on him."

"That makes sense," Joyce conceded. "What about this Reggie? Can't you have him arrested?"

"Come on, Joyce, you know better than that. Packer's gone, and even if he wasn't, all I've got is his word. Which is basically worthless."

"So we're just going to wait for somebody to try to kill Mack and hope that one of the neighbors stops him? Is that what you're saying?"

"Oriole's a small town, honey; it won't be so easy for an outside hit man to show up without somebody knowing about it. That's probably why Reggie chose Packer in the first place."

"Maybe he'll try somebody local again."

"I doubt it. Next time he'll use a guy he's sure won't walk with the money."

"Okay, then what? When the guy he's sure of shows up?"

McClain squared his big shoulders. "Then I'll take care of business," he said.

"You're retired," said Joyce. "I don't want you doing anything stupid."

McClain reached out and pulled Joyce to him. "Sorry, honey," he said, stroking her soft brown cheek. "You should have thought of that before you married me."

Twenty-seven

It took Herman Reggie a month to realize that he was out twenty-five thousand dollars. He discovered it when his cousin Jeff phoned from California.

"Green called Ligget this morning."

"Who?"

"Andy Ligget, the Hollywood front man. Green told him the book will be finished in ten days. Oh, and he told him he moved—he's not living with the cop anymore."

Reggie called Packer's house, and a woman answered. "May I speak with Mr. Packer please?" he said.

"No, you may not," trilled the woman. "He no longer resides at this residence."

"Can you tell me where I can reach him?"

"No I cannot."

"My name is Mr. Reggie. Did he leave a message for me?"

"He didn't leave a thing, except a couple of half-paid-for electrical appliances."

"Didn't say when he'd be back?"

"Mister, one morning he got in his car and drove away from home. That's all I know."

"He owes me money," said Reggie.

"Me, too," said Jean sadly. "You find him, call me back."

Reggie phoned Arlen Nashua. "Buddy Packer's missing," he said. "Any idea where he might be?"

"I could find out," Nashua wheezed.

"Do that. Oh, and get me Mack Green's new address in Oriole and some details about when he's likely to be at home alone."

"How soon do you need it?"

"Day after tomorrow will be fine," said Reggie.

"I'll call when I know something."

"You can tell me in person," said Reggie. "I'm coming out there myself."

Reggie hung up and ran his hand over his bald head. He wasn't worried about Packer running off with the money—a guy who looked like him would be easy to track down. When he found him he'd turn him over to Afterbirth; the little fellow loved working on tall, lanky guys.

Reggie thought for a while about Packer's replacement. Soon he'd have the *Diary,* an unimpeachable suicide note. And with Green out of McClain's house, almost anyone could do the job on him. Suddenly he had an inspiration. Afterbirth was too shy to mention it but Herman knew he was desperate for a promotion. Give him the chance and he'd go out to Oriole for free, turning whatever was recovered from Packer into pure profit.

There was more than just money involved in Herman's calculation. Afterbirth was a valued subordinate who happened to have a physical disability. Helping him up a rung on the professional ladder would make him a happy man. It was a good thing to do because it was the right thing, the American thing. Herman Reggie, the bookie thought to himself proudly, Equal Opportunity Employer.

On the opening day of the baseball season, with the Tigers scheduled to play at home against the Red Sox, Mack awoke all alone in a strange bed. The strong scent of lavender on the pillow mixed with the used bourbon fumes in his nostrils made his head spin and his stomach churn perilously. "Jesus H. Christ," he moaned. "Where am I?"

There was no answer, just the sound of water running in a nearby shower. Painfully, he tried to reconstruct the events of the last twenty-four hours. He remembered finishing the *Diary*. He recalled slipping Wolfowitz's and Ligget's copies into cardboard boxes and dropping them off at Federal Express. He recollected stopping at Stanley's for a sandwich and a few celebratory cocktails. Vaguely he remembered calling Linda, who hadn't been home.

The water stopped and Mack struggled to sit up. He had called someone else after Linda. Packer's girlfriend. She said Buddy was gone for good and would he like to come over. That's where things began to go blank; he couldn't remember his answer. Maybe that's where he was right now, in Packer's bed. Serve him right, Mack thought, for pulling his stupid prank on McClain.

McClain. Suddenly Mack remembered they had a date for opening day. He looked at his watch, squinting with concentration, and saw it was 10:15. McClain was supposed to pick him up at the condo in an hour.

The idea of fresh air and loud, cheering voices nauseated him. Maybe it's raining, he thought hopefully. With a grunt he stumbled to the window, pulled back the heavy shade and got a blast of April sunlight that sent a dagger of pain through his skull. There would be a game for sure.

If he rushed he'd just make it, but first he desperately needed a cold shower. "How's it going in there?" he called to the mystery woman in the bathroom. "You almost done?"

"Hey, you're awake," she answered in a high, cheerful voice he didn't recognize. "I'll be right out. How do you feel?"

"Terrible," said Mack. "My head's exploding."

"I've got just the thing for that." After a moment he heard the sound of harmonica music echoing off the bathroom walls; it was "For the Longest Time." The song was off-key, but Mack didn't care. He still couldn't remember what had happened the night before, but at least he knew now who it had happened with.

Afterbirth Anderson arrived in Oriole at the wheel of a rented late-model Cadillac specially outfitted with hand controls and an elevated seat. On the passenger side he had a street map and a leather briefcase. In the case was a set of burglary tools, a pack of Necco wafers, a change of underwear and the untraceable Beretta Herman Reggie had given him that morning.

Reggie had booked a regal suite at the Pontchartrain and taken him out the night before, for a fine steak dinner and a final briefing. His instructions were simple. "All you have to do is drive out to Green's place, get inside, make him sit down, shoot him in the head with one bullet and put the gun in his hand. Then you leave and meet me back here," he said.

"Why does he have to be sitting down?" Afterbirth asked.

"The angle," Reggie explained. "If you do it while he's standing, you'll be shooting up. This is supposed to look like a do-it-yourself job."

"I could get up on a chair."

"No need for that," said Reggie. "You are who you are. Just be yourself, that's good enough for me."

All the way to Oriole, Afterbirth had savored those few words. They gave him a confidence and sense of worth that he hadn't known since boyhood. If there were more men like Herman Reggie, he mused warmly, the world would be a better place, not just for midgets but for everyone.

He arrived just before eleven, parked the Caddy in the condo's lot, took his briefcase and walked up a flight of outside stairs to the second floor. There was no one on the street or in the yard below. He rang the bell, knocked, rang again and then deftly let himself in.

He stood in the small front hallway, listening, but there was no sound in the apartment. He made a quick inspection tour—living room, kitchen, bedroom, bathroom—saw that no one was home, and went back to the living room to wait. His gaze fell on a small footstool next to an overstuffed television chair and he smiled to himself. He wouldn't be needing the footstool. Now that he was working for Herman Reggie full time, his climbing days were over.

McClain was standing in front of the full-length mirror in the hall, a Tiger's cap on his head, watching himself take a few opening day swings with an air bat, when the phone rang. He whipped around and hit one last imaginary fastball on a line into deep center field for a triple, bowed to his image in the mirror and picked up the receiver. He expected Mack; instead he heard the gravelly voice of Ducky Brokowski.

"I just looked out my window and saw some little fucker break into your condo," Ducky said.

"What kind of little fucker? You mean a kid?"

"More like a dwarf. Mean-looking mohumper with a barrel chest and a big-ass head. He's not from around here, I can tell you that."

McClain remembered the midget wrestler with a weird name in Reggie's FBI file. "He's there for Mack," he said. "You gotta grab him."

"Mack's not home," said Brokowski. "His car was gone when I got home from my shift at seven, and it's still gone. I figure he's shacked up someplace."

"I was supposed to pick him up in a little while," said McClain. "We're going to opening day."

"Maybe it skipped his mind," said Brokowski. "Pussy will make a man forget baseball every time."

"Probably he's on his way over here."

"Yeah. Look, John, you want me to go over and scoop this turd up for you?"

"No," said McClain. Ducky was a good cop, but he had a tendency to shoot people, and McClain wanted to talk to the midget. "I'll be there in ten minutes. If he tries to go, grab him, but if he stays put, leave him for me."

In the next five minutes, McClain got halfway to the condo; Ducky sat on the toilet reading a *Free Press* story about the Tigers' pitching rotation; and Mack came home just in time to shave, change his clothes and keep his date with McClain. He was three steps into the front hallway when he felt a hunk of hard steel thrust roughly between his legs and heard a voice from behind say, "Hands on your head, Green, or I'll blow your balls off." He raised his hands as the barrel prodded his scrotum. "Now, turn around slow."

He turned and found himself looking down at Afterbirth Anderson. A rush of adrenaline cleared Mack's head as he realized with an amazed detachment that Packer had been telling the truth after all.

"I'm not Green, you dumbfuck," said Mack said in a calm, slightly irritated tone that shocked him; he had no idea why he had said it, or what was coming next.

"No? Then who are you?"

"I'm Detective John McClain," said Mack. Now he understood what he was trying to do.

Afterbirth blinked in confusion. Reggie had shown him a picture of Green taken from a book jacket, but it was twenty years old. Besides, although he hadn't admitted it to Herman, regular-sized men looked a lot alike to him. "Show me some ID," he said.

"We don't carry ID off-duty, Afterbirth," said Mack, slipping easily into McClain's gruff style.

"Hey, how'd you know my name?"

"Because Reggie sent me over here to get you, hotshot. The hit's off."

"I just saw Reggie two hours ago at the hotel."

"I know that," Mack said impatiently. "I called down there fifteen minutes after you left to tell him they picked Green up for drunk driving. He's in the tank right now. Herman told me to get over here and send you back."

"I thought you said you're a cop."

"Herman and I are old friends," said Mack. "Business friends. I helped him set this thing up."

"How do I know you're not bullshitting me?" asked Anderson, his gristly features contorted in confusion.

"The hit on Green was originally supposed to be done by Buddy Packer. How would I know that unless Herman told me? Think about it."

Suddenly they heard the sound of a key turning in the lock. "It's Green," Mack whispered urgently. "They must've let him out."

Afterbirth looked wildly from Mack to the direction of the door. "You go in the living room and stay put," he said, gesturing with his pistol.

Mack stepped back into the living room as McClain opened the door. He heard the midget say, "Freeze," picked up the footstool and tiptoed in the direction of the hall.

"Hands on your head, Green," said Afterbirth to McClain, as Mack slowly raised the stool into striking position.

"I'm not Green, you dumbfuck," he heard McClain say.

"Nobody's Green around here," Afterbirth protested as Mack sprang at him from behind, bringing the footstool down on his head. The midget crumpled to the floor, his body lying between Mack and an astonished John McClain.

"Took you long enough to get here, hotshot," snapped Mack.

McClain gave him a sharp look. "Looks like I was right about Packer," he said.

"Yeah, it does," said Mack, fading out of his McClain character. The hangover headache was back, pounding at the tops of his eyes. "What do we do with him?" He nudged Afterbirth's prone form with his foot.

"Help me get him into a chair," said McClain. "I'm going to show you how to conduct an interrogation."

Herman Reggie was in his suite, leafing through a copy of *Forbes,* when the phone rang. He expected Afterbirth, reporting on a job well done. Instead, a voice he didn't know said, "Herman?"

"Who's this?"

"Mack Green."

"Oh?" said Herman. "I'm sorry, do I know you?"

"That's what I was wondering," said Mack. "I'm down in the bar. Why don't you meet me and we can talk." There was a long pause and Mack added, "I've got Afterbirth."

"I'll be down in two minutes," Herman said.

"Good. I'll just stay on the line until you get here. You weren't planning to use your phone, right?"

When Reggie entered the bar he saw Green and a powerful-looking old man sitting together. He recognized Mack from his picture; the old guy he made for a cop from fifty feet away. Wordlessly, he walked over to their table and sat down.

"I've never seen you before in my life," said Mack, squinting at him.

"That's true," said Reggie. "Listen, can I get you fellas something to eat? Club sandwich, maybe, or a chef salad?"

"No thanks," said McClain, his eyes fixed on Reggie. "We didn't come for lunch."

"I know that," Herman said, "but since I'm the one staying at the hotel, that makes me the host."

"You've got balls," said McClain.

"You need them in my business. Yours, too. Detroit PD?"

"Oriole, retired."

"Ah, you're John McClain," said Reggie, extending his hand. "I've heard a lot of good things about you."

"Thanks," said McClain, taking the hand and giving it a shake.

"Excuse me for interrupting," said Mack, "but I was wondering why you tried to have me killed this morning."

"I'm sure you don't expect me to admit something like that," said Reggie. He turned to McClain. "What brings you down here?"

"Well, it's like Mack says, we want to know why you tried to kill him. And to make sure you don't try again. If you tell us, you can have Afterbirth and go back to New York. If not, I'll have him charged with attempted murder and you named as an accessory."

"Is he all right?" asked Reggie with real concern.

"You've got a loyal employee there," said McClain. "Feels real bad about letting you down."

"This will be tough on him," said Reggie. "He didn't have much self-confidence to begin with."

"Well, nobody bats a thousand," said McClain.

"I'll tell him you said that. If that's all right."

"Go right ahead," said McClain.

"Jesus, I can't believe this conversation," said Green.

"This deal you're offering, are you speaking for Mack here, too?"

"Mack?" said Green. "What am I, a friend of yours?"

"Yeah, I'm speaking for both of us," said McClain.

"Word of honor?" asked Reggie, staring into McClain's eyes. The big man nodded and held out his hand again; Reggie took it in a solemn grip. "That's good enough for me."

"How about explaining what this is all about," said Mack. "Just for the fun of it."

"I can see how you'd be curious," said Reggie. "It all started out when Tommy Russo couldn't repay an eighteen thousand dollar debt—"

Mack sat listening in agitated disbelief as Herman Reggie described the plot to turn his novel into a multimillion dollar snuff diary. By the time he was finished, Mack realized that he had been sold out by Russo; stalked by a guy in a blue Mitsubishi he couldn't remember seeing; set up by a sham Hollywood producer; and that only a moment of inspired invention at the condo stood between him and the J. D. Murphy Funeral Home.

"—so that's it," Reggie concluded. "The whole story. From my point of view it's close, but no cigar."

"It was quite a scheme," said McClain with what sounded to Mack like admiration.

"A hell of a scheme," Reggie agreed. "No hard feelings, I hope."

"Not if you get out of town and stay away from Mack," said McClain. "Of course, he keeps the hundred thousand from the movie offer."

"A deal's a deal," Reggie said.

"The way I look at it, this Russo owes you for that," said McClain.

"Plus the original eighteen and the vig," said Reggie.

"And don't forget the twenty-five you gave Packer."

"That was my mistake," said Reggie. "I'll collect that one separately."

McClain nodded at the fairness of Reggie's distinction. "Come on, Mack," he said, rising. "Let's get back to Oriole."

Reggie reached out and caught McClain's arm. "I'd appreciate a private word with you first," he said.

"Private word my ass," said Mack.

"No, it's okay," McClain said. "Mack, wait for me in the lobby."

Green frowned, started to say something and then walked away, shaking his head.

"Nice young man," said Reggie. "You obviously have a good relationship."

"What can I do for you, Herman?" asked McClain.

"Let me know when Buddy Packer gets back," said Reggie. "It'd be worth 20 percent—three thousand, six hundred dollars. Interested?"

"Not if you're planning something like today."

"No, it's just debt collection," said Reggie. "I can't promise it'll be nonviolent, but it won't be lethal."

"In that case, leave me your number," said McClain. "I don't want the money, though; giving you Packer will be my pleasure."

"In that case, I'll owe you a favor," said Reggie.

"Yeah," said McClain. "You will, won't you?"

Twenty-eight

John dropped Mack off at home and drove over to the Nutmeg Village Day Care Center, where Joyce was fingerpainting with a bunch of four-year-olds. "Honey, I've got to talk to you," he said.

"Can't it wait?" she said. "It's playtime."

"No," said McClain. "We were wrong about Mack's diary. It's just a novel."

"I know," said Joyce, wiping her hands on a rag.

"Which means Wolfowitz scammed me. All this time I've been sending—what do you mean, you know?"

"Linda told me."

"And you didn't tell me?"

"I didn't want to trouble you," said Joyce. "I didn't see the point."

"You didn't see the point," McClain repeated, enunciating each word distinctly.

"John, don't you take that po-lice tone with me."

"Sorry," McClain muttered. "It's been a tough day. Herman Reggie made his move this morning, over at the condo."

"Oh—"

"Don't worry, Mack's all right," said McClain quickly. "As a matter of fact he did great."

"Where's he now?"

"Home, sleeping off a hangover."

"Where's Reggie?"

"I let him go," said McClain. "In return for a promise to leave Mack alone."

"And you believed him? Just like that?"

"Joyce, he's famous for keeping his word."

"The man made a big impression on you, I see."

"There's something about him," said McClain. "Anyway, now I've got to tell Mack about me stealing his book."

"I wouldn't worry about that," she said. "When he knows why you did it, he'll be grateful. Linda thinks so, too."

"You told Linda about me and Wolfowitz?"

Joyce looked at her husband steadily. "Yes, I did."

"Jesus, this thing is out of control," said McClain miserably. "Now I don't know what to do."

"What we're going to do is drive over to the mall and pick up Linda, go find Mack and get everything on the table. Everybody's going to tell everything they know about everything. We've all got to get on the same wavelength."

"I guess you're right," said McClain reluctantly.

"And then," she said in a quiet, angry voice, "we're going to put our heads together and see about Mister Wolfowitz."

Three days later, Mack, Linda and the McClains flew to New York. Mack wanted to book a suite at the Waldorf, two double bedrooms connected by a sitting room, but Linda insisted on staying alone. "I'm here as your lawyer, not your girlfriend," she told him.

"When this is over, I want to get married," said Mack. He was sitting on the bed, watching her unpack.

"Let's not go into that right now," said Linda. "We've got enough to deal with as it is."

"On your terms."

"Since when?"

"Since I realized that everybody I ever trusted has betrayed me in some way. Wolfowitz, Tommy, John and Joyce—"

"They're different," said Linda. "They thought they were doing it for your own good."

"—even you. You knew about Wolfowitz and didn't say anything. And you dumped me for a quarterback."

"That was a lifetime ago."

"Maybe, but it was my lifetime. I've been thinking about it, wondering how I could have been so oblivious to what's going on around me, and I realized you're right—I do see my life as a novel. Everybody's my character, so how can my characters be doing something I don't know about? I didn't get it before, but I do now."

"All of a sudden."

"People change, Linnie. You did. You're not the same person you were in California."

Linda stared at Mack. "I hope you're not saying all this just to screw me while we're in New York," she said.

"Linnie, honest to God—" Mack said. Then he saw her crooked grin and pulled her down on the bed.

They split up after lunch. Joyce and John took a cab up to Harlem. Linda walked over to the Gothic Building on Fifth Avenue to see Carter Lang, Gothic's in-house attorney, about setting up a meeting. And Mack went to the Flying Tiger, were he met Otto and Walter T. Horton for a drink. Then he went to see Tommy Russo.

Mack brushed past Russo's secretary and found the agent in his office, talking into a speaker phone. When he saw Green he smiled and frowned at the same time.

"Mack!" he called, shutting off the machine, leaping from behind his desk and bustling toward him. Green plopped down on the sofa, leaving Russo in the middle of the room with his plump arms outstretched and a tentative expression on his dark face.

"Tommy!" said Mack, in a sour imitation of the agent's greeting.

"Hey, something the matter?"

"You could say that. I had a visit from my agent the other day," said Mack. "Herman Reggie."

Russo went back and sat behind his desk. "I guess I better explain what happened," he said.

"Herman already explained," said Mack. "Just after he tried to have me killed."

"Wha'?"

"He figured my diary would make a better movie if it was nonfiction. He was right, too. I'm surprised you didn't think of it yourself—you could have sold me for more than eighteen thousand bucks."

"Mack, this is crazy. Honest to God, I don't know what the hell you're talking about. I mean, yeah, I gave your contract to Herman, it was either that or get beat to death, but the rest of it, him trying to kill you, on my mother's eyes, I had no idea."

"I guess you had no idea about Wolfowitz, either."

"What about Wolfowitz?" said Tommy. He was sweating now, and he shifted uneasily in his chair.

"I was just over at the Tiger. Otto and Horton told me about Walter T.'s new book. They say he told you all about it Christmas Day."

"I didn't think he was serious," said Tommy. "I mean, the guy was dead drunk."

"What did Wolfowitz say when you asked him about it?"

"I, ah, never talked to Wolfowitz," Tommy said. "I didn't see any reason to. I mean, what was I gonna say, ya know?"

"You think if you keep talking long enough I'm going to start believing this bullshit? Wolfowitz has been screwing up my books all along, hasn't he, Tommy?"

"You're the one who wanted him," said Russo. "Remember, I told you you'd be better off someplace else."

"But you didn't tell me why. Just like you didn't tell me about Horton. Wolfowitz was setting me up for a plagiarism thing, wasn't he?"

"I don't know that."

Mack stared at him, holding his eyes until the little agent sighed and looked away. "You don't know because you didn't want to know," Mack said. "You sold me and you sold me out."

"I had to do business with him," said Tommy. "I never meant for you to get hurt, honest to God. I thought after all this time Wolfowitz had gotten over it."

"Gotten over what?" asked Mack.

"I told you the first time we ever met, a guy screws another guy's wife, there's trouble."

Mack stared at Tommy. "Another guy's wife? You mean Louise?"

"Yeah, Louise."

"Jesus, that was more than twenty years ago. Even then it didn't mean anything."

"It meant something to him, Mack."

"And you just sat there all this time and said nothing. How could you have done that to me?"

The mildness of the rebuke caught Russo off guard; he felt tears well up in his eyes. "I'm sorry, Mack," he said. "I'm ashamed. If I could make it right I would, but it's too late. I can't even ask you to forgive me."

"I'm not doing one of those 'te absolvo' scenes, if that's what you've got in mind, but I'm not looking for any revenge, either. What I want from you is a written statement, everything you know or even suspect about what Wolfowitz has been doing to my books. Have it at the Waldorf by five."

"I'd feel better if you kicked my ass. I deserve it."

Mack rose, walked to the door and paused. "Don't worry, Father Tomas, you'll pay for this," he said.

"My Catholic conscience," said Tommy.

"No, your Catholic bankbook. You may not know it, but you owe Herman Reggie a hundred and eighteen thousand dollars."

Twenty-nine

When Mack and Linda arrived at Gothic, they were greeted in the reception area by an effusive Stealth Wolfowitz. "The book's great," he said. "You've really got your old touch back."

"I'm glad you think so," Mack said noncommittally.

"Is everyone here?" asked Linda.

"Floutie and Carter Lang are in the conference room," said Wolfowitz. "And Fassbinder. Jesus, Mack, I don't know why you insisted on him being here. This better be important."

"It is," said Linda.

"Before we go in, would you please tell me what's going on?" said Wolfowitz to Mack.

"It's a surprise," Linda replied.

Wolfowitz gave Linda a wintry smile. "I see you've got a new spokeswoman," he said to Mack.

"Sorry. This is my lawyer, Linda Birney."

"I hope you're not here to renegotiate Mack's contract," said Wolfowitz. "The book is terrific, but we've got a deal."

"Oh, nothing as painless as that," said Linda breezily, returning the editor's false smile. "Let's get started, shall we?"

They followed Wolfowitz down the long hall to the book-lined conference room where Floutie, Fassbinder and Carter Lang, Gothic's chief legal counsel, were seated on one side of the big mahogany table. Floutie and Lang rose graciously, but Fassbinder remained seated, glowering at them.

"Well now," said Linda briskly.

"I wonder if you'd be good enough to begin with an explanation of why we're here," said Floutie. "The purpose of this meeting is rather obscure."

"I'll see if I can't clarify it for you," said Linda, catching the rhythm of Floutie's fake Oxbridge tone. It was hard for Mack to repress a grin as he recalled how, only a few hours before, this self-possessed attorney in her severe black silk suit had been tumbling around with him, wild eyed and panting, in her king-sized bed at the Waldorf. "There are several items on the agenda. Let's begin with Mr. Wolfowitz's criminal bad faith."

"Bad faith?" asked Wolfowitz, spreading his hands in a gesture of innocent confusion. "I have no idea what you're talking about."

"I'm talking about your arrangement with Walter T. Horton."

Wolfowitz stared at her and shook his head. "Sorry, I don't know what you mean."

"Well, I thought you might not remember, so I've gone to the trouble of getting a notarized statement from Mr. Horton." She snapped open her briefcase and slid copies across the table to Lang and the others. "Why don't you all take a minute and read it. It's not too long. Or too complicated."

The men bent their heads over the paper. Lang was the first to finish. "According to this, Mr. Wolfowitz asked Horton to write an alternative version of *The Diary of a Dying Man,*" he said to Linda in his Virginia drawl. "Is that correct?"

"What do you mean, 'correct'? It's a crock," Wolfowitz interrupted hotly. "This guy Horton's a psycho. He's dying from AIDS for Christ's sake, he was probably zonked on some kind of medicine when he signed this. If he even did."

"He signed it," said Linda calmly. "And he wasn't, in your empathetic phrase, zonked on anything."

"Why would Wolfowitz make such a deal?" asked Floutie. "Particularly for another publishing house?"

"Because he owns a part of the house," said Linda. "As to why—maybe Mr. Wolfowitz would like to answer that."

"I'm not answering a goddamn thing," said Wolfowitz. "I'm not on trial here."

"Very well, then I'll answer for him," said Linda. "It was part of a personal vendetta against Mr. Green. He also undermined my client's last two books for the same reason."

"Now I know you're nuts," said Wolfowitz, throwing up his hands in outrage. "Vendetta! What am I, the Cosa Nostra? Green's books don't sell and I'm responsible?"

"Not you, Gothic. After all, you are the editor in chief," said Linda.

"I get it now," said Wolfowitz, looking past Floutie to Fassbinder. "This is some kind of shakedown. Jesus, Mack, I'm disappointed, I really am."

Green cleared his throat, but Linda placed a restraining hand on his arm. "Let's cut the crap. Who's actually in charge here?"

"I am the publisher of Gothic Books," said Floutie, with heavy dignity.

"That's right," said Fassbinder ominously. "Floutie here's the head rooster. Anybody gets it in the neck, it's him."

Once again Linda reached into her briefcase, produced a thick sheaf of papers and handed them to Floutie. "This is a copy of Walter T. Horton's manuscript. It's based on Mack's idea and patterned on the pages Mr. Wolfowitz obtained under false pretenses from John McClain of Oriole, Michigan. Mr. McClain, by the way, is not a psycho or even an AIDS patient. He's a retired police detective." She looked at Lang. "I have his statement right here if you'd care to see it. And another from Tomas Russo, Mack's agent."

"Please," said Lang, taking a copy of the documents.

"So," said Linda sweetly, "allow me to summarize the situation. The editor in chief of Gothic Books has been engaged in a conspiracy to defraud my client, and he has engaged in a similar conspiracy on at least two previous occasions."

"These alleged previous instances, would you care to be more specific?" asked Lang.

"Not really," said Linda. "Mr. Wolfowitz knows what I'm talking about, he can fill you in. Naturally, you'll get all the details during discovery."

Wolfowitz rose so suddenly that his chair tumbled backward. "I've heard all I'm going to listen to," he snapped. "Carter, you're a lawyer, tell this bitch she can't come waltzing in here making wild accusations. There are libel laws, slander laws—"

"I don't care for your language, Arthur," said Floutie. "I apologize, Ms. Birney."

"Who gives a shit what you care for?" snapped Wolfowitz.

"Calm down," said Lang in a surprisingly strong tone. He leaned over to Floutie and cupped his hand to the publisher's ear. "Douglas, as Gothic's counsel it is my duty to tell you that our interests may now be in conflict with Wolfowitz's," he whispered.

Wolfowitz overheard the remark. "You're selling me out, is that it? Harlan, tell these Ivy League faggots what's what—"

Fassbinder ignored the demand. "This thing gonna cost me money?" he asked Lang.

"There's no need to discuss that here," said Lang.

"Big money," said Linda, who had listened to the byplay in silence. "And that's the least of your problems."

"I'm not taking any more of this crap," shouted Wolfowitz, stalking to the door. "I'll get myself a real lawyer and sue you for slander and defamation of character."

"I can't even remember what she was like," said Mack quietly. It was the first time he had spoken, and it brought Wolfowitz up short.

"What?"

"I can't remember what Louise was like in bed. All this trouble and I can't even remember."

Wolfowitz stared at Mack, threw open the door and stormed out. There was a moment's silence and then Carter Lang said, "I think it would be a good idea if we took a fifteen-minute recess."

"We've got 'em running scared," Mack whispered to Linda and squeezed her hand.

She returned the pressure and chuckled. "You think they're scared now, wait till they see what's coming next."

By the time Wolfowitz reached his corner office he was already calm enough to begin analyzing his situation. Things weren't nearly as bad as he had first thought. The legal threat was bogus— all they had was Horton's statement, the word of an alcoholic on medication. Besides, with luck Horton would be dead in a few months, making him a poor witness. As far as McClain was concerned, well, it was McClain who had contacted him. How was he to know that Mack wasn't really thinking about killing himself?

He might have to leave Gothic, although he had a chance to talk Fassbinder around after the others were gone. But even if he couldn't, he had plenty of money and a company to run—the small house that was going to publish Horton's novel.

The more Wolfowitz thought about it, the better things looked. He'd bring out Horton's novel anyway, and if Mack or Gothic made a stink, well, there was nothing like a literary scandal to stir sales. In fact, he could blackmail Walter T. by telling him that he wouldn't publish his book unless he dropped his statement. Then, with the right publicity, Wolfowitz could still make it look like Mack had stolen Horton's idea and cooked up an implausible story about a vendetta to save his own skin.

Wolfowitz gathered some private papers, put them in his brief-case and glanced lovingly at the picture of Louise on his desk. He wasn't finished with Mack yet, not by a long shot. He walked down the corridor to the exit with a light step. He was a man with a mission, a happy man. He would have whistled if there had been anyone around to hear him.

McClain met Reggie on the northwest corner of Park and Sixty-fifth, only a few blocks from Gothic headquarters. They shook hands and McClain said, "We're the two biggest men on the street."

Reggie looked around at the other pedestrians and nodded in agreement. "We've got a lot in common," he said. "A certain kind of chemistry. I sensed that in Detroit. You did, too, didn't you? I could tell."

"Yeah, I did," said McClain. "Look, there's something I need to talk to you about."

"Let's walk while we talk," said Herman, taking McClain's arm and guiding him in the direction of Central Park. "What's on your mind?"

"Wolfowitz," said McClain. "Mack's editor. And a guy named Walter T. Horton."

"I've never heard of Walter T. Horton," said Reggie.

"He's a guy Wolfowitz hired to copy Mack's book. When his comes out, it's supposed to look like Mack plagiarized him."

"Why would Wolfowitz do that?"

"It's complicated, but what it comes down to is, he's jealous 'cause Mack screwed his wife."

"Not much of a reason," said Reggie. "Not that I approve of adultery. But what's it got to do with me?"

"I figured you'd want to know. I mean, after all, you still own 10 percent of Mack's book. And if Wolfowitz doesn't screw it up, that'll be worth a lot of money."

"What makes you think so? Aside from loyalty?"

"Inside information," said McClain. "Gothic's going to put a lot of money behind it, make it a bestseller."

"I thought you said Wolfowitz was going to publish this other one instead."

"With a different company. Unless somebody stops him."

Reggie led McClain across Fifth Avenue and into the park.

"He might not be easy to stop," said Reggie. "He sounds like a determined man."

"If it was going to be easy, I wouldn't be here right now," said McClain.

"I see," said Reggie. They walked in silence for a while and then he said, "Mack might not like the idea of having me stay on as his agent."

"He's the one who suggested it," said McClain. "He said, 'if I'm going to be represented by a crook, at least I want one who's on my side.' "

"And he figured I could take care of Wolfowitz for him?" said Reggie.

"No, that's my idea. Mack thinks that getting him fired will stop him. He's a great kid, but when it comes to dealing with bad men, he's a little naïve."

"I admire that in him," said Reggie. "There's such a thing as being too cynical."

"Yeah, you wouldn't call him cynical," McClain said. "So, are you interested?"

Reggie stopped and extended his hand. "Tell Mack I'll do my best for him," he said.

"I've got Wolfowitz's address in case you need it," said McClain.

"No, I'd rather see him away from home," said Reggie. "He's a married man, and Afterbirth tends to have an upsetting effect on wives. Don't worry, though; I'll catch up to him."

"Speaking of which, I almost forgot. Packer's not going to be back," said McClain.

"More inside information?"

McClain nodded.

"Do you happen to know where he is?"

"Someplace they speak Spanish," said McClain. "If I were you, I'd write him off."

"No offense, but I don't write anyone off. Would you like a hot dog?"

"Sure," said McClain. "My treat."

"No, it's on me," said Reggie. He walked over to the Sabrett vendor and came back with four hot dogs smothered in onions. "Two each," he said. "The big man's order."

"Good dog," said McClain, taking a large bite. "I wish they made 'em like this at the Elks. That's my hangout these days."

"How old a man are you, if you don't mind my asking?"

"Mid-sixties," McClain said.

"And that's what you do? Hang out at the Elks?"

"I told you, I'm retired."

"A man reaches his prime and they discard him," said Reggie, shaking his big bald head. "It's a criminal waste of talent."

"I can't disagree with you there."

"I wonder if you'd consider coming to work for me? I could use a vigorous senior citizen in my operation."

"Naw, my wife would kill me," said McClain, unable to suppress a grin. "I appreciate the offer, though. It's nice to feel wanted."

The meeting at Gothic was reconvened by Douglas Floutie. He had just begun to explain his position on the question of corporate liability when the door flew open and Joyce came in, accompanied by a very large, very dark man, dressed in a jeweled turban and a flowing African robe. He took a seat next to Linda and nodded amicably to Mack. Fassbinder glowered at him, and he returned the look with an intensity that obviously disconcerted the old man. "Who the hell are you supposed to be?" he snapped. "Mau-Mau home delivery?"

"Allow me to introduce my friend Joyce McClain and Minister Abijamin Malik, my spiritual adviser," said Mack.

"Oh-oh," murmured Carter Lang.

"Pleased to meet you, Reverend," said Floutie with an elaborate courtesy that barely masked his sense of glee. Finally, after years of humiliation, Wolfowitz's departure had put him in a position to demonstrate to his father-in-law that he was capable of running the affairs of Gothic Books.

"Douglas, I think we ought to take another recess," said Carter Lang.

"That won't be necessary," said Floutie, with a magisterial wave of his hand. "Ms. Birney, assuming for the moment that what you say is true, permit me to assure you that Gothic Books had no knowledge whatsoever of any irregularities on Mr. Wolfowitz's part."

"Doesn't matter," said Linda. "As far as we're concerned, Wolfowitz *is* Gothic Books. The liability belongs to the company."

Floutie looked at Lang, who nodded almost imperceptibly. The publisher clasped his hands in a donnish manner and smiled at Mack. "I'm certain that nothing has happened that can't be rectified," he said. "After all, ah, Mr. Green is an artist, not some litigious businessman. His paramount concern is, I'm sure, the publication of his new novel."

"Don't say anything, Mack," cautioned Linda. "Mr. Floutie, do I hear an implied threat in that remark?"

"Not at all," said the publisher, glancing once again at his father-in-law to make certain he wasn't missing this masterful display. "I do, however, want to point out that *The Diary of a Dying Man* hasn't yet been accepted for publication. And, as you know, under the contract, Gothic Books has the right to determine its satisfactory delivery."

"That's true," said Carter Lang, seizing the point.

"Obviously, we would find it unsatisfactory to publish a book by an author who was, shall we say, hostile to our interests," Floutie said smoothly.

This was the gambit Mack had anticipated. With his track record, a rejection by Gothic would be fatal. No matter how good *The Diary* was, when word got out that it was a turkey—and that would be Gothic's story—no other publisher in town would want it.

Mack saw the smug look on Floutie's face, waited a beat and then nodded slightly to Roy Ray, who abruptly stood, pointed an accusatory finger at the three men on the other side of the table and began emitting loud squawking noises.

"Is your friend all right?" asked Floutie.

"Ask him. He speaks English," said Mack.

"Are you all right?" Floutie said.

"When is the black man all right in an America that's all white?" demanded Roy Ray.

"Mr. Green's a white man," Lang pointed out in a reasonable tone.

"Yes, but he has a black heart. A black heart and a black soul. He's got the soul, you've got the control."

Floutie coughed politely. "This is all very interesting, I'm sure—"

"White man treat the black man like an animal," Malik continued, ignoring the interruption. "Worse than an animal—worse than them inferior, overpriced, disease-making, money-taking, flavor-faking, no-good-for-baking, profit-raking chickens that this old white man here sells in the ghettos of our benighted nation."

"What the hell's the matter with my chickens?" demanded Fassbinder, the vein on his wattled neck throbbing.

"Chickens is nothing to the white man," proclaimed Malik. "The white man eats filet mignon in his fancy clubs, while the folks up in Harlem got to scrape the meat off the scrawny bones of them low-rent Fassbinder poultry they sell in the store."

"Nothing you can do about that, Reverend," said Mack with a grin.

"Oh yes there is too," Malik said. " 'Bout time somebody put a boycott on them ad-lying, no-frying, bad-buying, baby-dying, race-denying birds old man Fassbinder be peddling to our people."

"Baby-dying?" asked Lang, mesmerized by the litany.

"Them things is pumped full of all manner of nasty chemicals," Malik said.

"Race-denying?" said Floutie. "How can a chicken be race-denying, whatever that means?"

"How many black people work at Fassbinder Poultry?" Malik demanded. "All y'all do is take our cash and sell us trash."

"Be interesting to know how many black people work for Gothic Books," Joyce mused. "I sure didn't see any today. Might even be a civil rights violation."

"Maybe we need to add this here to our boycott," said Malik, swinging his arm in a wide arc that took in the boardroom. "Or don't y'all think black people can read?"

"This is preposterous," said Floutie. "If you think you can come in here with this extortionary tactic and—"

"Shut up, Floutie," said Fassbinder. The vein in his neck was throbbing more powerfully now and his face was red, making him look even more like one of his own roosters. "Carter, get this dumb-cluck professor out of here and these others, too. I want to talk turkey with this little lady."

"I stay," Mack said. "It's my book and my life."

"Fine, but the rest of you, scat," said Fassbinder. He watched them file out of the room, Floutie with a crestfallen expression, Lang a study in bland uninvolvement, Joyce with a small smile on her face, Malik still loudly denouncing the racial injustice of the poultry business.

"Jesus on the mountain," the old man said to Linda, "you're a pisser, you are. What's this gonna cost me?"

Linda reached into her briefcase and produced a list. "It's all right here," she said.

"Read it to me," said Fassbinder.

"All right. First, we want a written commitment that *The Diary of a Dying Man* will be published on schedule, with an appropriate promotional budget. Appropriate in our view is five hundred thousand dollars."

Fassbinder took a small notebook from his pocket and wrote down the figure with a blue ballpoint.

"Second, we're asking that Gothic reissue each of Mr. Green's two previous novels, accompanying each release with a further half million dollar promotional campaign."

"Half a million each, or half a million for both of 'em?"

"Half a million each," said Linda. "Furthermore—"

"Just a minute," said Fassbinder, "I can't write that fast. Each. Okay, what else?"

"Third, compensation for personal suffering, loss of income and professional standing. Figuring conservatively, I'd estimate two million dollars."

"Two million," said Fassbinder, writing down the number. "Okay, anything else?"

"I can't think of anything," said Linda. "Mack?"

"That covers it, more or less."

"All rightee," said Fassbinder. "Let's see, one million five hundred thousand for publicity, another two million in damages, that comes to, check me on this now, three million, five hundred thousand."

"Exactly," said Linda. "Of course, the money for publicity is really an investment. Mack's books will make that much and more if they aren't being intentionally sabotaged. So it's really considerably less. Chicken feed for a man like you."

"Well now," said Fassbinder. "Supposing I just kick your asses out of here? Then what?"

"Then things get messy," said Linda in a matter-of-fact tone. "We go to court, in Oriole, where the demographics pretty much ensure us a black-and-brown jury—if you don't know what that means, check with Lang—and we'll see how a group of unemployed auto workers and welfare mothers feel about a big New

York company trying to ruin a local boy's life. Believe me, it'll cost you a hell of a lot more than what we're asking."

"If you're so blamed sure, why don't you take me to court?" asked Fassbinder.

"Turn me down and I will," said Linda.

"What about the goddamn chicken boycott?"

"I think I might be able to influence Minister Malik to reconsider," said Mack. "We're old friends."

"I get the picture," said Fassbinder. "You two stay right here, I want to talk to Lang."

"Take your time," said Linda, glancing at the bookshelves. "We'll browse while we wait."

Fassbinder was back within five minutes, accompanied by a grim-faced Carter Lang.

"Okay," said Fassbinder, "you got a deal. The papers and a check will be ready by the end of the week."

"Of course we'll need a release from further claims," said Lang. "And a confidentiality agreement."

"Of course," said Linda. "Nobody's looking for publicity here."

"I have one question," said Mack. "Just out of curiosity, what are you going to do about Wolfowitz?"

"Don't worry about him," said the old man, a look of pure malice on his mottled face. "By the time I get through with him, Arthur Wolfowitz is going to be one dead duck."

Thirty

McClain was waiting at the Waldorf when they returned, anxious to hear an account of the meeting at Gothic. Linda told the story, and when she came to the part about Roy Ray's tirade, McClain laughed so hard he turned red.

"Flavor-faking, no-good-for-baking," he sputtered in his east side accent. "Baby-dying, race-denying. I wish I could have been there. How did Wolfowitz take his ass-kicking?"

"Not too bad," said Linda, with a smile. "Considering he's unemployed and Louise has probably changed the locks already."

"You really think she'll leave him?" asked Joyce.

"In a minute," said Linda.

"A minute would give her time to pack," said Green. "Losing his career and his wife in one day. I almost feel sorry for him."

"The man tried to ruin your life," said Linda. "In my opinion, he's getting off easy."

McClain stared at his napkin. "A guy like Wolfowitz, you never know what nasty little surprises might still catch up with him."

"Speaking of surprises," said Joyce, "in all the excitement I forgot to give you this." She took a small package from her purse.

"It's from Packer," said Mack. "I recognize the handwriting."

"No return address," said McClain.

Mack noticed that the envelope had been opened. It contained an audiocasette.

"I've got a recorder, if you want to hear it," said Linda.

Mack slipped the tape into the small machine. After a moment they heard the sound of sharp inhalation, a cough and then Buddy Packer's flat, sardonic voice. "Hey, Macky, what's happening? It's just past noon and I'm still in bed. Here on my right is the lovely Juanita. Next to me on my left is her sister Juanita. It's Juanita season down here—"

"Your best friend," said Linda.

"—and they're biting. All you have to do is use the right bait which I've got, thanks to Reggie. Not a bad fo-ray, if I do say so myself." There was the sound of another toke, another cough and then, "I'm getting a toe-lick from one of the Juanitas, so I'll make this quick. Irish Willie's got a championship bout in Detroit next month and he needs me in his corner. I figure by now McClain's taken care of Reggie. I'll call you on the twenty-third over at Uncle John and Aunt Jemima's, just to make sure, and then I'll be back for a few drinks and a few laughs. Viva la Gamers!"

Mack looked at Joyce. "The twenty-third was the day we left for New York," he said. "I wonder why he didn't call."

"Oh, he called," said Joyce. "I talked to him."

"You did? Did you tell him the coast was clear?"

"Not exactly."

"Well, what did you tell him?"

"That you had disappeared," said Joyce sweetly. "And that there was a warrant out for his arrest."

• • •

That night, after a long nap, they all went to the Flying Tiger to celebrate. It was a little before nine when they arrived and the place was almost empty. The jukebox was playing Edwin Starr's "Agent Double O Soul" and Otto was leaning against the old-fashioned cash register, watching a Knicks game on the silent television. He smiled broadly when he spotted Mack. "Hiya kid, how'd it go?" he said.

"Great, thanks to you," said Mack.

"I never trusted that Russo," said Otto. "He was in here this afternoon, by the way. Wanted me to tell you he was getting out of the agent business."

"Maybe he's going back to the priesthood."

"Chaplain in a casino, maybe," said Otto.

"Yeah, well. Say hello to some friends from Michigan."

Otto came from behind the bar and shook hands all around. "What about you?" he asked Mack. "You back for good?"

"Just until tomorrow. Then we're flying out to Oriole. That's home now."

"In that case, first drink's on the house," said Otto without evident emotion. "What'll it be?"

McClain and Linda ordered scotch on the rocks, Joyce a Campari-and-soda. "I'll have a cold Heineken," Mack said, watching Otto's eyebrows rise.

"Turned into a beer drinker out there, eh?"

"Cutting down on the hard stuff," Mack said. "Just to give my liver a little rest. And bring us some menus. I want to show these tourists what real New York greasy-spoon fare tastes like."

"Drinks and grease coming up," said Otto.

"Good man," observed McClain when the bartender left them. "Not your type, hotshot. He seems like a normal human being."

"Thanks."

"I like this place," said Linda, surveying the dingy barroom.

"It's not exactly the Russian Tea Room, but it suits you. Sort of funky."

"That's me, funky," said Mack. "I'm a blue-collar writer."

"Not after today," said McClain. "You just moved into the upper classes."

The food arrived, McClain ordered a second round of drinks and Mack went over to the jukebox and put in a handful of quarters. "See if you remember this one," he said. The Chantels' "Maybe" came on and he held out his hand to Linda. She rose, stepped into his arms and they began to dance slowly in the narrow aisle. Behind the bar, Otto Kelly smiled—he hadn't seen Green dance in years—but Mack didn't notice. He had his eyes closed as he softly sang the words in Linnie's ear. "May-ay-be, if I pray, every day, you will come back to me—"

"Are you trying to seduce me with that crooning?" Linda laughed.

"I want you back, Linnie," said Mack.

"I'm already back," said Linda. "Did you forget last night? And this morning?"

"I'm not talking about that. You still haven't said you'll marry me."

"And live happily ever after? Is that the way this story's supposed to end?"

"Aw, Linnie, not that again—"

"Open your eyes, Mack," said Linda. When he did, he saw the crooked pirate grin on her face. "I was kidding. Okay, I'll think about it."

"But you'll probably say yes, right? Eventually?"

They danced for a while in silence, Linda rubbing her cheek against Mack's chest. Finally she looked up at him and smiled. "Yeah, maybe, Mackinac," she sighed. "Maybe."

As they were getting ready to leave, just before eleven, Mack saw a group of the young writers come in. They nodded to him and he returned their vague greetings; he recognized a few faces, but didn't know a single name.

Mack took out his checkbook and walked over to the bar. "We're out of here, Otto," he said. "I'll come by next time I'm in New York."

"Nice to see you looking so happy," Otto said. "That girl-friend of yours is a beauty."

"Yeah, she is, isn't she?" said Mack. "We're getting married."

"Congratulations," said Otto.

"You got a pen?"

"Does Sam have Dave?" He smiled and produced a ballpoint. Mack took it and wrote Otto a check for five thousand dollars.

"What the hell's this for? You don't owe me any money," said the bartender, staring at the check.

"It's a scholarship fund from an old grad," said Mack. "For writers who are waiting for a great idea. Just tell them to hang in there, something will come up. And that in the meantime, the drinks are on the Oriole Kid."

ABOUT THE AUTHOR

ZEV CHAFETS was born in Pontiac, Michigan, and moved to Israel at the age of twenty in 1967. He is the author of *Inherit the Mob*; *Double Vision*; *Heroes and Hustlers*; *Hard Hats and Holy Men*; *Members of the Tribe*; and *Devil's Night: And Other True Tales of Detroit*. Chafets currently lives in Tel Aviv, Israel.

ABOUT THE TYPE

This book was set in Bembo, a typeface based on an old-style Roman face that was used for Cardinal Bembo's tract *De Aetna* in 1495. Bembo was cut by Francisco Griffo in the early sixteenth century. The Lanston Monotype Machine Company of Philadelphia brought the well-proportioned letter forms of Bembo to the United States in the 1930s.